JENNIFER A. NIELSEN

RISE OF THE WOLF

—— • MARK OF THE THIEF • ——
Book Two

WITHDRAWN

SCHOLASTIC PRESS · NEW YORK

Library of Congress Cataloging-in-Publication Data

Nielsen, Jennifer A., author.
Rise of the wolf / Jennifer Nielsen. — First edition.
pages cm. — (Mark of the thief ; Book Two)
Summary: Now a driver in the chariot races, Nic is still a target of the Praetors because of the magical amulet he found, and they will do anything to get their hands on it — and meanwhile Atroxia is beginning to wake up.
ISBN 978-0-545-56204-1 (jacketed hardcover)
1. Magic — Juvenile fiction. 2. Amulets — Juvenile fiction. 3. Conspiracies — Juvenile fiction. 4. Dragons — Juvenile fiction. 5. Chariot racing — Juvenile fiction. 6. Rome — Antiquities — Juvenile fiction. 7. Rome — History — Empire, 30 B.C.-476 A.D. — Juvenile fiction. [1. Magic — Fiction. 2. Amulets — Fiction. 3. Conspiracies — Fiction. 4. Dragons — Fiction. 5. Chariot racing — Fiction. 6. Rome — History — Empire, 30 B.C.-476 A.D. — Fiction.] I. Title.
PZ7.N5672Ri 2016
813.6 — dc23
[Fic]
2015015920

10 9 8 7 6 5 4 3 2 1   16 17 18 19 20

Printed in the U.S.A.   23
First edition, February 2016
Book design by Christopher Stengel

A note to readers: Latin words will be italicized upon their first appearance in the text.

To Mrs. Behunin, 3rd Grade,
who planted books within my heart

❧ · ONE · ❧

My life no longer made sense. At least, not according to the usual rules of logic. But the absence of logic didn't bother me. A strange feeling of peace had come over me once I accepted that the only person I could trust in this world was also trying to kill me.

My grandfather, General Flavius Radulf.

Since he made no secret of his plans for my death, I didn't figure he had much of a reason to lie about anything else. Awful as his plans were, in some ways I was worse than him. Because he'd be a fool to trust me, and he knew nothing of my plans.

Though for now, those plans would have to wait. For, at the moment, the chariot I was driving required my full concentration.

Chariot racing had been Radulf's idea. He got the idea two months ago when he saw me riding the horse in the amphitheater. Back then, all I had cared about was surviving Rome's *venatio*, and I'd needed an obedient horse to do it. Competing in the chariot races one day had been the furthest thought from my mind.

Yet here I was, driving a team of four horses around the circuit for a practice race and loving every moment of it. Other teams were practicing too, which meant there were several hundred spectators in the audience, hoping for a good show. Hoping to see blood.

My blood, possibly. Because even in practice, I intended to win, and winning drivers always pressed toward the innermost track, where it was fastest, and most dangerous.

Although greens and blues, or even whites, were more popular, I rode as part of the red faction — Radulf had friends there. Since I was new and had an unfortunate reputation for destroying things, such as the great amphitheater, no other team would even consider me. I wasn't sure what it had cost Radulf in threats or bribery, but while on the track, I wore the red toga. A couple of other red teams were riding today, but they were already behind me.

With eight other teams, the track was crowded, but not as bad as it'd be during the circus, when twelve teams would race for glory, honor, and a small sack of gold. So I took advantage of the lesser numbers and pushed my team of horses inward. A white-cloaked charioteer just ahead glared back at me, and I smiled in return. If he was irritated, then I was doing something right.

Despite my relative inexperience, my practice races had all gone well, though I had yet to be tested in a real race. The *Ludi Romani* was coming up in a couple of weeks. It was the grandest of all festivals, honoring Jupiter, the highest of the gods, so most

Romans would attend at some point. I had to prove myself to be accepted there. If I worked hard to improve my skills, perhaps within a few years I'd be good enough for that race.

The chariot's reins were tied around my waist, which helped me control the horses more instinctively. That was fine, unless we overturned, in which case the horses would drag me to my death. I had a knife in my belt to cut free if necessary, though that wouldn't keep me from being trampled by other teams of horses. Trampling was hardly the way I intended to die, so I had to pay attention now. The man ahead of me shouted some sort of insult as I edged him farther out from the center of the track. Based on his expression, he'd be happy to see me fall. I had few friendships anywhere, but none in the circus.

The man's footing on the floor of his chariot was less secure than he wanted me to believe. I saw him fight for balance every time we made a turn. I didn't struggle with that as much. Back when I'd worked as a slave in the mines, my master, Sal, had often forced me onto steep and narrow paths. I hadn't fallen then, and I wouldn't fall now. Or that was my plan, anyway. The heavy bag hanging from my belt might change things.

I turned again, and the bag swung hard to the left, shifting my weight. My first instinct was to use magic to regain my balance, but I didn't. I couldn't. Once the chariot had straightened out, I reset my feet in the center of the chariot and rode on even harder.

Radulf had stolen my *bulla* after we fought in the amphitheater, which had taken that magic from me. But he hadn't taken everything. Since our battle, the Divine Star on my shoulder had come to life in ways I'd never felt before. I rarely used the magic from that mark — I couldn't trust what Radulf would do if he knew I still had magic — so instead I contained it within me except for the smallest uses, such as comforting my horses. But never to correct my balance. That was far too risky.

"I saw what you did in the amphitheater!" a white-faction charioteer shouted as he tried to pass me. "Will you destroy the circus too if you lose?"

I smiled and urged my horses to block him. "Probably not, since I don't intend to lose!"

"Your chariot is too heavy with that bag. Stupid slave boy, the lead is worth nothing!"

Not to him, it wasn't. But things were different for me. The lead in this bag might save my life.

Romans were fiercely loyal to their preferred factions, possibly even more so than to the empire. Though it was illegal for other games, they often placed bets on the chariot races. To improve their team's chances of winning, they created curse tablets, lead slabs with curses scratched into them. Then they'd nail them to the wall of the circus or bury them in the dirt beneath the track. I collected as many as I could each day, and told Radulf that if the gods didn't see the curses, then the gods couldn't enforce them. It was a stupid lie, but I told it every single night, straight to his face.

Radulf hated that I wore the bag. We'd fought over it since the first day I brought it to the circus, but I didn't care and I wouldn't give in. He'd become convinced that it was a superstition for me, which was far from the truth. There was no room in my life for superstitions. Reality was already dangerous enough.

"Carrying that bag around is ridiculous, and embarrassing for the grandson of a general," he'd said only last night. "Besides, the gods have already cursed you. What more could they possibly do?"

I knew the answer to that question. The gods could stop providing me with curse tablets each day.

Still shouting insults, the white-cloaked charioteer tried to force my team against the wall. I calmed the horses with a wave of my hand and urged them even faster, earning some cheers from the audience. I turned to thank the crowd, and then someone caught my attention.

My younger sister, Livia, was in the stands, behind the senators' box. Her golden curls always stood out in a crowd, and they did now, as bright as ever. Still, I was surprised to see her here. Since we had come to Radulf's house two months ago, she and I had never been allowed outside at the same time. Radulf thought it would make us more likely to run. I hadn't gotten far in arguing that with him, mostly because we both knew that's exactly what we'd do.

So why was Livia here now, and on her own? As my chariot came closer, she turned to speak to a woman next to her and I realized it wasn't Livia after all. But for the difference in their ages, it was someone who could have been her twin.

My heart lurched into my throat. Only one other person could look so much like Livia. That was my mother, I was sure of it.

"Control your horses or I'll have you thrown off this track!" another charioteer shouted as he passed me by.

"What? Oh — sorry." I shifted attention back to my horses, who had wandered into the outer track, and then I looked for the gates to pull out of the race. They were behind me, requiring almost a full circuit, so I kept an eye on my mother as much as possible while the next turn came closer.

I realized now that my mother wasn't in conversation with the woman beside her — she was serving her. And looking at the track whenever she could. Did she recognize me and know I was down here? Or was it simple curiosity about the practice? Maybe the answer didn't make any difference — after all, she couldn't speak to me without the permission of her mistress. And with Radulf in the stands, it wasn't a good idea for me to approach her either. But for the past five years, I hadn't seen her once, or even known anything about her new life. There was no chance I would let her go now.

The white-cloaked charioteer had edged ahead of me and looked back, yelling, "This will teach you a lesson, boy!" And he steered his team of horses directly into mine, pushing us hard into the wall. My lead horse stumbled, and would take the others with him when he fell. Seven other chariots were behind me. At least one would trample me. Probably on purpose.

I glanced at where I had last seen Radulf, but couldn't see him any longer. Though it would require a greater use of magic to save the horses, it was a necessary risk. As the horses tangled with one another, I brushed my hand sideways, and they immediately regained their footing. It was a relief to release a portion of the magic bottled up inside me, a little less pressure to contain. On the other hand, if Radulf noticed what I'd just done, I would pay for this.

By then, I was able to pull off to the gates, and when I did, I used the knife to cut myself free from the chariot, removed my helmet, and leapt to the ground. While handlers took over the care of my horses, I sprinted off the track, dodging other horse teams when necessary. Then I ran up the stone steps into the stands, toward where my mother had been. But though my heart was pounding and I was completely out of breath, I hadn't been fast enough. I could not see her anymore, nor the woman she had served. Those seats were empty, and no matter how hard I looked, I could not see them anywhere. My mother was gone.

✣ · TWO · ✣

N ic! Why'd you quit the race?"

That was Aurelia's voice, and I turned to see her hurrying toward me, wearing a deep yellow tunic. Her light brown hair was pulled away from her face in a complicated braid that signified her newfound wealth. To see how nice she looked now, it was hard to believe she had once lived in the sewers beneath Rome.

I knew that I had missed her over the last two months, but until this moment, I hadn't realized how much she had become part of my life. It was rude to stare back at her, but I couldn't help it. The fire in her eyes was as bright as ever, as striking as always. Had she asked me a question? I couldn't remember.

"Nic? Are you awake in there?" She was in front of me now, smiling and waving a hand in front of my face.

It didn't make sense, seeing her now. The last time we had been together was after I had fought Radulf in the amphitheater. Senator Horatio, Aurelia's father, had died there. Maybe she didn't blame me for that after all, as I had believed. Because her smile suggested that we were still friends. Was that possible?

"What are you doing here?" I finally asked. A part of me hoped Aurelia would say she had come to see me race. Actually, *every* part of me hoped that.

"I came . . ." she stammered. "Er, *we* came —"

"We?"

"Is everything all right? The practice was going so well." That was Crispus, who walked through a nearby archway and stood beside Aurelia. She only gave him a casual glance, telling me far more than I wanted to know. They had come here together. And whatever anger she had supposedly felt toward Crispus before had clearly vanished.

My anger had not.

"I have nothing to say to you," I muttered to Crispus. Then I turned and marched away from him. Now things were beginning to make sense, but not in a good way.

Aurelia hurried down the rows and crossed directly in front of me. "We came to talk to you," she said.

"You came with him?" I pointed to Crispus, still standing several rows above us. "The last time we were all together, he nearly got both of us killed. He succeeded with your father's death, and had me blamed for it."

"Crispus didn't do all that," Aurelia said. "It was his father."

There was truth in her words. Crispus's father, Valerius, had planned it all so he could become the Senate's presiding magistrate, a position of great power that had previously belonged to Senator Horatio. More important, the position also allowed Valerius to inherit the key to unlock a magical amulet he called the Malice of Mars. I didn't know much about it, other than that it would give its bearer victory in battle and that it was hidden somewhere.

The problem was that Valerius never got that key. Everyone seemed to believe Horatio had given it to me before he died, but he didn't. Radulf believed I had it too, one of only a few reasons he was keeping me alive.

Crispus stepped toward me, though he still kept his distance. "You were right to be angry, Nic, and it's understandable if your feelings haven't changed. But even if you disagree with what my father did in the arena, that doesn't make him your enemy."

"Without Radulf's protection, the empire would've executed me by now, all because of your father." I squinted into the sun to finally look at Crispus. "So tell me how he isn't my enemy."

"He came here to save your life." As if to prove it, Crispus pointed across the circus to the imperial box, where Radulf was sitting in close conversation with Valerius.

I swerved on my heels and began marching over to them. I wasn't sure whether Crispus followed me or not, but Aurelia almost immediately caught up to me.

"Believe it or not, Valerius is trying to help you," she said. "It does us no good to be angry with them."

"Us?" I scoffed at that, then said, "Since when did you become friends with Crispus? Was it the same night Valerius had your father killed, or did you wait a whole day first?"

"How dare you?" Aurelia punched my shoulder, and crossed in front of me, forcing me to stop. "My whole life, all I wanted was to get back to my father. You know better than anyone how much I wanted a family! But I walked away from him, because of his terrible plans for Rome." Her tone softened. "Because of his terrible plans for you, Nic. I did that because we are friends. I went into the arena to help you fight, and all I've done since then is try to figure out how to get you away from Radulf."

If that was true, then why hadn't I seen or heard from her? I knew she had tried to help me that day, but she couldn't possibly understand how difficult the last couple of months had been.

I shook my head and walked past her. "So your friendship with Crispus is to help me? Or does he help you instead?"

She caught up again, and this time grabbed my arm. "What is that supposed to mean?"

I checked behind us. Crispus was following, but at a safe distance. It wasn't far enough, though.

I turned back to Aurelia and said, "I know why you're so friendly to him."

She folded her arms. "Really? Why is that?"

"When your father died, he left behind a large fortune. Enough to take care of you for the rest of your life. Except Radulf told me Horatio's will only provides for you under one condition."

"You know about that?" The way she said it should've been a warning to me to stop talking. But I wasn't that wise.

My eyes darted to Crispus and then back to her. "There's only one way for you to keep your inheritance."

"You still think I only care about money? After all you and I have been through together?"

"We're not together." I nodded toward Crispus. "You came here with him."

"To help you! Nic, I'm trying to be your friend. I *am* your friend. Why can't you see that?"

My throat tightened, and for a moment, it was hard to speak. Finally, I said, "You were more free when you had nothing. You gave up that freedom for a life of comfort."

She groaned. "And you're any different? The last time we talked, you were going to leave Rome and be free. Now you bask in the comfort of Radulf's home, racing chariots and dining on the finest foods money can buy."

I brushed past her again. "You don't understand."

"Don't I?" She continued at my side. "Why is it wrong for me to have a friendship with a senator and his son when you agreed to live in the home of the man who nearly killed you in the arena? You accuse me of giving up my freedom for comforts, but you have done the very same thing!"

Aurelia took my hand, forcing me to turn back to her. I tried to pull free, but she redoubled her grip. Then as she got a better look at my wrist, her gaze sharpened. "Oh, Nic, what's this?"

I yanked my arm away. "It's nothing."

She grabbed it again and held it up to study it closer. The wrist was red and slightly swollen with scars that never had enough time to heal. "What caused these wounds?" When I wouldn't answer, she said, "Tell me."

"That's me, agreeing to live in Radulf's home."

"Oh. I see." Her voice softened, and for a moment, it was possible to believe that she really did care about me as a friend. "So this isn't your choice."

My eyes darted away, to where Radulf and Valerius were speaking. They glanced over at me, then returned to their huddled conversation. I considered pulling my hand away from Aurelia again, but she was brushing her fingers over the wounds in such a tender way, I suddenly didn't mind that she was holding it.

"We should meet in private tonight and talk," I said. "In the sewers, if you can find the place where I need to meet you."

"I can find it," she said. "Where?"

"Below Radulf's home." Then in a whisper, I added, "Bring the *crepundia.*" That necklace had meant everything to her, once. For her whole life, it had been her only connection to her father. It surprised me that she no longer wore it.

Her brows pressed together, more suspicious than curious. "Why do you want the crepundia? My father's dead. It's meaningless now."

By then, Crispus had caught up to us, less wary of me than he had been at first. "I want us to be friends too," he said. "You don't have to trust my father, or even me, but is there enough friendship between us that you'll listen to me now?"

Probably not, but I still asked, "Why is your father talking to Radulf?"

Crispus frowned. "Aurelia already told you. He's trying to save your life."

"From what?"

"From the real enemy to Rome. The Praetors are coming, Nic. We don't know if it's to kill you or control you, but they are coming. You're in terrible danger."

❧ · THREE · ❧

Officially, the Praetors ran the government of Rome, as clerks and judges and tax collectors. Unofficially, their loyalties ran much deeper than the empire, in service of a cause that made Radulf afraid of them. If the Praetors were coming after me, that made me equally nervous.

When I first stole the bulla, I'd had no idea of the trouble I was bringing into my life. Indeed, I had heard Julius Caesar's own whispers from the grave, warning me that the bulla would become a curse. And the reality of that curse was playing out here as I stood in conversation with Crispus and Aurelia.

"Once my father took control of the Senate, the Praetors did follow him," Crispus said. "But not for the reasons he'd expected. The Praetors are secretly dedicated to much higher powers."

"They serve the gods?" I asked. "So does all of Rome."

"They serve only one. Diana, the goddess who powered your bulla."

Instinctively, I reached for it at my side, though I found nothing. The bulla hadn't rested there for two months.

Aurelia leaned in closer. "When Caesar first had the bulla, who gave it magic?"

"Venus was the first." I shrugged. "But after Caesar abandoned it, Diana gave it power."

"Did you ever wonder why Diana did that?"

I shrugged again. Once I stole the bulla, everything had spun so quickly out of my control, there was no time to think about *why* anything was happening.

"It's because Diana intends harm against Rome, and against the other gods," Aurelia said. "And the Praetors are sworn to help her to do it."

"How?"

"They want the three amulets here in Rome," Crispus said. "The bulla is powerful, of course, but not nearly as powerful as the Malice of Mars. The Praetors followed my father because the presiding magistrate has always held the key to unlocking that amulet. But he never got it. Before his death, Horatio gave it to someone else." His eyes drifted to mine.

"He never gave it to me," I said firmly. "The Praetors will find sugar in the salt mines before they ever find me with that key."

"My father believes you have it too," Crispus said. "Everyone believes it."

"Everyone is wrong," I said. "Radulf has searched me many times. If I did have the key, he would've taken it from me. So tell the Praetors to capture him instead and leave me alone!"

"Is the key in that sack at your waist?" Crispus asked. "Every time we've come to these practices, I've seen you carry it."

"No." I bunched the sack in my fist, as if he might try to take it. "How many of my practices have you been to?"

"Several." Crispus looked back to the track. "My father is a big supporter of the blue faction. Just like the emperor."

"The blue faction races like they were pulled by kittens," I said.

"Can we focus on an actual problem?" Aurelia touched both of our arms. "The Praetors want more than just the key. There's a third amulet."

"The Jupiter Stone," I breathed.

"They know how to create it," she said. "But they need someone with magic to attempt it. You."

"Radulf took my magic in the arena," I said. That much was true, and I wondered if not saying anything more made it a lie. "Even if he didn't, I wouldn't help the Praetors make a Jupiter Stone."

"The Praetors don't want it for themselves," Crispus said. "They want it for Diana. With it, she will become invincible, even to the other gods."

My eyes narrowed. "I won't help them. I won't allow Diana that much power." The ridiculousness of such a statement did not escape me. I was still a runaway slave. She ruled in the heavens.

"You might not have any choice," Crispus said. "If they —" Then he stopped, like his words had slammed into a stone wall.

With little patience left, I asked, "If they what?"

Crispus sighed. "You have to trust me and my father, no matter how they try to force you. Because if the Praetors succeed, it could mean that all of Rome is destroyed."

My temper warmed, but I kept my voice low. "Why won't I have any choice in helping them, Crispus?"

I looked to Aurelia for answers, but she only glanced down. Muttering a curse under my breath, I left them and walked over to Valerius and Radulf, still in conversation. Their backs were toward me, so they didn't see me approach, and I heard their argument as I came closer.

"You must believe me," Valerius was saying. "Nic is in grave danger."

They turned when they heard me coming. Valerius stood, his face creased with lines of worry. But Radulf leaned back and smiled. He said, "Welcome to the conversation, Nic. Sit down."

"I want you both to leave," Valerius said to Crispus and Aurelia, who had followed me.

"No," I said. "I want them to stay." Or at least, I wanted Aurelia to stay. I wasn't sure about Crispus.

Hesitantly, Valerius consented, and they took seats behind me. I glanced back at Aurelia, who brushed her fingers against my shoulder as a sign of support. I hoped Crispus saw it.

When Radulf had my attention, he nodded at Valerius and said, "I told the senator you'd never run from a fight."

On the contrary, I would gladly run from a fight if the option were ever given to me. I had no training, not even in magic, and lacked the cold disrespect for life that one would expect from a warrior. On the other hand, I had never backed down from Radulf's challenges. Not until he threatened my sister's life if I refused to join his house. Since then, I had not defied him once. Or at least, not as far as he knew.

"What's the fight?" I asked.

Valerius cleared his throat. "The Praetors are in rebellion against me, and soon will rebel against all of Rome. I blame you for this, Nic."

"When did your poor leadership become my fault?" I was nothing to Rome, less than a speck of dust on the boot of the lowest soldier. Or at least, that was how Radulf described me each night when I was sent to my room. One of the men sitting before me was wrong. Either I mattered to the empire, or I didn't.

"You brought magic to Rome," Valerius continued. "The Praetors have waited nearly three hundred years for someone to find Caesar's bulla."

I glanced over at Radulf and only briefly met his eyes. He'd taken the bulla from me when I joined his house, and I had not stolen it back. Well, not yet.

"The Praetors will not get the bulla," Radulf said. "Only I know its secrets."

I nearly burst out laughing. Since I came to his home, Radulf had spent almost every night desperately trying to create magic from the bulla. He claimed he could still sense its magic, but I suspected what he actually sensed was the magic returning to me, because the bulla no longer had its powerful gemstones. I had removed those before our fight in the arena. If Radulf were less prideful, he would ask me for help. And if I were less stubborn . . . well, I had no intention of helping him, ever. Radulf was on his own.

Valerius was too focused on Radulf to notice my reaction. Speaking now to Radulf, he said, "The Praetors aren't concerned about the bulla. It's the Malice of Mars they want, and they'll come to Nic for the key to unlocking it. If he gives it to them now —"

"I DON'T HAVE THE KEY!" I yelled. Only the gods knew how many times I had denied having the key, and they probably quit counting weeks ago. Lowering my voice only a little, I added, "Horatio never expected to die, so he had no reason to give away the key. Even if he did give it away, he'd never have chosen me. He hated me, and he believed Radulf would kill *me* in the arena, not him."

I heard a chuckle and looked sideways at Radulf, who had somehow found my words funny.

"But Horatio told everyone he gave it to Nic," Crispus said from behind me. We turned, and he added, "Besides, whether he has it or not, the Praetors will treat Nic as if he has the key. He must be protected."

Valerius leaned forward. "Radulf, you must make Nic give up the key, then take him as far from Rome as possible. Leave the empire if you can, though I doubt even that will be far enough."

"If he can't outrun the Praetors, then there's no point in leaving." Radulf smiled over at me. "Nic will not leave Rome, and he certainly will not give them the key. After he defeats the Praetors, I will take the Malice of Mars for myself."

"How?" I asked. "Even with the key, nobody knows where the Malice is hidden." I was still looking at Crispus as I spoke, and Valerius tossed him a warning glance. That made me curious.

Valerius tried again. "Please, Radulf, do not seek the Malice. It can only end badly. We need to give the Praetors the key and then get out safely, all of us. Lives depend on it."

Now I understood, and it didn't improve my opinion of Valerius much. "That's why you came here," I said to him. "You're not interested in saving my life, or in saving Rome from the Praetors. If you don't give them the key, they'll kill you."

Before he could answer, his eyes widened, and then he raised a shaking hand and pointed behind Radulf. We all turned and saw a group of Praetors entering the circus. They were dressed in the robes and togas of the upper class, but each of them had a thin silver band in the shape of an arrow wrapped around his arm. It was proof of their loyalty to Diana, who, according to Crispus, was in rebellion against the other gods. Every head in the circus turned my way.

A lump formed in my throat as I tried to figure out what to do. Valerius said they intended to take me.

"Give them the key," Valerius said, grabbing my arm. "Please, Nic. It's your only hope."

"He'll do no such thing," Radulf said, standing. "Nic, get behind me. The rest of you had better find a place to hide."

And in his hand, I saw a flame spark into a ball. While Aurelia, Crispus, and Valerius raced away, I braced myself for the fight.

✠ · FOUR · ✠

Until coming to Radulf's home, I had always kept the bulla with me, and would've loved the chance to use it now. Since he had taken it for himself, Radulf had shown far more caution. He hid the bulla in his room, thinking it was safe from the Praetors or thieves. Or me. Still, the magic in the mark on Radulf's back was exceedingly powerful — it would be enough to fend off the Praetors.

Even so, when I saw them enter the circus, the Divine Star on my shoulder sparked to life and burned like a cold flame, but I could not let Radulf know that. Having used magic to save my horses during the chariot race was already too risky. If I did anything here, he might take my magic again. I wouldn't survive that degree of pain a second time. So I curled my hands into fists, hoping that would be enough to hold the magic inside, and tried not to look at the Praetors.

They approached from the top end of the circus, nearly fifty of them. Every one of them had his eyes directly on me. I felt the weight of their glares like boulders on my chest; these men had power and wealth I could not imagine, almost as much as the senators of Rome, and they were no friends of mine.

Most of the onlookers who had been here before sensed the coming fight and were quickly clearing out. Even the charioteers had stopped their practice and turned their horses toward the stables. Valerius, Crispus, and Aurelia were gone too, leaving Radulf and me alone with the Praetors. I hated cowering in his shadow, but if it was true that they were here to get me, I had only two choices: To fight them and reveal my magic to Radulf. Or to cower.

"Stay close to me," Radulf said. "Let's hope the Praetors keep their distance."

"They have powers?" I asked.

"No, but they —"

"General Radulf, we mean you no harm," a Praetor in front said. He was both taller and younger than Radulf, with hair as curly as Crispus's, but as dark as night. His eyes were also dark and looked as if they'd been lined with soot. I recognized him from when Radulf and I had fought in the amphitheater. He was the man who had ordered Radulf to stop taking my magic. Though he might have saved my life then, I couldn't help but think as I looked at him that he regretted letting me walk away from the amphitheater as easily as I had. He had come here now to fix that mistake.

He said, "My name is Decimas Brutus, and I am a judge of the Roman Empire. We need to talk to that boy behind you, about crimes he has committed."

My shoulder flared again with pain, and I gasped and fell onto the steps, then clenched my teeth together in hopes Radulf wouldn't hear. Magic from the Divine Star was filling every vein of my body, begging to be released.

"I am the commanding general of all the armies throughout Rome," Radulf said. "If this boy committed any crimes, there is no one better than me to punish him."

Brutus came closer, his cold eyes on me. "Our new emperor, Florian, is still fighting in Gaul, but he has asked for an evaluation of the boy."

"If he wants to remain emperor, then Florian had better keep his distance from me, and my family," Radulf said.

"Is that a threat, General Radulf?"

"Yes, it is." Radulf didn't even flinch as he spoke. "Our last emperor, Tacitus, dismissed me too easily. I hope Florian will not do the same."

"Florian is your ruler!"

"We'll see about that." Radulf gestured to me. "Florian needs no evaluation of this boy. Neither do you."

"I disagree," Brutus said. "The empire must understand the extent of his powers, his ability to destroy Rome."

Radulf chuckled, whispering under his breath, "Or your ability to help *them* destroy Rome, eh, Nic?"

"I won't go with them," I whispered back. Radulf was a terrible person, and his intentions for Rome were just as bad as the Praetors', but at least I had some claim upon him as my grandfather. The Praetors would wring me inside out without a care for my life.

"What's in that bag?" Brutus asked, nodding at my waist. "A key, perhaps?"

"Sunshine," I told him. "And roses."

"Really?" Radulf scowled. "Must you anger them?"

Then he raised a hand and pushed it toward Brutus, who fell onto the stone steps. Instantly, every Praetor in the circus drew swords and spread out, encircling us. They blocked all of the exits, probably even in parts of the circus I could not see.

Brutus shouted, "Get the boy!"

"Horatio never gave me the key!" I shouted back. "I'm of no use to you!"

Brutus smiled. "Let us determine that."

Radulf twisted, repelling another Praetor who had come up behind us and gotten close. I felt the magic race through his Divine Star as it emptied. It seemed impossible that he didn't feel mine whenever I used magic.

"Don't let them touch me." Radulf sent magic toward yet another Praetor who was edging closer to us. "If they do, I can't protect you anymore. They'll take the key." I started to protest, and he looked at me long enough to say, "You have it, even if you don't know it."

He shot out more magic to keep the Praetors back, but I sank deeper into my thoughts. It was a partial attempt to distract myself from the pressure inside me, but I also had to ask myself if it was possible to hold the key to the Malice and not even know it. Had Horatio given me anything, even if it didn't look like a key? No, he never did, I was sure of it. But Crispus had been correct before — Horatio himself did say that he had given me the key. Why tell such a lie?

Radulf grabbed my arm and swung me behind him as he rotated yet again. His punches of magic were becoming fiercer, but the Praetors were also coming in faster. He couldn't get them all.

Suddenly, a dozen Praetors rushed at us, all at once. Radulf sent out enough magic to fell most of them, but the rest kept coming and more were hurrying toward us, some with their swords out.

I noticed a few small rocks scattered on the steps and picked them up. My aim was true and I hit a couple of men who were rushing up the steps toward us. What little good that did also distracted me from noticing the Praetors who had been above us in the stands. With Radulf focused on those directly in front of him, two men grabbed me by the arms. One put a knife to my throat while the other picked up my legs. I squirmed and tried to get a hand free enough to do magic. With the energy contained inside me, I knew I could drop these two men to the ground faster than hard rain.

But something had happened. The instant one Praetor's hand grabbed my wrist, the magic drained out of me. It was gone, all of it. I tried sending out anything I could, just as a test, but nothing was there.

"Nic!" Radulf turned around, but the man holding the

knife against my throat pressed it closer to my chin, and Radulf lowered his hand. I kicked with one leg and felt the knife cut. It wasn't terrible, but it did stop my squirming. The next cut might not be as lucky.

"You want something from me," I said. "So I know you won't kill me."

"We need that mark on your shoulder," the Praetor hissed as he slid the knife to my arm. "Not much else of you."

Then that same man suddenly howled in pain, dropping the knife and my hand that he'd been holding. I twisted around as he turned, revealing an arrow deep in his backside.

The Praetor holding my feet dropped them too, and I tumbled to the steps, landing hard on my side. That Praetor ran back down, clutching an arrow lodged in his arm.

I rolled to see Aurelia at the top of the steps with a bow in her hand and another arrow nocked. She nodded at me only momentarily, and then released the arrow toward a Praetor near Radulf.

At some point, the sack with the lead tablets in it must've been cut, and it had fallen down a couple of rows. I scrambled down to it and heard Radulf shout for me to get up to him instead. I would, in a moment.

With the Praetors at a distance, magic was starting to fill my body again, something I couldn't quite understand. But I had no time to contemplate it before Radulf was at my side.

"That sack doesn't matter as much as your life," he said.

Actually, this sack might save my life, but there was no time to argue. Instead, I mumbled, "There're still more Praetors."

"Try to breathe normally," he said. "This hurts a little."

And then with his hands on my shoulders, I was sucked into darkness, and the circus disappeared before my eyes.

❧ · FIVE · ❧

We returned to Radulf's home, built amongst the military camps in the northeastern part of the city. Far from nearly everything, except his soldiers.

Once I came back to myself, I immediately pulled away from Radulf's firm grip. I was still bleeding from where the Praetor had cut me, but he had no concern for that and only said, "Go to your room. I have work to do."

"No!" I shouted. My left arm stung from the vanishing, or reappearing, or whatever he had done, and magic still surged through me. In the past hour, I had seen my mother, and then Aurelia — with Crispus — and then I'd narrowly escaped capture by Brutus and his Praetors. The tumult of emotions within me sounded like anger.

"You will obey me, boy!"

"You almost got me killed just now. Valerius warned you they were coming, and your only response was that you welcomed the fight?"

"I want the Malice. If we have to fight a few Praetors along the way, then so be it!"

"I can't fight those Praetors for you, Radulf, nor will I. What difference does it make if they destroy Rome, or you do it?"

"Because," he hissed, "they don't care if you are still standing when this is all over."

With my body square to him, I shook my head. "And you do? I'm nothing but a tool for your treason!"

He smiled. "If I win, then I write the history books. We will write them, together."

I darkened my glare. "You won't win without me. And I won't have any part in your plans."

I turned on my heel and marched to my room, slamming the door shut behind me. I wished I had somewhere else to go. This wasn't really a bedroom. Before I'd come, Radulf had used it as a place to plan his military strategies, and it looked the part.

The frescoes on the wall were images of the goddess Minerva, just as fierce a warrior as her half sister, Diana. When he first brought me here, Radulf had described a ten-year war in which the giants had fought the gods. Minerva fell into battle with a dragon, an enormous serpent the Romans called a draco. As the serpent twisted around to kill Minerva, she threw the dragon into the northern skies, where it instantly froze. Painted on the ceiling was the draco coiled around the constellation, its forked tongue lashing out in anger. Looking up at it was hardly the most pleasant way to fall asleep each night.

I avoided that image now as I paced in my room, reviewing the dozen things I wished I had said to Radulf, and then kicked at the door, in case he had somehow missed my anger.

My eyes fell upon a wax tablet near my bed. After cleaning up my neck and changing into a new tunic, I sat with the tablet, attempting to concentrate enough to practice my writing. Radulf had me tutored every day in reading and writing, and I was working hard to become as educated as any other boy my age. It was a steep goal, but I was making tremendous progress. As frustrating as it could be to create words out of the shapes I scratched into the wax, the ability to learn had become as exhilarating as when I first took control of the bulla's magic, and perhaps for the same reason. Knowledge was raw power.

Soon after, Livia slipped into my room. Deep wrinkles lined her brow, evidence of her worries for me. Since we'd come to Radulf's home, I'd seen those worries increasingly often. "I heard you yelling," she said. "Even the gods in the heavens would've heard that."

I handed her the sack of lead tablets, as I had all the others I'd collected since I began racing. "There weren't as many as I hoped for," I said. "We ran into trouble, or I'd have gotten more."

"What happened at the circus?" she asked. "Everyone is asking questions, but *Pater* won't see anyone."

She still called him that, hoping if she treated him like a grandfather, he would stop treating us like prisoners. It was a foolish wish. I doubted whether Radulf felt any emotions at all other than greed and envy. Certainly there was no room for love of his grandchildren.

"We're leaving," I whispered. "Tonight."

Livia's eyes widened. "Why? Why now?"

There was so little I dared explain to her. Telling Livia I had seen our mother would give her false hope. Explaining anything about the Praetors would terrify her.

"Because we're out of time." I nodded at the curse tablets. "Do we have enough?"

"There's no way to know. But they'll have to do."

My door opened, and one of Radulf's pig-snouted servants filled the frame. "The general asks you to join him for a private supper."

There was little difference between Radulf asking me to do something and ordering it. All I could do was nod in reply.

"Your sister will eat alone tonight," the servant said.

All the better. She had an important job ahead. Livia nodded to the servant and said, "Please have some food brought to my room." She took the heavy curse tablets with her when she left.

With that, I followed the servant to Radulf's *tablinium*. This area was usually reserved for him to work, so when he brought me there to eat, I understood why: I was work for him, not family. This wasn't our first supper in private, though I had spent most of them refusing to say a word to him. Tonight was different.

We had no sooner been left alone when I asked him, "How did you make us disappear?"

"It's not complicated magic. I think of where I want to go, picture it as if I were already there, and then let go of my surroundings. It feels like jumping off a cliff at first, but you get used to it." Then Radulf drummed his fingers against the table while he looked me over. "It takes practice to master, but of course, without magic, that trick will be impossible for you. Won't it?"

The way he said it worried me. Did he know my magic had returned? If so, why didn't he say something? Surely he knew I would never volunteer such dangerous information.

Which also meant I couldn't ask the biggest question on my mind — why all of my magic had vanished when the Praetor grabbed me.

So instead I said, "Without magic, I'm no good to help you destroy Rome. There's no point in keeping me here."

Radulf smiled as if he knew something I didn't, then sat back to eat and invited me to do the same. I remained where I was.

I said, "Crispus told me that Diana is in rebellion against the other gods."

"Valerius told me the same thing. It's a secret the Praetors have guarded for three hundred years." Radulf grimaced. "For the sake of the gods, Nic, sit down and eat."

This time I did, and reached for some bread and dipped it in warm honey. Maybe I was a prisoner in Radulf's home, but I was a well-fed prisoner. If it wouldn't have made him suspicious, I'd have loaded my arms with every bite of food at this table, in preparation for Livia's and my escape.

Radulf continued, "Because he had descended from Venus, Emperor Julius Caesar was a favorite of the gods. Venus powered his bulla, which he used to achieve glory. With every victory of Caesar's, Venus also gained even more honor, and Diana became jealous. After all, Diana had descendents in Rome too, and they'd been given no special treatment. So when Caesar abandoned the bulla — his protection — Diana launched her war. She wanted Caesar dead."

"Caesar was stabbed to death by Marcus Brutus." I finished the bread and reached for fish now. "That Praetor who tried to take me from the circus was named Decimas Brutus."

"That's no coincidence." Radulf finished chewing his bread, then added, "Decimas is from the same family as Marcus, and Marcus comes from —"

"Diana," I breathed. "Marcus was her descendent."

"Decimas comes through the same family line." Radulf leaned forward. "Diana stole the Malice from the heavens and gave it to Marcus, who used it for the murder. Then Diana filled the bulla with her powers, expecting it would also fall into Marcus's hands. She poured into it her strength, her anger, and her jealousy."

I thought of the jealousy I had felt when seeing Crispus and Aurelia together earlier that day, or really, any time I had ever seen them together. It was one emotion of Diana's that I completely understood.

"Upon Caesar's death, a war erupted in the heavens, between those who favored Venus and those who felt Diana had been wronged." Radulf leaned forward and locked eyes with me. "The war followed to this earth, where the Praetors are still fighting Diana's battle. Nic, when Valerius spoke of the Praetor War, this is it. We are only pawns in the war of the gods. To lose means death, but to win —" Radulf's smug smile widened. "My boy, this is why I am keeping you here. Winning will make us gods as well."

⚜ · SIX · ⚜

I barely breathed as Radulf spoke. My mind couldn't absorb so much this quickly. "Then Diana's rebellion isn't over?" I whispered.

"It was," Radulf said. "As king of the gods, Jupiter stepped in to make peace between his children. Two amulets of the gods had been given to Rome, and he could not change that. So to appease Venus's followers, he placed Apollo's griffin in the cave to guard the bulla."

Caela. I had not seen her since I came to Radulf's home. I wondered if she was still in the empire or if she had returned to her master in the heavens.

"Then to appease Diana's followers, the Malice was hidden, and said to be guarded by a wolf, the sacred animal to Mars," Radulf said. "But the key to finding the Malice was given to the presiding magistrate of the Senate, so that only a person loyal to Rome could ever access it. We must find that hiding place first, before the Praetors get to it."

I shook my head. "Even if we had the key — and we don't — and even if we knew where the Malice is — and we don't — we'll never get past a wolf belonging to the gods. Without the bulla, I can't speak to animals anymore. You still can't."

Radulf threw down the bread in his hands. "The bulla doesn't work anymore. Perhaps Diana abandoned it too."

"It worked perfectly well for me." It was a taunt to him, and we both knew it. "Give the bulla back and I'll use it."

Radulf's laugh was false and mocking. "You were a slave when you stole it, a nothing. The bulla was never meant for you."

"Yet I could power it, and in your hands, it's useless."

"You've tricked me somehow."

I arched a brow. "A Roman general is tricked by a boy worth nothing? Is that how history will write about you?"

"Enough!" Radulf stood and called for his guards. When they arrived, he said, "Take my grandson to his room. He'll be there for the rest of the night."

No, I wouldn't.

They led me away, though by now I was so used to this routine that I only walked along beside them. I was allowed a few minutes to prepare for the night, then they brought me into my room. I sat on my bed and held up my left wrist, the one Aurelia had been so concerned about before.

A guard cuffed my wrist with a chain already attached to the bed. It was too tight — thus, the sores on my skin — and too thick for me to escape. At least, without magic.

For the first week that I was here, I had fought the guards each night until I finally began putting together a plan for escape. Radulf's doors were well guarded, with soldiers stationed at every exit. I also knew I couldn't leave without Livia, or without the bulla. And once I used magic to break free from this chain, Radulf would know it, so we needed a quick way out of Radulf's home. Finally, I was ready to put my plan into action, and I just hoped it wasn't an utter disaster.

I lay on the bed for several hours, wide awake and counting the minutes. Radulf had sent me to my room earlier than usual, so I'd had to wait through the long evening when he was still awake.

He was in his room, trying to make the bulla work again. I knew because I could feel him using his magic, and it only made me laugh. Even if he bounced on his head to make it work, it never would. And because I could feel that magic, I also had some idea of when he gave up and settled in for the night. I waited a long time after that, even after the entire household had quieted down. Because I was chained, Radulf never worried about posting guards at my door, and he never chained Livia or had her guarded. He figured she would never escape without me. Two great mistakes.

Finally, it was time to go, and I sat on my bed and laced up my sandals. I had spent every minute of my time here holding back the magic I felt in the Divine Star on my shoulder. Even now, I didn't dare use any more of it than was absolutely necessary, but it definitely wanted to release. I would have to be careful.

Once I was free, I didn't want any of the chain left binding my wrist. So I pressed my thumb down on the lock, wishing if I had any key at all, it would be this one. Then I closed my eyes and focused on the Divine Star.

Whenever I had used the magic from the bulla, it came through me like a flood, so much more than I could control. And most of the time, the bulla also overpowered any feeling from the Divine Star's magic, which wasn't quite as strong, and not nearly as difficult to control.

At my command, the magic flowed from my shoulders down my arms and into my hands. The bulla had always been warm, even hot, but the Divine Star was cool, like river water. When I felt it in my thumb, I twisted it against the lock, and as I had hoped, the lock turned too and the cuff snapped open. I was free.

Free of the lock, at least. I paused a moment to determine if Radulf had perceived my use of magic. On the rare occasions when I had used bits of it, he didn't seem to have noticed, and I had only used another bit of magic just now. But I had to be sure.

There was no response from Radulf — none of his voice crashing into my head as he used to do before I came to his home. Maybe that was the trick, to work so close to his own magic that he could not tell the difference between my magic and his.

I tiptoed to my door and inched it open. Still, it didn't sound as if anybody was awake, which seemed curious to me. As leader of all the armies in Rome, Radulf was noticeably absent from the battles the new emperor, Florian, was fighting in Gaul. Did he think there would be no consequences for that? That Florian would not have his revenge? Radulf's home was usually far more guarded than this.

Or maybe that wasn't necessary. Radulf had ordered the last emperor's death. If Florian was smart, he would celebrate being as far from Radulf as possible.

I was in the atrium now, grateful for the rain pouring into the pool and the sound of raindrops overhead. It would provide some cover for whatever noise I made.

Radulf's love of the dragon was everywhere here, in frescoes and statues, and even carved into the columns as serpents climbing the walls. They were Radulf's reminders to visitors that he remained a general of the empire. Whenever they rode into a battle, the military carried banners of the draco's head attached to wind socks. They helped the archers determine wind direction but also served as a reminder to the enemy that the gods were on our side. The carvings seemed to stare at me now, warning that they favored Radulf, not me. A fact I already understood perfectly well.

I crept toward Radulf's room. I had only been inside it once, when I snuck in to figure out where Radulf hid the bulla. Radulf had caught me there and my punishment for being in his room had been fierce. But it didn't matter. I had found his hiding place.

I opened Radulf's door as slowly as possible. I had no idea how deeply Radulf slept, but there was no reason for me to get close to him. One of the marble squares of his floor was loose, and he hid the bulla in a cavity beneath it.

I got to all fours and crawled there now, near the window of his room. Outside, the rain had begun falling heavier, which I appreciated as I gripped the edge of the marble and tilted it upward. It gave way without too much noise, but when I reached down for the bulla, I found nothing there. I looked inside, certain there must be a mistake, but no, it was empty.

And when I lowered the marble again, Radulf stirred. This time when he rolled, I saw the bulla, loosely clutched in his hand. The snake had gone to sleep with it!

I cursed under my breath, then crawled to the edge of Radulf's bed. It was made of ivory and gilded with gold insets and draped with golden cloth. If the gods slept, then I doubted it was in a bed as fine as Radulf's.

I wrapped my hand over the face of the bulla. The gold had gone cold now, which made me want it all the more, because I knew how to make it work again. The side of the bulla facing me had a griffin engraved on it. I thought again of Caela and how easy my escape would be if she were here now.

His sleeping hand easily released the bulla, but the chain was wrapped in the other. Careful not to make the slightest sound, I unwound it from his fingers, then crouched low to pull the last link free.

When I did, his hand curled over the chain, and the other hand reached out and grabbed my tunic at my neck.

"So," he snarled, his eyes fully open, "after all I've done for him, my grandson is still a thief."

 ·SEVEN ·

I put both hands on the bulla to prevent him from pulling it away from me, but did so at the expense of my neck, which he was choking in his clutch.

"You fool of a boy!" he said. "Did you think I couldn't sense your magic? In the circus today, when you nudged your horses to safety, and all the times before when you've used it. When you freed yourself just now."

Then I really was a fool, because of course he would know. He had been waiting all this time for me to try something just like this.

"Did you think I wouldn't guess you were coming here to steal my bulla?"

"*My* bulla!" I said through gasps for air. "I'm stealing it back!"

He tugged at the amulet, and I pulled harder at it, though his grip tightened around my neck until splotches of darkness filled my vision. I was going to faint. Which meant I was going to lose, and that made me furious.

"I brought you into my home," he said. "Fed you, clothed

you, gave you the horses for the chariot races. I gave you and your sister everything."

"Everything but freedom," I said. "Which is all I ever wanted."

And with that, I sent magic from the Divine Star toward him. It hit him in the chest, throwing him against the far wall. Both the bulla and my neck were free, so I turned and started running.

He threw a ball of magic at my heels, and I fell to the ground when it hit me but scrambled to my feet again to stumble into the atrium. Then I sent out more magic to collapse his doorway.

By then we had made enough noise that every guard in his house was running toward me. I shot out magic at anyone who got in my way, though I wasn't practiced enough with the Divine Star to do much more than trip them or cause a vase or marble bust to fall in their path.

Radulf's baths were at the far end of his home. His *tepidarium* wasn't nearly as nice as the one Valerius had, but I had practiced in it whenever possible to get better at swimming. For all those efforts, I was still a miserable swimmer, but at least I knew enough to keep myself from drowning.

Livia was waiting for me at the far end of the pool with two sacks in her hands. I knew how heavy they must be, so it had been no small thing for her to quietly drag them all the way in here. Her eyes were wide as she saw Radulf's guards on my heels.

"Jump in!" I yelled at her. "Livia, jump!"

She immediately dove in with one sack while I raced around the pool for the second one.

"Stop!" a guard yelled at me. "Or you will die."

I did stop, but only long enough to say, "I have no plans to die today."

Then I grabbed the second sack and dove with it into the water. The sacks were filled with the lead curse tablets that I had gathered from the circus, and with their combined weight, I sank like a rock to the bottom of the deep pool. Livia was already there, and I was sure she needed air soon.

I aimed the last of the magic in my shoulder toward the plug for the pool. Radulf had the water changed out every month, and I knew from watching it drain that Livia and I could fit through the pipe, if we had enough weight to carry us out.

Once the plug exploded from its place, the water began flowing. Livia was carried first through the pipe, and then I followed behind her. It was a tighter squeeze than I had expected, but I held the lead-filled sack ahead of me, which kept pulling me lower.

My lungs finally burst apart, and I had no choice but to swallow in water, which hurt like I was exploding from within. The pipe was longer than I had anticipated, or else we were moving slower. No, we really were moving slower. Maybe the pipe was narrowing, or the pressure of the water above was lessening, even with the leaden sacks. Or maybe there was a grate below that would trap us in the pipe. The water would eventually empty, but if we survived this, we'd be forced to climb back up through the pipe and into Radulf's home. I could only imagine what he would do to us then.

It was a grate. Livia landed on it first, and I landed on her. She was thrashing around below me, and my heart fell with a sense of my carelessness. Because even as my own life was fading, I knew hers must be fading also, and I felt terrible. I had done worse than fail to save her. I would be the cause of her death.

I wanted to send magic to open the grate, but for whatever it mattered now, I worried it might hit Livia. Besides that, I had exhausted my magic and all my energy on getting us this far. There was nothing left now.

Livia continued moving, up and down, almost angrily. Then as if there had been another explosion below us, the grate opened and we fell from it into the sewer water below.

I coughed on water as it emptied from my lungs, not caring about the sewage around me or the total darkness that we had entered.

Beside me, Livia put a hand on my back. "Not everything is done by magic."

So she had kicked the grate away. She had saved us, in a way my magic could never have done, and I nodded to thank her.

Ahead of us came a voice, and it brought a wide smile to my face.

"I should've expected that," Aurelia said, lighting a small torch in her hands. "Now I know why you wanted to meet here."

⚜·EIGHT·⚜

It took several minutes before I was strong enough to say more than a few words of welcome to Aurelia. She returned my gratitude by saying, "You both are going to smell horrid, and now I'll smell too. Honestly, Nic, I'm beginning to wonder what your attraction is to sewage."

"It's not what attracts me down here as much as what repels me up there," I said. Despite being covered in filth I didn't even want to think about, I felt only happiness for being here now. This was the second time the *Cloaca Maxima* had saved my life. And much more than the second time that Aurelia had come to save me.

I stood and helped Livia to her feet. She was obviously disgusted by the smells around us, but hid her revulsion as well as anyone could. When she faced Aurelia, I made the introductions.

"Your brother has told me so much about you," Aurelia said with a polite bow to Livia.

Livia bowed back. "And the same for you. From Nic's descriptions, I feel as if I already know you."

"He described me?" Aurelia glanced my way with a broad grin. I felt myself blushing and hoped it wasn't visible in the torchlight.

"This is a terrible place for such silly talk," I said. "Let's go."

Aurelia and Livia began walking, with me trailing them. "What did Nic say about me?" Aurelia asked.

"That you're loud and you ask too many questions," I replied before Livia could speak.

Livia giggled. "No, that wasn't it."

Then Aurelia giggled too, which left me thoroughly confused. What did giggling mean anyway? It sounded happy, but it certainly wasn't making me feel any better. Considering they had just met, what unspoken joke could they already have in common?

Oh. It was me.

Aurelia led us through the sewers as easily as if she were strolling a garden path. She knew the turns and the dangers and even the places where freshwater poured in, giving us a clean shower. Somehow, when I had been lost in here before, I had missed all of that.

After another mile, she pointed out a freshwater basin ahead that had gathered in last night's rainstorm. Livia went there and began cleaning herself again. While she did, I caught up to Aurelia. She had snuffed out her torch to conserve it for the night, but the moonlight still came in through the grate overhead. With that light, I could see her plenty well. She was in a shorter, plainer tunic than she'd worn in the circus and her brown hair fell loosely over her shoulders. This was the Aurelia I remembered. Over the last two months, I had thought about her constantly, though I'd never admit that. More important, I saw the crepundia around her neck, and I couldn't help but stare at it.

"Thank you for being here," I said. "We wouldn't have made it out otherwise."

"You're welcome." Her eyes darted to Livia and then back to me, more serious than usual. If there were things she wanted to say, I wondered if she wanted to do it privately and so I took Aurelia's arm and we went a little farther away.

Livia took the hint. "I'm tired, Nic. Is it all right if I rest for a while?"

Aurelia answered for me. "No one will search for us down here, so this is where we should sleep. We can get an early start in the morning and be out before anyone else is awake."

Then she and I sat together on a wide ledge above the water with our backs to Livia. In a hushed voice, Aurelia said, "Crispus wanted to come and help. He's worried about you."

"You told Crispus I'd be here?" I scowled. "Why?"

"I couldn't just disappear and leave him wondering where I was."

"Now Crispus will tell his father about me, and then his father will tell the Praetors. Are they planning to meet me here too?"

"I told *Crispus*, nobody else! You forget that he's done nothing to you. Your quarrel is with his father."

"My quarrel is with half the Roman Empire." I glared at her. "Maybe you too."

"You are so busy with building your list of enemies that you've forgotten you also need friends!"

"Friends like Crispus, and his father?"

"Yes, actually, you do need them. But not only them. I'm trying to help you, Nic. I owe you that much, but you're not making it easy."

My glare darkened. "You owe me nothing. And if you're doing this for Crispus and Valerius, I don't want their help."

"But you need it!" Then more quietly, she added, "They aren't the reason I'm here."

From the corner of my eye, I saw Livia roll away from us. Even if she had wanted to sleep, she'd hardly be able to. I knew she could hear us fighting.

I looked back at Aurelia and lowered my voice too. "Why did you come?"

She only sighed, as if the answer should have been obvious. Unfortunately, the only obvious thing to me was that I hadn't finished saying things I was sure to regret.

"Will Crispus approve of our friendship after you marry him?"

Her eyes widened. "Who said I was going to marry him?"

"It's the only way you can inherit your father's wealth. Clearly, you need Crispus's friendship too."

"We are friends, yes. But that's all."

Was that true? Maybe I had misread the situation between them, in which case I owed her an apology. "So you're not planning to marry him?" I asked.

She hesitated, not a good sign. "Things are . . . complicated. You're right about one thing: My father's will only grants me his inheritance if I am married."

"You'd marry someone just to keep your money?"

"It's not about the money, not directly anyway. Remember those children who were hiding here in the sewers with me? I used my father's money to buy their freedom, every one of them. And I'll use my last *denarius* to buy freedom for anyone else I can find. But if I lose the inheritance, then I'll have no way to help them anymore, or to even help myself."

The muscles in my face were tightening again. "Then marry Crispus. Use his last coin too."

"I don't want to marry Crispus! Not if I can marry someone else, someone I really care about." She shifted closer and touched my arm. "Give me another option. Please, Nic."

"Like what?"

Her eyes fell, unable to look at me. "Don't make me say it. Surely you must know what I want, why I came here to meet you."

My heart was pounding, but I had nothing to say. As confused as I was about her feelings, I certainly understood my own. I knew what I wanted to ask.

But who was I to offer her anything? I was nobody, with no future but running from half the Roman Empire, and with nothing in my possession but an empty bulla. She deserved better.

"Fine," she said to my silence. "Thanks for nothing." Then she removed the crepundia from her neck and held it out to me. "Why do you want this anyway?"

She was already angry, so I dreaded having to tell her now. I took the crepundia and opened the pouch in its center. I had worried that if Aurelia had opened it already, she would have recognized the real gems and sold them. But as soon as I saw them, I knew they were the ones I had put inside it before my fight in the arena. They glowed for me, while the mark on my shoulder caught the scent of magic nearby and sparked to life.

I opened the bulla as well and switched the gems with the crepundia. Immediately, power flowed into the bulla, with the same strength as I remembered from before. This was Diana's power, her magic, as she stood in rebellion against the gods. Understanding why she had powered this bulla made me more nervous than ever to hold it.

When I looked back at Aurelia, her mouth was pinched into a thin line. Anger was an inadequate description for the heat I felt coming from her.

"Tell me you didn't —"

"I couldn't let Radulf get the bulla's magic."

"So you left me with it? If the Praetors had sensed it — they've been there when I wore the crepundia!"

"They don't have magic, so they couldn't sense it. It was safer with you than if I'd kept it."

"Why didn't you warn me?"

I snorted. "When would I have done that? While I was battling Radulf with one hand and your father with my other — maybe I could've yelled out a warning that you were holding the real power of the gods?"

Her eyes narrowed. "You, and that magic in your hands. It's all you care about."

"That's not true!" Livia shouted. We turned, and she was standing behind us, hands on her hips. She stepped forward and addressed Aurelia. "If you knew how terrible Radulf is, what he'd do to Rome if he got hold of that bulla, then you would understand why Nic had to switch the gems. And Nic cares for me, and even for Crispus, though he won't admit that. He cares a lot for you too, Aurelia, so deeply that he doesn't even know the right words when he talks about you. Even if he won't say how he feels, I know he cares, and so do you."

There was silence for a moment, then Aurelia asked, "Is this true, Nic?"

I wanted to answer, to tell her that I had thought about her every single day while at Radulf's. That whenever I had practiced writing, or swimming, or racing in the circus, it was always in the hopes of making her think better of me. I wished she understood that I had waited to escape from Radulf's home until I'd had a chance to talk to her first and ask her to come with me.

But now that Aurelia was here, I didn't know how to say all that. The words that trickled through my mind sounded weak and ignorant. If I had Crispus's gift for speaking, then I could make her understand me better. As it was, I could only stand here, looking ridiculous and feeling even worse.

I kicked my sandal against the ground, but felt Aurelia take the bulla from my hands and place it over my neck. "You're a difficult friend," she whispered. "But always my friend."

The bulla's warmth immediately began to fill me, and only then did I realize how cold I had been since losing it. It would take a while to absorb the full effects of its magic, I supposed, though I was already stronger than before.

Now that she had moved closer to me, Aurelia touched my neck. "What are these bruises?"

I felt their tenderness with my fingers and shrugged. "Radulf wasn't happy about us leaving."

She smiled softly. "You do have a gift for making people angry. What will you do about the Praetors?"

I shook my head. "Nothing, for tonight. Maybe we should get some sleep and figure that out in the morning."

She lay down near me, using her arm for a cushion. I would've offered her mine, but so much magic was flowing through it already, I didn't think it was wise.

"Thank you for coming," I whispered.

At first, she didn't answer, and I was sure she must have already fallen asleep. Then she whispered back, "I will always come, Nic."

❧ · NINE · ❧

If I slept at all over the next few hours, then it was only for minutes at a time. The bulla's growing magic kept me restless, the smell of the sewers was nearly unbearable, and worst of all, I could not get Aurelia out of my mind. It was true that I had endured some difficult things in my life, but thinking about her while she was so close by was an entirely different kind of problem.

The earliest hints of light were in the air when Aurelia awoke. Not far away, Livia was still asleep, but she looked cold and I worried that she might not have slept well either. Before lying down, I should've checked to be sure she was all right — Livia rarely complained. I wanted to help her now. With the Divine Star, I could send a little warmth to her, but then Radulf would know and could find us. With the bulla, I'd do too much, probably send a fire through the tunnels and up through every toilet opening in the city. Hardly the way any Roman wants to start his day.

Aurelia rolled toward me and said, "I can see why you love her so much. Livia seems like a wonderful sister."

"She's better than I deserve."

Aurelia's smile was gentle and kind. "I can't argue with that."

"Forgive me for not warning you about the crepundia . . . about my trick with the gems." I hardly dared to continue looking at her, but I did anyway. She was only nodding and seemed to be in a good mood, so I added, "You were right last night, about almost everything."

"Not *almost* everything." Aurelia giggled a little when she said it, and I smiled too. There was quiet between us for a moment, and then Aurelia added, "I'm also right that you should trust Crispus. And his father too."

"They would've let me die in the amphitheater. How can I trust them again?"

She pressed her lips together, then said, "Two days ago, I was having dinner with Crispus when Decimas Brutus came to the home, asking for Valerius. They went into a private room, but Crispus and I crept to the door to listen. Brutus demanded to know where you were."

"And Valerius told him I'd be at the circus."

"Valerius told him nothing." Now Aurelia sat up on her arm. "You have no idea how furious Brutus was. He threatened Valerius in every possible way. He wanted to know where the Malice of Mars was hidden, telling him that as soon as they got control of you, they were going to make you open the door. Valerius tried to convince him that my father died with the key and that it was lost forever, but Brutus insisted Horatio would not have been so careless."

"Maybe he was," I said.

Aurelia shrugged. "Maybe." But she obviously didn't believe it. "When Brutus left, he said that if the key wasn't found soon, he would place the blame with Valerius. The very next day, Valerius went to the circus to see Radulf and warn him. He's risking a lot to protect you."

I nodded wordlessly. It felt like Aurelia wanted me to say something, but I wasn't sure what.

Finally, she said, "Valerius is right, Nic. You should leave Rome, as soon as possible."

"Livia and I might need help in leaving." I licked my lips. "Someone good with a bow and arrow, perhaps?"

Aurelia's smile fell. "That's what you want from me? A hunter? Or a guard?"

"A friend." My eyes met hers. "Livia and I don't have many friends at the moment."

"You're leaving today?"

"No, not yet." I looked over at Livia, making sure she was still asleep. "First, I have to find my mother."

Aurelia sat up all the way, so I did too. "Nic . . ."

"She's not far away. I saw her yesterday in the circus." Behind us, Livia gasped. I should have looked more carefully. This wasn't the way I had intended for her to find out.

"Why didn't you tell me?" Livia asked. "You speak about trust and wouldn't even trust me with that?"

"I'm sorry," I whispered. My second apology of the day, and no doubt, several more were coming.

"You need to forget about finding your mother," Aurelia said. "Please, believe me, and leave Rome."

Impossible. That was like asking me to forget my own name, which I'd sooner do than abandon my mother. "Why?"

She sighed. "There's something I need to tell you."

"About my mother?"

Aurelia only frowned. Yes, it was about my mother. And I already knew that it was bad.

✄ · TEN · ✄

Before talking any further, we agreed to go to the surface. If we waited too much longer, people would be on the streets and would surely notice us coming above ground. Besides, I didn't like the stuffiness down here, or the smell.

After a final washing, we climbed a ladder that took us into an area not far from the Pantheon. This temple was different from the others since its interior was rounded with an oculus on the top. When he took me there last month, Radulf had described the overhead opening as the eye of the gods. If that was true, then I refused to go inside now — I didn't want to guess at which of the gods was watching me.

So Aurelia, Livia, and I sat on some grasses nearby to dry off in the sunlight and watch the city awaken. The merchants arrived first with their wares. If I'd thought about it last night, I should've stolen some money when I stole back the bulla. Since I was committing one crime, a second wouldn't be so bad, or at least that's what I told myself when I stared at the merchants' food. But it was too late for that, so I let go of the thought and instead turned to Livia and Aurelia.

"Tell me about our mother," Livia said. "She can't be far from here."

"Why do you think she was in the circus?" Aurelia asked. "Of all places in Rome, and at the very time Nic was practicing?"

"Lots of patricians come to watch the chariots practice," Livia said. "It's how they plan their bets for the races."

"A million people live in Rome, but your mother was taken there for Nic's practice. Can you really believe that was only a coincidence?"

"Why else —" Then I understood, with a reality that felt like a hard blow to my chest. "The Praetors have her."

"Decimas Brutus began looking for your mother shortly after your battle in the arena. He found her a few days ago. You can guess why."

My mouth went dry. "To lure me to him. Brutus wanted me to see her in the circus."

"Once you ended the race so abruptly, they knew you had seen her and took her away," Aurelia said.

"Crispus knew about this yesterday," I said. "This was what he didn't want to tell me."

"He's worried that you'll decide to rescue her."

"He was right — that's exactly what I'll do." I glanced over at Livia, who nodded in agreement.

"Then I shouldn't have told you now." Aurelia sighed. "Listen to me, the Praetors want you, not her. If you leave Rome, there's no reason for them to keep your mother. Maybe they'll let her go."

"Or maybe they won't," I countered. "Brutus has no interest in mercy. Not for me, and not for her."

Aurelia leaned forward. "You can walk away this minute and never have to deal with the Praetors or Radulf or anyone ever again. I know what you went through to make Livia safe, and all you risked to get here now."

"Then you also know he would never leave our mother in the hands of the Praetors," Livia said.

"Your mother would agree with me!" Aurelia said. "Nic, if you stay here, think of how they want to use you. And what happens to Livia if they succeed?"

"What happens to Mother if we leave?" Livia turned to me. "I won't go without her. And I'm stronger than you think."

She said something else, but I didn't hear it. Instead, a familiar cold swept over me, one I had dreaded since stealing the bulla back.

"You can never run from me, Nic."

Radulf's voice entered my head, as unwelcome as leprosy. It had never been a question of whether he would find me, only how long until his icy presence returned.

I stood and looked around. With morning here, the street was filling with people, many of them women and children. "Everyone leave this area!" I shouted. "Now!" In case they hadn't heard me, I sent out darts of magic, hoping to frighten them enough to run. And for the most part, it worked. The panicked looks they threw back at me were familiar from when I'd caused all the destruction in the amphitheater.

Aurelia stood too, clearly alarmed. "Nic, what are you doing?"

I took Livia by the hand, and walked her closer to Aurelia. "Take care of each other, please. Get out of here, now."

Aurelia shook her head. "What's going on?"

"Radulf."

He appeared directly behind Livia, and immediately put an arm across her shoulders, holding her in place. I raised my hand toward him, already filled with so much magic that if I wasn't careful, I'd explode half of this street. I had forgotten how strong the bulla could be. Beside me, Aurelia had raised her bow at Radulf, but his attention was entirely upon me.

"Give me that bulla," Radulf ordered.

My eyes darted sideways at Aurelia. If she fired that arrow, he'd have to move to block it. Could I shoot something at him without hitting Livia?

"Let my sister go and we'll talk," I said.

"Go now," Livia said. "Pater won't hurt me."

"Do you believe that too, Nic?" Radulf swung his spare hand toward Aurelia, who was thrown backward on the street. Her bow and its arrows scattered around her. "I want the bulla."

I backed up and tried to make myself disappear, the way Radulf had done with me yesterday. Then I could reappear directly behind him and give myself the advantage. But I couldn't picture the street in my head when I was seeing it even more plainly with my eyes.

Radulf seemed to sense what I was doing. "You're relying too much on the bulla's magic," he said. "There's more power in the Divine Star, if you'll trust it."

It had taken me a long time to understand my grandfather. Why he would encourage me to develop the magic he had once stolen from me. Why he would advise me in my attempt to trick him. I still couldn't answer those questions, not really, but I did know this: The only thing Radulf cared about was getting the three amulets so that he could bring Rome to its knees and rule over its ashes. With the amulets, Radulf would make himself a god, and he needed me to do it.

I closed my eyes this time, focusing on the Divine Star and what I wanted to do. And perhaps I did start to fade, a little, but then Aurelia yelled my name, and at the same time, Livia screamed.

I looked, and men in Praetor robes had Radulf on the ground, one with a sword at his chest. They had come up so quietly, that from here I hadn't heard them. Apparently, neither had he.

"Livia, run!" I yelled.

And she did, toward Aurelia, who cried, "Nic, they're behind you too!"

I twisted around and shot magic toward a group of five men who had been sneaking toward me as slyly as they had overtaken Radulf. Where my magic hit, the ground beneath them collapsed, creating a wide gulf between us.

Still, there were others, surrounding us as they had done in the circus. I shot magic toward the men closest to Aurelia and Livia, throwing the Praetors back almost as far as the Pantheon. Despite the danger here, it felt good to use magic again, like I had been crippled and finally could walk again.

I ran to Aurelia and Livia, and said, "You two must go together. I'll find you when it's safe."

Livia shook her head. "Let's all leave together."

"I can't let them take Radulf." Even now, he was shouting curses at them as they bound his hands and feet in chains. "I can't let them win."

"After all he's done to you?" Aurelia asked. "He'd leave you behind if they got you first."

"No, he wouldn't." I was firm on that point.

"You are playing into their hands," Aurelia yelled. "With your mother, with Radulf. You are doing everything they want you to do!"

Which was probably true. But no other choice was acceptable.

Aurelia grabbed my hands and looked down at them as if she could feel the sizzle of magic inside me. When she met my eyes again, she asked, "Let's do what you want, Nic. Let's leave Rome, you and Livia." She swallowed hard. "And me."

I felt her words like a press on my heart, but only because I had to refuse her the very thing I most wanted. "Get Livia to safety," I mumbled. "I'll find you as soon as I can."

Then I lit a line of flame away from us, forcing everyone nearby to back away from it. The fire immediately burned out, leaving Livia and Aurelia a clear path to run from the area. Though where they would go next, I did not know.

I would find them soon. But first, I had a job to do.

❧ · ELEVEN · ❧

More Praetors were arriving now, some of them on horses and one with a wagon of iron bars. That's where they'd put Radulf, and perhaps where they planned to put me. Well, they'd never get me in there. Never.

I whispered to the horses carrying the Praetors and sent it through the morning breeze. Responding to my words, they bucked hard, throwing every man off his horse. The men landed on the stone road, confused at what had caused their animals' disloyalty.

"You all smell very bad!" I shouted to the Praetors. "Perhaps your horses couldn't take it anymore."

Next, I created a shield around me. It was effective, but exhausting, more tiring than I had remembered, and with my next step, I stumbled to my knees. In my short time without the bulla, I had lost most of my strength to use magic.

"Nicolas Calva, we don't wish to fight you."

I looked up and saw Decimas Brutus coming toward me. My hands curled into fists. Maybe he didn't want to fight, but I certainly did.

"Run, you fool!" Radulf yelled, then took a kick to his side for it.

I was nothing if not a fool. He was right about that.

"That girl who just left," Brutus said. "We know who she was before she got her father's fortune. She was a sewer rat, and if you don't cooperate, we'll make her one again."

"You know about sewer rats, then?" I grinned, and used magic to create a hole where the gulf in the road had been. The stench from the exposed sewer rose in the air like a fog.

Brutus stepped backward. "Don't you dare."

Not only did I dare, I was looking forward to it. One by one, I used magic to sweep the Praetors into the sewer, all except for Brutus. Though it was quickly sapping my strength, I held him at the edge of the hole, where he dangled in an uneasy balance. "Where's my mother?" I asked.

Now it was his turn to smile. "What we want is simple. Give us the key to the Malice of Mars and we'll set your mother free. Then you can both walk away and live as free citizens."

That was a lie. They needed me to unlock the Malice, and to use it and the bulla to create a Jupiter Stone. Then they would give it to Diana to succeed in her rebellion against the other gods. That was hardly a simple matter.

Brutus reached his hand toward me. "Give me the key, Nicolas. Give it to me now and be finished with us."

I did not have that cursed key, and my disgust at having to explain that for the hundredth time was punctuated with a blow

I sent in a wave of magic. His arms rolled in circles to keep from falling into the sewer gulf.

When he looked up, his eyes had darkened and his anger was so thick that it came at me like a punch to my gut. Still, I held my place and refused to flinch before him.

"You have no right to hold magic!" he screamed. "How dare a slave boy wield the power of the gods!"

"I wield it against the enemies of Rome," I yelled. "Against you!"

He chuckled. "Listen carefully. You have exactly one day to turn over the key to the Malice or you will never see your mother again. And once I'm finished with her, I'll go after your sister, and then that sewer girl, and then anyone else I must destroy until you cooperate with me. In the end, I will win."

"Impossible," I said. "Because I intend to win this war, and I do not share my victories with cowards."

He smiled. "I will have you on your knees before the week is out. You will beg me to spare the lives of those you love."

Then he widened his arms and took a step backward, willingly letting himself fall into the sewer water. Which should have meant he had lost our fight, but somehow, I felt as if I was the one who had lost.

A hand gripped my shoulder, and I swung around, raising my hands to confront the next Praetor. Magic flew to the tips of my fingers, and once I recognized who had grabbed me, it was all I could do to keep the magic inside.

"It's over!" Radulf released me and backed up to show he was posing no threat. The chains that had bound him lay on the ground where he had been, but they were split apart like they'd been made of dried reeds. His magic had returned.

He started to approach me again, but I backed away from him too. "Lower your hands," he said. "I'm not your enemy."

"Aren't you?" Still angry with Brutus and anxious for my mother, I needed to empty the magic inside me and wanted nothing more than to use him for target practice.

"The problems you face are of your own creation," he said. "Not mine!"

"I never wanted this!" I yelled. "None of it!"

"Maybe you did." His tone was as sharp as the edge of a knife and felt like cuts across my chest. "I warned you not to wear the bulla in Caesar's cave, but you stole it and called it yours. You stood between me and Horatio to take a key that I would've gotten from him on my own. Every time I tried to keep you out of this war, you put yourself at the center of it."

"You *want* me at the center of this war!" Magic swirled inside my head. It was hard to think straight.

"I could've killed you in that arena, but I didn't. I could've let the emperor's guards arrest you afterward, but I refused to let him have you. I've kept you alive, Nic!"

"Only until you force me to make a Jupiter Stone, which will probably kill me!"

Surprisingly, his anger cooled. With a chuckle, he said, "Yes, I suppose that's true. It is risky to make a Jupiter Stone, but doing so is no more dangerous than facing the Praetors. So let's agree that if I'm an enemy to you, the Praetors are worse. You need me."

I swerved on my heel to march away from him. "I need you like I need to break out in boils."

He crossed in front of me. "Boils? Is that the worst thing you can think of? Then you don't understand the Praetors, or what they will do to your mother if you fail to bring them the key tomorrow."

"I don't have —"

"I know what you think about the key." He sighed and folded his arms. "Why didn't you run when the Praetors came? You didn't stay here to save me."

"Of course not," I said, though maybe I did. Nothing made sense anymore.

Radulf stared back at me, his eyes blinking far too fast. I scratched my cheek and finally looked away.

Radulf said, "I will help you save your mother. I owe you that, in gratitude for saving me just now. Are you all right?"

I was so tired that I barely understood his question. The swell of magic within me was calming, but I knew it would take a while until I could fight again. I only hoped he couldn't figure that out.

"Why did you need me to save you back there?" My brows creased together. "Why didn't you use magic to stop them yourself?"

Suddenly, I realized that we had begun walking back to his home. Still, I wanted his answer, so I continued to follow him.

"The Praetors have no magic of their own," Radulf said. "But they do have a way to stop us. Did you ever wonder why Marcus Brutus was able to kill Julius Caesar so easily? Shouldn't Caesar have had enough magic to defend himself?"

I shrugged. It had never occurred to me to wonder that, but it was a good question.

Radulf answered for me. "It's because the Praetors can disable magic just through their touch. The armbands they wear endow them with that power. Three hundred years ago, when Brutus killed Caesar, he grabbed him first, rendering the emperor unable to use any magic. After that, it was a simple thing to kill him. The Praetors would've killed me just now if you had not stopped them. By the time I realized they were behind me, it was too late."

"I felt the same thing yesterday," I said. "When they grabbed me in the circus, all the magic within me vanished." A quick glance at Radulf's smirk reminded me that he had known all along I still had some magic. Quickly, I continued, "It took a few seconds after they let go before I could feel it again."

"We are stronger than the Praetors," Radulf said. "But they have far greater numbers. If they get hands on both of us at the same time, we are finished."

ᴥ· TWELVE ·ᴥ

Two dracos were carved into the doorway of Radulf's house, intertwined as if in battle with each other. I took it as a warning against reentering.

Only yesterday, this home had been my prison, and just because I held the bulla didn't mean anything had changed between my grandfather and me. He'd stolen the bulla from me once, and I wouldn't be able to trick him a second time.

He knew all this, so he shouldn't have looked so surprised when I stopped on the road in front of his house, refusing to go any farther.

"Don't be a fool," he said. "Do you really believe you're safer out here?"

"I'm safer from you. And your house won't protect me from the Praetors."

"My home is well guarded — you know that as well as anyone. My guards will kill any Praetor who tries to enter, but here on the streets" — Radulf grinned — "much as I might want to, a hero of the Roman Empire can hardly go about shooting arrows at people just for walking past his home. It's unfriendly."

He missed the idea that once I was inside, he could more easily order his guards to shoot arrows at me. The bulla was mine again, and I knew that infuriated Radulf. If he saw even the smallest opportunity to steal it back, he'd take it. I knew that, because I'd fight just as hard to keep it.

I stepped back a few paces and shook my head at his invitation to enter. Valerius and Crispus had already betrayed me once, and obviously I could not trust the Praetors. But that didn't mean I had to trust Radulf.

My hand was on the bulla with my forefinger brushing over the griffin's image molded into the gold. If Caela were here, so many things would be easier. We could fly over Rome and search for my mother that way. I wouldn't have to worry about the Praetors getting too close. With Caela, it would be an easy thing to escape them. I thought about calling for her, just to see if she would answer.

"The griffin won't come," Radulf said, as if he had heard my thoughts. "Her task was to guard the bulla, but now that it's over, she's returned to the gods."

"My griffin would come if I called." Actually, I had no idea whether that was true, but I liked to say it.

"She was never yours," Radulf said. "It's arrogant to believe that an animal of the gods could ever belong to a human."

"Then I was hers!" I shouted. Radulf had never loved anyone or anything. He'd never understand. "If she were here, I wouldn't be within a mile of you right now!"

"But she's not here! No one is here to help you, except for me." Radulf reached for my shoulder, though I shook my head and pulled away when he did. "You must stop wishing that things were different than they are. Like it or not, you are a part of the Praetor War. The Praetors will never stop hunting you until they wring the key to the Malice from your fist. Or until you're dead." He drew in a slow breath. "And whether you like it or not, the truth is that I am your only chance of stopping them. Come inside, Nic, please."

"Let's talk about it now, right here."

He leaned in. "If you intend to defy the Praetors, then you need to know everything about the Malice. And about the Mistress who guards it for the gods. Do you want to learn these things from me, or from Decimas Brutus?"

"Who is the Mistress?"

He glanced around the street. "You cannot possibly expect me to discuss that out here."

My hand tightened around the bulla. "You'll steal this, take my magic again." I still cringed to think of when he had done it before.

"What I did is nothing compared to what the Praetors will do to get that key." Radulf smiled. "Besides, it appears that I'd have to kill you to take your magic entirely, and as you know, I need you alive to create the Jupiter Stone." He sighed, losing patience with me. "I give you my solemn vow. You may keep the bulla, for now. For some reason, I can't operate it anyway, and if the Praetors return, at least one of us should be able to destroy something with it."

"I don't have the key to the Malice."

"So you've said, probably a thousand times today alone. Stubborn boy, can't you see I'm trying to help you?" When I didn't respond, he said, "I have a gift for you in there, something I wasn't going to show you until the chariot races for the Ludi Romani next week. If you miss your griffin, you'll want to see this."

That tempted me, enough to finally give in and follow him inside. I knew there were several areas I had not been allowed to explore, so it was hardly a surprise that he might have secrets here.

We went through the atrium into his baths. I smiled when I saw how torn apart they were. Destroyed, really. Except for a few inches at the very bottom of the pool, the water was entirely drained out, and the concrete was missing large chunks. It was obvious where those chunks had flown up out of the water and crashed against his walls. Repairing this room would require almost an entire rebuilding.

"What happened here?" I didn't even attempt to sound innocent.

He laughed. "My grandson hasn't learned the proper use of a door apparently."

Even I had to laugh along with him, partially out of relief that I would not be punished for what I'd done. Looking at the destruction, I definitely deserved it.

But Radulf only led me past the baths to a door I'd wondered about every time I'd been in here. He gave a quick knock, two short raps followed by a pause, and then a third knock. Then the door was unlocked on the inside and opened by a small, hunched man who was dressed as a gardener.

He eyed me suspiciously and said to Radulf. "Callistus is for *him*? Are you sure?"

I tried not to take offense. After all, despite having washed before leaving the sewers, I probably still carried too much of its odor. And I'd just fought off several Praetors, which couldn't have improved my smell. *Callistus* meant "most beautiful." Whatever it was, I'd probably melt its nostrils. I was almost melting my own.

Radulf nodded, and we were allowed to pass through the narrow corridor into a fenced courtyard. I heard the snort of a horse and the glimpse of a white tail, which didn't surprise me. Radulf had already told me this was for the chariot races, so I figured he must have a powerful horse in his possession.

But it wasn't that. Not exactly anyway.

Radulf had a unicorn.

❧ · THIRTEEN · ❧

I felt myself walking forward, drawn to the animal as if from his will rather than my own.

"How is this possible?" I mumbled.

Radulf put his hand on my shoulder, pressing against the Divine Star that was there. I flinched when it sparked, and moved away from him.

"Do you remember how I got magic?" he asked me. "My Divine Star?"

Magic had to come from a creature of the gods, and the memory of how he had acquired his returned to me like a kick to my gut.

"It was given to you accidentally, as you killed a unicorn."

"The unicorn was a mother, and this was her colt. I named him Callistus." Radulf's voice bore no hint of sorrow or regret for what he'd done, which sickened me. "For obvious reasons, he won't allow me anywhere near him, and only my oldest servant can feed and water him." With his hand, Radulf pressed me forward. "But I suspect Callistus will like you."

The unicorn had his eye on me as warily as I was watching him. His fur and mane were as white as clouds, his eyes like the blue heavens from which he had come. But most notable was the spiral horn on his forehead, as golden as the bulla.

Since Radulf had trained me in chariot racing, I'd become comfortable with horses, but I still wasn't sure what to expect from a unicorn. He pawed at the ground a few times and arched his head, and then stared directly at the bulla, hidden again beneath my tunic. He knew it was there.

I withdrew the bulla, and this time felt its power with more intensity than usual. Of course I would, in the presence of such a magnificent animal. And Radulf killed his mother. I glared back at him, wanting him to feel the force of my anger for his crime.

But Radulf was past feeling anything. He only pointed to a leather saddle hanging over the fence. "This was made for Callistus. With the finest materials the empire can produce. Callistus is yours now, Nic."

No, this unicorn wasn't his to give. Callistus was a prisoner here, as I had been. Or maybe as I still was.

I reached out a hand, touching Callistus along the side of his neck first, and then slowly moving up to his head. I didn't dare touch his horn, but I sensed powerful magic in it, something I felt both in my shoulder and in the warming bulla. After a moment, Callistus nudged toward me, much as Caela used to do. I looked into his deep blue eyes and felt swallowed up in them.

Callistus truly was the most beautiful creature I'd ever seen, just as Radulf's name for him suggested. But even more, he was pure, like the fresh-fallen snow described to me by men who came here from the far north. And here I was, filthy from the sewers. I was a thief, a runaway slave, and a potential rival of the gods, his true masters. I was unworthy to ride him.

I withdrew my hand and turned to face Radulf again. "I cannot accept this gift," I said. "Callistus should not be owned, or made to serve anyone. Not me, and certainly not you."

"Callistus might save your life. His horn can heal the worst of injuries."

"The Divine Star can heal."

"At great cost. It nearly killed you to save the griffin. The Divine Star may not be enough for what the Praetors will attempt when they find you." Radulf put a hand on my shoulder again and steered me out of the courtyard. "But if you won't accept the gift, then let's get some servants to clean you up. After that, we'll eat. I'm sure you're hungry."

He was right about that, and after I'd been scrubbed down by at least five of his servants, I hurried into the dining room to eat. Radulf was reclined on his couch, waiting for me, but I was halfway through a bunch of grapes before he'd even reached for his first bite. Rather than eat anything, he sat up and studied me.

Finally, I stopped eating and looked over at him. "You obviously have something to say."

"I know what Brutus told you. By tomorrow, you have to give him the key or else they'll kill your mother."

With that reminder, I lost my appetite completely. "I don't have the key, I swear it upon the gods."

"What if the key is something that can't be held? Like a code?"

"I've considered that," I said. "But there was nothing like a code when Horatio spoke to me. Never."

"Well then, your mother has a big problem."

"You said you'd help me rescue her," I reminded him. "That's the only reason I came back here."

"And I will," Radulf said. "But since you don't have the key, to get her back we'll have to trick the Praetors."

"This is my mother. There will be no tricks and no games."

"Tricks and games are all we have left. You must trust me, Nic."

Which might be a problem since *my* plan had always been to trust nothing from him. Cautiously, I said, "What are you thinking?"

"First, you must leave the bulla safe here with me."

I snorted. "You've got to be joking." That was like leaving fresh meat in the safekeeping of a lion.

"If they capture you, then they capture the bulla, and everything you can do with it."

"And if I give you the bulla, then I know everything you'll do with it."

"Listen to me —"

"What about my mother?"

He sighed, then reached down and opened a box that had been near his feet. "The magic of the first amulet is stored inside a bulla, as common as any Roman boy would wear. The Malice of Mars is just as simple."

He pulled out an armband, similar to those worn by the gladiators in the amphitheater, except made of silver rather than the more common leather or bronze. Indeed, several of the statues of Mars in this city showed him with armbands very similar to what Radulf was now holding. Images of Mars holding his spear were carved onto the band, though most prominent was the head of a wolf.

"This is not the actual Malice," I said.

"No, but Valerius gave this to me yesterday. He had it made as an exact model of what he believes the Malice will look like."

"There's no magic in it. The Praetors will know this is a trick."

"The Praetors cannot sense magic, so they can be convinced. Besides, we don't need to trick them for long. Just until we get the real Malice of Mars on our own."

"We can't get it without the key."

"We should try! But in the meantime, we can use this trick to bargain for your mother."

I stood, feeling my temper rise. "We cannot risk my mother's safety."

"The Malice is worth the risk! It contains powers you cannot imagine!"

"Then perhaps I should've bargained for your life this morning. Would you risk yourself?"

Radulf shook his head. "I already did, outside the Pantheon."

"No, I risked myself, to save you."

Radulf opened his mouth to speak, then closed it. After a moment, he whispered, "Yes, you did. Why, Nic?"

My eyes darted sideways, and I unclenched my fists. There was no answer to his question. I only said, "I already lost my father. I might need your help to save my mother."

"You lost your father — my son — *because* of her! He was too hasty in believing he could create a Jupiter Stone, but he attempted it in trying to save her. We can succeed where your father failed."

"You're wrong. I saw the lightning bolt that killed him. We can never win against it. And I was wrong to have come here."

I stormed from the room and headed toward the baths. Using the bulla, it was nothing to open the locked door to the courtyard, which flew apart at its hinges. Callistus was standing in the center of the courtyard as if he had been waiting for me.

Radulf ran in behind me. "You'll never save her on your own. And worse still, you'll let them destroy you too."

I grabbed the saddle from the fence post and set it on Callistus's back, then whispered my apologies for asking such a humble task of him. In response, he arched his head and angled toward me, making my job easier.

Radulf stepped closer. "I am the only one who can help you."

"You've already helped me too much," I said, climbing into the saddle. "And my greatest hope is that you never help me again."

With that, I released enough magic from my hand to break open a hole in Radulf's courtyard. As usual, the bulla's overflowing power collapsed most of the wall and leveled several trees in my path. I gave Callistus a brief pat on his neck, and then we rode away.

Radulf released a flare of magic as I left, lighting a tree in his courtyard on fire. I wasn't sure if that came from his anger or his frustration at not being able to control me. And I really didn't care.

❧ · FOURTEEN · ❧

Chariot racing had taught me better control of horses than I might have otherwise learned in a lifetime, but I quickly discovered that Callistus needed none of that training. I didn't have to speak to him, as I did with Caela. He knew my thoughts, and understood instinctively that I needed his help to find Aurelia and Livia again. And after that . . . well, I didn't know what.

Aurelia always had everything fully thought out before the first breath of an idea had ever entered my mind. So I already knew that she would find a safe place to hide Livia. But though I had a good idea of where she wasn't, I still had no idea of where she would be. Would they return to the sewers? I hoped not, because I couldn't find my way through them and didn't like the idea of going there yet again. My present goal was to limit my sewer visits to no more than once a month.

Aurelia probably had a thousand places to hide in Rome, which was a good thing for both her and Livia. If I didn't give the Praetors a key tomorrow, my mother would pay the price for it. Livia was next on their list. Aurelia would follow.

As I considered my options, it bothered me to realize that there had been some wisdom in Radulf's plans. Without a key to give the Praetors, there really was no choice but to trick them. I closed my eyes, trying to imagine what I could come up with by tomorrow. The Praetors were no fools.

But I certainly was, a truth I felt running through every vein of my body.

Was it possible that Callistus knew about the key to the Malice? There was no reason he should, but if the key had come from the gods, and so had this unicorn, then maybe he knew something. But when I asked, Callistus only snorted, which I took as a sign that I was still on my own.

The biggest problem I faced was in convincing everyone that I didn't have the key. If they knew the despicable way Horatio had treated me every time we were together, they would understand why he never would have chosen to give it to me. The only thing Horatio had ever given me was a handful of insults and a nasty sword wound from his soldiers. Even after I tried to warn him that Valerius wanted him dead, Horatio went into the arena anyway. Despite my best efforts, Valerius succeeded with his plan. If Horatio gave away the key before he died, it wasn't to me.

Then why did he announce in the arena that he had?

Shortly before he sent me into the arena, Horatio told me he had the key with him at all times. We'd exchanged a few more words before he actually sent me into the arena, but that was all, just meaningless words. No codes, no cipher, and certainly nothing I'd consider a key. Up through the moment he entered the arena, Horatio planned to give the key to Radulf, right after my death. But much to his frustration, I had lived, so I doubted Radulf ever received the key either.

No, what Horatio had announced in the arena was that he had given me the key, *and* kept it for himself. What did that mean?

I became so absorbed in thinking about Horatio and the key that the clatter of Callistus's hooves against the paved stone road had become background noise. When it quieted, I realized we had left the road and were now far from Radulf's home. Callistus had us outside the center of Rome, in an area that might not have been familiar to most people, but I knew it well. Callistus was bringing me to Valerius's villa.

I didn't want to go there, which surely Callistus already knew, and yet despite my attempt to prod him back to the road, he was intent in his course. Then it occurred to me why. If anyone in Rome knew where Aurelia might have gone, it was Crispus.

That thought dug into me like a knife. For all I knew, Aurelia was staying here in his home. It wouldn't be frowned upon for her to have her own room here . . . if she were viewed as his future wife.

But Aurelia didn't seem to want that any more than I did. She said she would leave Rome with me. Maybe they were only words to get me to leave the fight with the Praetors. But maybe not.

The only thing I was certain of was that Crispus did not deserve her.

For that matter, neither did I. Yet she had eaten dinner with him, and had come to the circus with *him*.

Callistus suddenly reared up, and I realized I had wound his reins so tightly around my fingers that they were pulling against him. Why was I so angry? It was jealousy obviously. The jealousy Diana felt toward Venus was flowing through the bulla and into me.

Either that, or Diana had nothing to do with this. Maybe the beat of my heart whenever I saw Aurelia had nothing to do with magic.

I whispered an apology to Callistus, who began running again, and in only minutes, we were at the property at the rear of Valerius's home, a place I had not been for the past two months. I saw his villa in the distance, already lit from within. If Aurelia was in there, I wanted to find her at once. Or alternately, never have to see her again, where I'd be forced to face my own stupidity. I wasn't sure which was worse.

At least here in Valerius's fields, I could hide amongst his many rows of vines, which were thick with ripening grapes. In another few weeks, I'd have filled my belly with them, but for now, I had to be content with inhaling their delicious scent.

Valerius had a vast amount of property. Most of it was these thick vineyards at the far end, but off to one side was a wooded area on a hill, and nearer the villa was an empty field. That was where I had first experimented with controlling my magic. Back when Crispus and his father had seemed like friends to me. And when I had been naïve enough to believe there was an easy way to gain my freedom from the empire.

While we were still on the outskirts of the field, I asked Callistus to halt. A sound had caught my attention; I could've sworn I'd heard something. Quiet as a breeze, but deeply disturbing.

A woman was crying. Not in sobs, but in sharp breaths as if she'd been crying for a long time. I put my hands over my ears, testing whether I could still hear, but that only made it louder. Sure enough, this was happening inside my head. No one else would be able to hear it.

I gently slid off the unicorn's back. "Wait here," I told him. "Don't let yourself be found by anyone but me."

Then I started to walk away, but hesitated midstep and removed the bulla from my neck. Radulf was also right about that part of his plan. If the Praetors found me, I couldn't risk them getting the bulla too. I knotted it to a dangling cord on Callistus's saddle and then tucked the amulet beneath the saddle. Even if someone found Callistus, they would never notice the bulla, and Callistus wouldn't let anyone come near him anyway.

Night was approaching, but enough light still remained to see my way through the fields. As I followed the sound of the crying, it grew louder, so I knew I was getting closer. I didn't dare call out to the woman — if this was a trap, the last thing I wanted was to announce myself. I could hear her better now, and the desperation of her tears worked its way deeper inside me and weighed me down. It was the saddest thing I'd ever heard, as if the woman had lost everything she loved.

My mother might have shed tears like that, perhaps when we watched my father die, or when she was sold away from Livia and me. She would cry the same way tomorrow if I didn't come up with a way to save her.

So maybe that was it, then, what I was hearing.

What if these were the cries of my mother?

ᛘ· FIFTEEN ·ᛊ

I f my mother was so close, then suddenly, finding Aurelia was no longer the most important reason for being here. I ducked low behind the last row of vines, surveying the open field. The tree I had accidentally toppled two months ago was gone, though a few innocent sticks from its massive branches still remained. There was also the same pile of rubble a little farther on. If Valerius had his servants carry away the broken tree, it surprised me that he would allow the rubble to remain. Maybe that was related to the Roman worship of the gods. If their temples were sacred, perhaps the rubble from their temples was equally sacred.

The crying started again in my head, a little louder now, and I scanned the area, confused as to why I couldn't see who it was coming from. Nor could I find a spot where someone might be hiding. I crept forward to get a better look around, which led me right into the center of the open field, a virtual trumpeting of my presence if anyone was watching. But having to listen to so much sadness was twisting my insides and boring deeper into my mind. Knowing it might be coming from my mother only made it worse.

The problem was that now, no matter what direction I went, the sound became softer. How was that possible? Nothing was here. No one.

I walked over to the rubble, which was really just a pile of fallen stones. A column lay on its side; if a second column had ever been here, it was gone now. There was certainly no place for anyone to hide.

Then why did it seem as if the cries were coming from this exact place?

A new sound replaced the sobbing now, this one a low growl to my right. I turned and caught my breath in my throat. Facing me was a large black wolf with yellow, glowing eyes. It was crouched low, and the fur stood high on its arched back. Probably not a sign he wanted us to be friends.

If I still had the bulla, I could speak to him, maybe convince him to bare less of his sharp teeth. But the bulla remained with Callistus. Crispus had once told me a wolf lived on this property. I should have remembered that and been more cautious now. I still had the Divine Star's magic, which I could use if necessary, but I didn't want to, not if it risked harming him. I was an intruder on this wolf's territory, not the other way around.

So I lowered my eyes, showing the wolf I was no threat to him, and slowly backed away. The wolf continued to growl, though he didn't follow me.

"Nic?"

Lights were hurrying down the hill from Valerius's villa. A moment later, Valerius stepped into the field, holding a torch. He was the one who had spoken. Crispus stood directly beside him with another torch. I turned back to where the wolf had been, but he was gone.

"What are you doing out here?" Crispus asked.

I didn't know how to answer. It felt stupid to ask about Aurelia, and even stupider to suggest that a unicorn had brought me here on his own.

"Whatever your reasons, you need to leave," Valerius said. "The Praetors watch this land very carefully."

"Is it because of the crying woman?" I asked. "Is she my mother?"

"You hear someone crying?" Crispus looked over to his father. "He hears the Mistress."

"Who?" I remembered that Radulf had mentioned the Mistress too. But I had left his home before he'd had the chance to tell me about her. Based on the tight expression on both Crispus's and Valerius's faces, perhaps I should've been more willing to listen.

Valerius immediately doused his torch and ordered Crispus to do the same. Then he grabbed my arm and shoved me forward until we were in the vines.

"You have the key to the Malice," Valerius said to me.

"I don't!"

"Lower your voice." Nervously, he looked around the field. "Come back to my home. It's safer there."

I snorted. "Not for me."

"It'd be safer to throw you overboard a ship than to leave you in that field." He nodded at Crispus. "Lead the way, but keep your head down."

I followed, more out of a curiosity to learn about the Mistress than anything else. We walked in darkness and in total silence back to his villa. The crying woman — the Mistress — continued to wail, so loud that I didn't understand how Crispus and Valerius couldn't hear it too. The cries had been joined by a kind of pounding sound, like fists beating on a door. It was hard to think straight with her desperation filling my head.

I stopped and put a hand to my forehead. It was as if she had begun pounding there.

Valerius touched my arm. "She's asleep, Nic."

"She's not."

"Keep walking. Soon we'll be out of her reach."

By the time we approached his villa, I couldn't hear the woman anymore. Yet while Valerius immediately called for servants to bring us food and drink, I remained restless. Even if Valerius was right and she was asleep, I didn't see how we could dine here and relax while she obviously needed help.

"We can explain everything," Crispus told me. "My father will answer your questions. Come in to eat."

"I'm not hungry." That wasn't entirely true — I was always hungry. What I should've said was that at the moment, I wasn't starving.

"But it's private in there," Valerius said. "Come in."

I followed them to a small dining room where servants were busy setting food onto his table. I took the same seat where I used to eat when I had stayed here. Aurelia had always sat right beside me. I wondered again where she and Livia had gone.

The door had barely shut behind us when Valerius began to speak. "Listen to me and answer as honestly as you can. When you were in my fields two months ago, you heard nothing, correct?"

"She wasn't there before."

"Nothing has changed in that field. But *you* have changed, Nic. The only way you could hear the Mistress is if you had the key. Think of everything Horatio gave to you —"

"Nothing, I swear it!"

"— or said to you. Even if it didn't seem significant at the time. An unusual choice of words perhaps."

There was something. It had nagged at my memory ever since riding here with Callistus. But whatever Horatio had said was out of my reach now. In the last few minutes when we stood together beneath the amphitheater, he did speak to me briefly, but I had been far more focused on entering the arena to fight Radulf. Listening to Horatio had never been my priority, though obviously, that was a mistake.

"Father, Nic needs to know about the Mistress," Crispus whispered.

Valerius looked at me. "Can you hear her, right now?"

"No. It was only in the field."

"What you heard is just an echo, a memory locked in the Mistress's dreams."

"Who is the Mistress?"

"She was a *vestalis*," Crispus said. "A sacred woman, like the woman who allowed you and Aurelia to take sanctuary in Caesar's temple. But the vestalis you hear right now is named Atroxia, and she lived three hundred years ago, in Caesar's time. Atroxia joined the Praetors in Diana's war against the gods. She supported Caesar's assassination."

"Atroxia had to be punished for her crimes," Valerius said. "No one in Rome receives honors like a vestalis. Which means, when necessary, no one receives their punishments either."

Based on the cries in my head, I already knew what the punishment must have been, but asked anyway, hoping I was wrong. "What happened to her?"

"Atroxia was buried alive, and she was buried with the Malice of Mars, according to Jupiter's plans for peace amongst the gods. The Praetors believe in exchange for Atroxia's service, that Diana put her to sleep, not to awaken until her tomb is opened." Valerius met my eyes to be sure I was listening. "That cannot happen, Nic. She cannot be awakened."

"Why not?"

"Because in order to keep her alive all this time, Diana had to curse her. Whatever she is now, Atroxia is no humble vestalis. She is the Mistress of the Malice and bound by the curse to return that Malice to Diana. My hope is that when we give them the key, the Praetors will remove the Malice without waking Atroxia."

"I have no key," I said. "But if I did, I still wouldn't give it to them."

"Not even for your mother?" Valerius asked.

My eyes fell as my heart pounded. Yes, to save my mother, I would give them anything they wanted.

✦ · SIXTEEN · ✦

We talked for a long time after that, though most of it was similar to what Radulf had already told me. About Caesar's assassination, Diana's rebellion, and Jupiter's attempt to stop a war amongst the gods. Things bigger than I'd ever expected to deal with when I was in the mines. Back then, I had been responsible for my sister's life and for keeping two steps ahead of my master, Sal. Now I had a role to play in a war between the gods. And greater still, the life of my mother depended upon me giving the Praetors a key. A key I did not have.

"Radulf suggested we trick the Praetors tomorrow," I said to Valerius. "Using that fake Malice you gave him."

But Valerius only shook his head. "I'd have tricked the Praetors myself if I thought it'd work. I'm told there is a scent to magic, no? So subtle that few people in Rome might ever detect when it's near, but Decimas Brutus has dedicated his life to obtaining the Malice, as his fathers have since the time of Julius Caesar. He will know the Malice is fake, because it will have no scent to it."

"Then what can I do?" I asked. Night was closing in, but no answers had come with it. The frustration within me had swelled so much that if I'd had the bulla, I'd have accidentally exploded something by now. The bulla was safer with Callistus, though I could only hope he still had it.

Valerius sighed. "After three hundred years, the Praetors know the bulla has been discovered, which means they've become obsessed with unlocking the Malice. I've tried talking to the Praetors, to convince them to leave you alone, but they're not listening anymore."

"You started this," I said. "You had Horatio killed, thinking you would get the key."

"If I had not done that, Horatio would have given the key to Radulf, and Rome would be in ashes by now."

My eyes fluttered as I looked away. That much was true. Someone had to stop Horatio.

Crispus added, "We never expected Horatio to announce that he had given you the key instead. But when he did, the Praetors realized they didn't need my father, and didn't even need Radulf. All they need is to control you."

My heart was pounding, but still I asked, "Where is the door to the Mistress's tomb?"

"You must not open it," Valerius said. Which was not an answer to my question. Whenever he was hiding something from me, his right eye twitched, and right now it was quivering like a hummingbird's wings. I was a terrible liar, no doubt, but he was worse.

"I can't run from the Praetors forever," I said. "But if I could retrieve the Malice and destroy it, then I could be free."

"It's too risky." Valerius got to his feet. "For your sake, and for the sake of all of Rome, I won't help you find the door. But I am sorry you have to be part of this war, Nic. I beg you to forgive me for not keeping you out of it."

I shook my head, dismissing his apology. "I'm the one who stole the bulla. No one deserves blame for that but me. And the rest is just the consequences of the choice I made in the cave that day."

Valerius sighed. "Nicolas Calva, there is more nobility in you than in any patrician I've met in a lifetime."

I sat forward. "Then help me win this, sir. Please. Where is the door?"

But Valerius wanted nothing to do with that question. He only clasped his hands and yawned. He didn't even bother pretending it was a real yawn. "It's getting late and I am tired. Crispus, Nic's old room is still available. When he's ready, please take him there."

Crispus stood and nodded. "Yes, Father."

After Valerius had left — or really, after Valerius escaped having to talk to me any further — Crispus sat back down. "I don't know where the door is," he said before I could ask. "I'm not even certain that my father knows. He's never admitted that to me."

"You saw the way he acted just now," I said. "He obviously knows more than he's telling."

Crispus nodded, but his face was somber. "The Praetors are going to kill my father. Brutus all but promised that. He said that once they had you, they wouldn't need him anymore."

"Why?" I asked. "I'm a threat to them, and so is Radulf. But not your father."

"He's trying to help you now. He feels he owes you that much, after what happened in the amphitheater, and the Praetors don't like that." Crispus had the ends of his toga bunched in his fist and was twisting the fabric into knots. "My father already asked the Senate to let me apprentice with them until I'm old enough to run for office. He's worried about my future without him here."

"Do you want to be a senator?" I asked. The only two senators I'd ever met were Valerius and Horatio. Horatio was a snake, in my opinion, even if he was Aurelia's father. And Valerius was trying to be a good man, though he wasn't always successful. At least I knew he was loyal to Rome.

"It doesn't matter what I want," Crispus said. "It never does."

I shrugged. "What if you didn't become a senator?" I asked. "What's the worst that could happen?"

Now it was his turn to shrug. "I don't know. I wish I could make plans to leave Rome, as you are doing."

I couldn't understand that. If it weren't so dangerous for me and Livia, we'd never leave this great city. Meanwhile, Crispus could stay here, surrounded by every possible comfort and without any need to worry about where his next meal was coming from. I doubted Livia and I would have that kind of luxury once we left the empire.

"Why would you want to leave?" I asked.

"I want freedom, just as you do." He was looking off in the distance when he said it, then he turned directly to me. "I want to be in control of my own life."

"Then you shall be," I said. "When my family leaves Rome, we want you to come with us."

"You didn't feel that way after the amphitheater. You asked Aurelia to come with you, but not me."

"Well, she's prettier than you are." Then I cocked my head and grinned. "Also, I remember being angry about your father nearly getting me killed."

Crispus chuckled, and then quickly became serious again. "You always hated the chains they made you wear as a slave. I understand how they must have felt. Because sometimes, I think I'm in chains too. Invisible ones made of duty and honor."

"I wear different chains now," I said. "Mine is a scar on my shoulder that does magic, and a key to an amulet that I do not have." I sighed and looked over at Crispus. "Maybe we're more alike than we realized."

"We're not alike at all," Crispus said. "I will never have your strength or courage."

"I'm nothing special," I said, shaking my head. "My whole life bears the truth of that!"

Crispus only smiled. "Maybe your whole life was bringing you to this moment. I believe the most amazing things are still ahead."

And despite my worries, I suddenly realized that I was smiling back.

☙ · SEVENTEEN · ❧

After a while, Crispus walked me to my room. He didn't need to — while I had never claimed to be the cleverest person in Rome, I had somehow managed to remember the twelve steps it took to get there from the dining area. And I actually wished he wouldn't have come with me. I wasn't going to be here for long.

As we walked, I asked him, "Do you know where Aurelia might be right now? My sister is with her."

"I haven't seen her since the circus." Crispus shrugged. "Besides, Aurelia never tells me anything."

I liked hearing that. She rarely told me much about herself either, but there were some times when she had lowered her guard with me. The more I understood about the person she really was, the more I wanted to know her better.

"I thought you two were good friends," I said.

"We are," Crispus said quickly. "Or at least, I like her well enough. I'm just not sure what she thinks of me."

"I thought it was all arranged that . . . sometime soon . . . you and she would —"

"That we would marry?" Crispus snorted a hard laugh. "My father tried to settle that as part of her inheritance, just as a way of making up for his fault in her father's death. But Aurelia hasn't agreed to it yet." He glanced sideways at me. "You know why that is, I'm sure."

"I don't," I said, which was a lie. When we were down in the sewers, Aurelia had all but begged me to offer marriage to her. Maybe she thought I was ignoring her request because we were still young, but that wasn't it at all. No matter how I tried to wiggle free of my situation, there was little hope for my future. The people who wanted to control me, or even to destroy me, were powerful, and the list of their names was steadily growing. If something happened to me, I already had to worry about what would happen to Livia, and now my mother. I wouldn't bind Aurelia to my fate as well.

"Would you want to marry her, if she agrees to it?" I asked. "Or was this all your father's doing?"

"She's a beautiful girl," Crispus said. "That is, if you can get her to put down her bow long enough to dress like a proper girl."

I didn't need her to be a proper girl, and knew for a fact that I was in no position to judge what a proper girl was anyway. If anyone misunderstood the rules of proper behavior, it was me, not her. But maybe it was our shared ignorance about good behavior that made Aurelia and me friends. I wished I could know how she truly felt about me. Was I simply a convenient way for her to keep her inheritance? Or were we more than that?

"Wherever she is right now, I'm sure your sister is safe with Aurelia," Crispus said. "And until this is over, they're both better off far away from you."

But this would never be over. I was beginning to accept that, which was my answer to any questions about a future with Aurelia. Our problem had nothing to do with either of our feelings. The fact was that she was better off remaining as far from me as possible, not just now, but always. That was true for Livia too, and my mother, and Crispus. In fact, if it could be done, I'd be smart to stay away from myself, and let someone else entirely take over the disaster of my life. But I figured that for better or worse, I was stuck with the consequences of everything I'd ever done wrong. Of everything I was still doing wrong.

<hr>

I waited in my room for an hour, until the household quieted down for the night and to be sure Crispus and Valerius were asleep. Then I crept outside, much as I had done when sneaking out of the villa before, except this time I headed back down to the fields.

The Malice was hidden somewhere on Valerius's property. That was obvious, not only in his weak denials of knowing where it was, but also in the fact that I could hear the Mistress — buried with the Malice — whenever I was there.

It took a while to make my way down to the fields in the darkness. The skies were darker than usual tonight, probably threatening rain, and that alone made me nervous. In addition to the lightning that killed my father, I had created a lightning storm when I fought Radulf in the amphitheater — Radulf said that was proof that I had the key to the Malice, in fact. Lightning was no friend to me, and I didn't want to be out here if a storm arose.

My plan was to get the bulla from Callistus, assuming he was still where I had left him at the far edge of the fields. Then I would use its power to talk to the wolf I had seen earlier. If the Malice was hidden here, then the wolf probably belonged to the god Mars. He would show me the door. Although I had no key, I did have the bulla, which was capable of great magic. If I focused it on a single lock, using the full force of my powers, I should be able to get it open. Of course, any explosion large enough to destroy something sealed off by the gods was likely to awaken half of Rome, as well as every Praetor in the city, and that would be bad enough. It also might awaken the Mistress, which Valerius had begged me not to do.

So admittedly, my plan wasn't perfect. But I had no choice. Morning was coming fast, and I had nothing to offer the Praetors in trade for my mother.

Once I got to the end of the path from Valerius's villa, I hesitated in the shadows. Valerius had warned that the Praetors watched this property. So they also suspected the Malice was hidden here.

I stepped into the fields with every sense on high alert. Something rustled in the reeds behind me. It was the wind, perhaps, or a small animal? Dark shadows lay nestled within even darker shadows. Was it Praetors, lying in wait for me?

To get to Callistus, I would have to cross the open field and then sneak into the vines, where I could hide better. My instinct told me to run, that I should be out in plain view for the shortest time possible. But it was already hard to think straight. The Mistress was crying in my head again, and pounding on a door or on the wall of whatever tomb they had put her in. Despite what Valerius had said, it seemed impossible that I was only listening to an echo of the past. Because if this was real, if it was happening now, then no matter what he had warned, I wanted to get her out as quickly as possible.

The instant my foot touched down on the netting hidden beneath the grasses of the field, I knew I was in trouble. It released a spring that closed a claw trap over my leg. I cried out and summoned magic to open it again. But before I could act, a rope pulled tight, yanking me off my feet where I fell hard on the ground. I sent out magic intended to cut the rope, but it either missed or there was more than one rope.

I was dragged across half the field before I finally severed the rope, but getting the claw trap off my leg wasn't as easy. I sat up and used magic to separate the two pieces of metal. The spikes on them were short, so although they'd broken the skin, it wasn't a terrible injury.

And then I sent out a ball of magic into the weeds ahead of me. Someone over there had pulled on my rope. I heard the yelps of at least three or four men and smiled. If I had hit them hard, then it still wasn't half of what I had intended.

I gathered more magic, but then a voice behind me said, "We've got you, Nicolas."

And immediately, Brutus had a hand on my shoulder. Every feeling of magic within me went to dust.

❧ · EIGHTEEN · ❧

I had no magic, but that didn't mean the fight within me was gone. On the contrary, I lashed out like I never had before. I kicked, and threw punches, and even used a few choice curse words, in case that helped. But each time I got one hand off me, another hand took its place, and more Praetors were coming.

Finally, there were enough of them to force me down flat, facing the ground. I squirmed and rolled, trying to make it impossible for them to get hold of both my hands and feet together, but even then, I was failing.

"Put a hand directly on his shoulder," Brutus ordered. "That's where he's marked."

Someone ripped my tunic at the neck, and a hand came down on the Divine Star like a boulder landing there. It sent a wave of pain through me, enough to make me nauseous, and instantly, I lost all fight. I barely could move.

Brutus knelt on the ground and carefully the Praetors rolled me to my side so I could face him. Still, the hand never left the Divine Star. The pain from it brought tears to my eyes, but I blinked them away. I refused to let them think it hurt as bad as it did.

"This was easier than I thought it'd be," Brutus said.

"This isn't over," I said. "I'm letting you get comfortable before I end this."

"Oh, you already tried ending this, and failed." Brutus clucked his tongue. "I expected more from you, to be honest. After you dropped my men in the sewers, there were many injuries."

"Only injuries?" I muttered. "Then I should've dropped them harder."

"It did have some effect," Brutus answered. "I had trouble convincing everyone to come here tonight. Having seen for themselves what you can do, several of my men are reluctant to face you."

"So you brought the stupid ones," I said. "Because they haven't seen half of what I can do."

"What you *could* do," Brutus said. "Until we took it away just now, and if you don't tell me what I want to hear, I'll take everything else. Where's the key?"

"Where's my mother?" I asked. "You promised to trade her for the key, so she must be nearby."

"Oh, she is." He brushed the sweat-dampened hair from my face. "The key, Nicolas. We've waited almost three hundred years for someone with magic to hold the key — do you think I can't feel it with you now?"

"Before I give it to you, I have to see my mother. I demand to talk to her alone."

"Impossible," Brutus said. "Once I remove my hand, your magic will return, and you can understand why that puts me at a slight disadvantage." With that, the hand pressed deeper on the Star, reminding me that for all the power I had, it could disappear so quickly.

Disappear. If I could get to my mother, we could disappear.

"Do what you want to me," I said through gritted teeth. "Nothing will get you the key until I see my mother, alone!"

"It's not what I'll do to *you*." There was growing tension in his voice. "Remember what happens to your mother if you refuse to cooperate!"

"You will not touch her!" I yelled. "Take me to my mother!"

"Never!" Brutus shouted back.

"I'll stay with you." That was Aurelia. I looked up and saw her standing on a mound of dirt with a nocked arrow in her bow. Praetors were looking her way, hungry to grab her, but not wanting a poke from that arrow.

"Ah, the sewer girl," Brutus said. "I'm delighted to see you again, my dear."

In contrast, I wasn't at all delighted. Why had she come here? Why now?

"Keep me with you while Nic sees his mother," Aurelia said. "Then when he's had a chance to talk to her, he'll turn himself back over to you in exchange for my release."

I rolled my eyes. The whole idea of this plan was *not* to turn myself back over to Brutus. Maybe it was too dark for her to see the strain on my face each time Brutus pressed against the Divine Star, but surely she had heard the pinch in my voice.

"All right." Brutus removed his hand from the Star, and then at least I could breathe again. But he still held my arm and used it to pull me to my feet, where I nearly blacked out from dizziness.

The Praetors grabbed Aurelia and took both her bow and knife. She protested but that didn't get much sympathy from me. What did she expect they would do?

Brutus started walking me away from the villa but also farther from the vines and into the wooded area of land I hadn't visited before. The cypress trees here were tall and dense and filled with thick underbrush around our narrow trail. Once inside this grove, I saw at least a hundred Praetors staring back at me from a small clearing, all of them armed and every one happy to do whatever it took to get the key. And those were only the Praetors I could see. I had no doubt there were many more in the darker shadows of these woods.

Aurelia was allowed to catch up to me, and when she did, I barely looked at her.

"You're angry," she said.

"I didn't need you to sacrifice yourself," I muttered. "Did you think this would help?"

"It wouldn't make things worse, based on how you were managing on your own. Why did you go down there alone?"

"To get the ——" I paused, unwilling to say more.

But Brutus, still holding me, already knew. "You wanted the bulla that had been tied onto that unicorn. I'd heard Radulf had one, but never was sure. We saw it when we surveyed the property."

I turned to him, my eyes wide with alarm.

Brutus only laughed. "We saw the bulla, but the unicorn wouldn't let us anywhere near it and dodged our arrows. He disappeared for a while, but when we saw him again, the bulla was gone. It must've fallen off when he ran. My men are searching for it now. It's only a matter of time before they find it."

My heart sank. So it had fallen from where I had laid it beneath his saddle, and obviously my knot hadn't worked either, at least not well enough for Callistus to be chased through thickets and vines. This was why Radulf had warned me not to bring the bulla anywhere near the Praetors.

Beside me, Aurelia squirmed against the man escorting her. "Can you relax your grip just a little? I'm cooperating; you don't need to hurt me."

I wasn't sure if the Praetor loosened his grip or not but she stopped protesting, so I hoped he had. There wasn't much I could do anyway. I wasn't angry with her, not really. After all, she was trying to assist me. But I hated the feeling of being so helpless.

Up ahead, I saw a wagon with bars and nearly fifty Praetors around it. That's where we were going. My heart leapt into my throat. I was nervous, and terrified. And certain that if I wasn't careful, everything could go horribly wrong.

"We'll honor our agreement, that Nicolas can have some privacy," Brutus said to the men around him. "But keep the sewer girl where he can see her."

Aurelia was dragged off in one direction while Brutus turned me to face him. "Here are my terms. If you touch your mother or allow her to touch you, the sewer girl dies. If you raise a hand to any of my men, even just for a friendly wave hello, then the sewer girl dies. And when I call for you to return to me, you obey immediately, even if it means you walk away midsentence. If you do not —"

"Then we all join in a game of small ball? I understand the terms, Brutus."

He smirked back at me, then released my arm, cautiously, as if he intended to grab it again if I made that necessary. And though I felt magic start to flow again from the Divine Star, I wouldn't be using it. Not now. Aurelia was behind me and somewhere up ahead . . .

A woman had her face pressed to the bars and one arm outstretched through them. She was chained in there too; I could hear the metal when she shifted to get even closer to me. Despite all that — the dirt on her face, the shabbiness of her thin tunic, and the metal bars, caging her as if she were no better than the animals of the venatio, she was beautiful. More elegant than the finest woman any of these Praetors returned home to at night.

Everything else melted in my vision as I came up to the cage and smiled back at her. "Hello, Mother."

❧·NINETEEN·❧

My mother was crying. I hadn't noticed that until I came close enough to see the tears running in lines down her face. They washed through the dirt in streaks, yet they did nothing to diminish her beauty. Livia would grow up to become just as lovely, no doubt.

"You're alive," she whispered.

I nodded. Tears were welling in my own eyes, though I didn't want her to see them. I needed her to believe I was strong enough to finish the fight still ahead for me. Or more likely, *I* needed to believe that.

"And Livia?"

"She's better than ever." At least, I hoped that was true. I'd had no chance to ask Aurelia about her in private. I wouldn't risk asking while Brutus could hear us.

My mother smiled and more tears fell. "I knew you'd take care of her. I never worried about that." Then her smile faded. "I'm told you have magic, the Divine Star on your shoulder, just as your father once had. I've heard stories of what you've done, in the amphitheater, on the streets, at the baths outside the city. The stories are impossible, I know."

I took a deep breath. But it didn't make me feel any better, and what I had to say wouldn't help her either. "No, Mother, they're true."

She shook her head. "How can they be? Your father was capable of some great things, but nothing close to what I've heard about you."

"I have one of the amulets." *Had* one. The bulla was lost now and possibly already in the hands of the Praetors.

Mother's eyes widened. "No, those are curses."

"I know that. I'm trying —" I swallowed in a painful gulp. "I'm trying to make everything right again. But I can't just give up. If the Praetors win, they will do worse than bring down the empire. They will bring war back to the gods. Everything will be destroyed!"

"But what if it's you who is destroyed instead?" More tears streamed down her face. "Leaving you and Livia was the hardest thing I ever had to do. Don't let that be for nothing."

"I'm trying to fix this," I said. "But I don't know how. The harder I try, the worse things become."

She nodded. "You are so like your father. He loved us with all his heart. He loved you, Nic, so much that he thought nothing of risking his life in the hope of saving ours."

"He tried to create a Jupiter Stone," I said. "Why would he do that? Without the amulets, he must've known he would fail."

"He had no amulets, but he understood that a person can only create a Jupiter Stone for the good of others, not for himself." She wiped a stray tear from her eye. "That was all he wanted, to save his family." With her fingers, my mother motioned for me to come closer. "Has it really been five years? You've grown so much. Let me see you better."

I kept my feet where they were. "I can't come closer, Mother."

Though I wanted to. It tore at my heart to be so close, after so long, and to do nothing but stare at her. When I was younger, sometimes it would begin storming at night, and inevitably, I'd feel her hand on my back as I curled up in the corner on the floor, shaking with fear that what had happened to my father might one day happen to me. She always knew how to make me feel better, always. Then when Livia and I had been on our own, we comforted ourselves by imagining what our mother would have done if she had been with us. Even that helped.

If I had known how hard this would be now, I might not have demanded to see her. Seeing my mother right in front of me, yet still out of my reach, was horrible. But I wouldn't have traded this moment away either.

I lowered my voice. "Listen to me, carefully. The Praetors want something from me in exchange for your release."

"The key to the Malice, I know."

My eyes widened, but it was a relief not to have to explain it. "I don't have the key, or if I do, then I can't find it. I'm going to find a way to get you free, though."

She shook her head. "Listen, you must not give them the key." She pushed closer to the bars. "Yes, I know their terms for my life, but I also know how the Praetors work. Brutus is more than my captor; he is my master now. I know his plans for Rome."

"I'll get you free, Mother."

"No, you won't. The Praetors never give; they only take. If you turn over the key, they will find a new way to threaten you for the Malice, and then find a new threat until you create a Jupiter Stone. If you don't leave Rome now, before they are finished, you will share the same fate as your father."

My heart pounded as magic swelled in my veins. It would only take a little to break her free from this cage. Then the Praetors would attack, all of them who were here. I turned to look back at Aurelia. In the darkness, it was hard to see her clearly, though I knew she'd be watching me.

"I'll get you free," I repeated again.

"Do not," she said. "As soon as you can, get your sister and run. Leave the empire while there is still a world beyond. Run to freedom — that's all I've ever wanted for you."

"Nicolas Calva!" Brutus called. "Return to me, now."

"I love you," I said as I began to back up. "Do not give up."

"Do not give in," she replied. "If you do, then all that I've sacrificed is for nothing."

When I was steps away from Brutus, I raised my hand to him. Aurelia was in the distance, held now by three Praetors.

"Let my friend go," I said. "Then I'll surrender."

Brutus grinned wickedly. "Let's settle this now. Give me what I want, and I'll let all of you go free."

He was lying. My mother was right about the Praetors only taking. He had no intention of letting all of us go.

"Honor our agreement," I said. "When you do, I'll honor my part of the bargain and return to your control."

After a moment of consideration, Brutus ordered, "Release the girl! Nobody touches her!"

"Nic?" Aurelia called to me.

"Give a shout when you're free of the woods," I said. "I'll hear you."

"You're supposed to come with me."

"Will you just run?"

And she did. While I waited, with my hand still held up to Brutus, I let the magic build inside me. Praetors were surrounding me, but I was ready for them. All I needed was to hear Aurelia's voice, that she was safe.

She ran fast, because it wasn't long before I heard her cry, "I'm out, Nic!"

And I lowered my hand. "There's no shield?" Brutus asked. "I can touch you."

"Yes." I kept my expression steady. "If you want to."

He did, but immediately yanked his hand away with a cry.

"What's the matter?" I smiled as I stretched out my arm. "If you don't accept my surrender, that's fine. I won't offer twice."

And other Praetors grabbed me too. I felt the spark as they

tried to take the magic, but they couldn't hold on long enough to do any serious damage.

"His skin is like fire." One of them scowled, cradling his burned hand in his arms.

The heat I was generating made me nauseous and sweat emptied from every pore in my body. But for now, I was untouchable.

I turned and started to run back to the caged wagon. Once I got my mother, I couldn't generate this heat, but I could make us disappear somewhere. For her sake, I would not fail at duplicating Radulf's trick.

Except that she was gone. The wagon was still there but the door was open, and I had no idea in which direction they had taken her. More Praetors were coming down the hill from behind the wagon. Wherever she was, I could not follow. All I could do was run back toward Valerius's field and hope to escape from there.

I threw punches of magic ahead of me, brushing aside every Praetor in my way. I saved a special force of air for Brutus, knocking him into the shadows, where I hoped he landed on the back of a mother bear. She could teach him a lesson about why one should never threaten a mother.

And then I ran. I let the heat burn off me as I raced through the trees, throwing magic ahead of me to keep the path clear. These woods were littered with Praetors — so many that they rivaled Radulf's armies. How were we to defeat them all?

I got back into the field, startling the Praetors who were still there. I couldn't see Aurelia anywhere, so I hoped she had remained free once leaving the woods.

They immediately began closing in around me, but I wasn't finished fighting.

I ran into the center of the field. At least forty Praetors surrounded me and more had followed from the woods. I fell to one knee, then put my fist to the ground, releasing everything within me. Magic poured into the earth, creating waves from solid ground. If I'd had the bulla, it might've exploded the entire area, and me along with it, but the Divine Star merely sent out ripples, violent enough to topple every man standing in the field.

Once they went down, I tried to raise a shield, but too much of my strength was already gone and I stumbled.

No, things would not end so quickly. I forced myself to stand but felt an arrow pierce my thigh. The exact reason I had wanted a shield actually.

I collapsed again, hearing the laughter of the Praetors as those who were not injured got to their feet. I yanked out the arrow and put a hand to my leg, searching for enough magic to heal it. There wouldn't be time before they grabbed me again.

"You will not touch him!" Valerius yelled, scurrying down the path and into his field. "Praetors of Rome, I am the presiding magistrate of the Senate, your superior. You will obey my orders. Let that boy go!"

❧ · TWENTY · ❧

At that moment, Decimas Brutus emerged from the woods, to my disappointment, free of any bear scratches, although he did seem more tousled than usual.

Brutus faced Valerius directly, on opposite ends of the open field. "Walk away, Senator. You are useless to us now, and if you want to stay alive, then you will remain useless."

"Threatening a Roman senator is treason," Crispus said, walking into the field with the guards of his home. "You will leave at once, or our guards will arrest you and deliver you to the emperor himself."

I got to my feet. The wound wasn't completely healed, but I could walk without pain and I wanted to preserve what magic I had left.

"Those are personal guards of your father's, not Roman soldiers," Brutus said to Crispus. "I'm not bound to their orders."

"Surrender your weapons now," Crispus said. "If you prefer to see how their skills compare to the soldiers of Rome, I promise to impress you."

"And this is my promise." Brutus drew his sword and aimed it directly at Valerius. "If you do not order your guards to leave, I will carry out my threat to your father." He ran forward, swinging back his sword for a strike.

"Valerius, run!" I cried, sending a new wave of magic toward the Praetors closest to him. Then I began running in that direction as well.

Crispus sent his guards into the field, where a fight broke out between them and the Praetors. Meanwhile, with the battle as a distraction, I leaned against the grapevines and searched for my magic again. I needed to find the bulla. If I could get to Callistus, maybe he could lead me to where it had fallen. I didn't think anyone had found it yet. They would've announced it if they had. But how long would it take me to find Callistus? Valerius needed my help now, just as he had helped me.

I ran over to Valerius, who was crouched on the path leading back to his home. Crispus knelt by him, urging him to get back to the villa.

"Come with us," Valerius said.

"Aurelia is here," I said. "Have you seen her?"

"I'll find her," Crispus said. "You should go with my father."

The mark in my shoulder was alive once more, but rather than creating pain this time, it was filling me with energy. Again, its contrast from the bulla's magic amazed me. The Divine Star served me, and not the other way around.

"This is my fight," I said to Crispus. "But your father must leave, for his own safety."

"We can't leave you behind," Valerius said. "Yours is the most important life of all."

I glanced back. Fists and swords and arrows were flying in all directions, but not to our favor. One by one, his men were falling, and too many Praetors were still standing.

I turned to Valerius. "I'm the cause of this battle, now I need to be the solution to it. Please, sir, the threat against you is real. Go to where it is safe."

"Where are you, Nicolas Calva?" That was Brutus speaking. "Show yourself and end this fight."

Radulf must've heard it too, or sensed it through our connection of the Divine Star. He didn't speak to me, but I felt his concern, even his panic. If I didn't get away, I was in trouble, and we both knew it.

I had not been given the chance to help my mother disappear, but I could do that now. All I needed was to picture someplace else in my mind. I could take Valerius with me, and maybe Crispus too. Bring them to safety and then return to find Aurelia. And Livia too, if she had come here with Aurelia. I hoped she wasn't anywhere near this field.

I scanned the area and still couldn't see Aurelia. The night was too dark, and the feeling of approaching rain was growing. I hoped she was halfway to the other end of Rome by now, though I knew her too well to believe that.

"Where can we go?" Valerius asked. "The Praetors will follow us to the villa."

The *hypogeum* beneath the amphitheater — that's where I'd take them. No government official would descend into that filth, probably not even to find me. I pictured the animals' cages, the mazelike paths, and Felix's face as it would be when we appeared directly in front of him.

"Take my arm," I said to Crispus and Valerius as I knelt by them. "I'm going to get you two out of here."

"Can you hear Atroxia's crying, even above the sounds of fighting?" Brutus yelled. "The Mistress needs rescuing. Only you can help her, Nicolas."

"He's lying," Valerius whispered. "Shut her out of your mind."

That was harder than it sounded. Because, yes, the crying had returned in my head, louder than ever. As more men fell in the battle, I heard the Mistress's voice, begging the gods to forgive her crimes.

I closed my eyes again, and the hypogeum reappeared in my sights. According to Radulf, it was simple magic to disappear, so why was I struggling with it?

"Three is too many for you," Radulf said. "Let go of the senator and his son. Get yourself away from there."

That was not an option. I muttered for Radulf to get out of my head and do something useful instead. If he wasn't here to help, then at least he could remain quiet so I could concentrate.

"They're getting closer," Crispus said. "Whatever you're doing, Nic, please hurry."

The hypogeum. I began to see it, not as an image in my mind, but as if I were truly standing there. I smelled the animals and the acrid sweat of the slaves at their labors. I felt its suffocating heat like I was part of it again.

Then Crispus released my arm and, with a yell, stood and attacked a Praetor who had come upon us, bringing them both down to the ground. It pulled me back into the field, and I leapt to my feet too. Praetors were swarming this field like ants across spilled honey. Crispus's guards helped, but not enough.

Valerius was slower to respond. He rolled beneath the vines, putting his hands over his head, no doubt hoping that would be enough to save him.

I shot magic toward the Praetor entangled with Crispus, and then yanked Crispus to his feet. "Protect your father," I told him. "I'll do what I can to stop this."

I started running, headed away from Crispus, away from the vines. If they needed a distraction, then I was happy to provide it.

I sent a ball of fire near the vines, similar to one I had seen Radulf create once. Enough moisture was already in the air that it required more magic to maintain the fire, but the smoke was all I cared about. I needed another shield, which would protect me as I ran through the fire toward where I'd left Callistus. The Praetors could not follow me then.

However, I underestimated how much weaker I had become, and my still-injured leg tripped on a simple stray vine. The area was already filling with smoke, choking me.

I got onto all fours and searched within myself for any remaining magic. If necessary, I would crawl until I found the bulla.

I found a bit of magic deep inside, enough for a minute or two of protection. If I hurried, it would get me past the fire.

Crispus was running up the hill now, directly behind his father. And not far from me, a Praetor had a bow aimed directly at them. Rather than create a shield, I used the last of my magic to hit the Praetor, but it was a moment too late.

With the punch of magic, his arrow released at a different angle than what had been intended and missed Crispus. But it did hit someone.

Valerius was shot.

⫷ · TWENTY-ONE · ⫸

I rushed back through the Praetors, slick with sweat and refusing to be taken again. I wanted to send magic at all of them, to cause the same hurt and pain that was now swelling in me. But for the moment, I couldn't feel even a whisper of magic from the Star.

By the time I reached the place where Valerius had rolled after he fell, Crispus was at my side.

"There's a unicorn," I said between breaths. "At the edge of your property, there's a unicorn. Bring him here . . . his horn . . . I can't heal this alone."

Crispus nodded and ran in the way I'd directed him.

Valerius clutched my hand. "I'm so sorry, Nic. For everything I've done to you. Everything that will still happen to you. I'm so sorry."

"I've got to pull this arrow out, sir," I told him. "It's going to hurt, but then I can heal you."

"No, don't . . . Use what you have . . . fight."

I shook my head and put my hands on the shaft of the

arrow, but Valerius put his hands over mine and pulled them down.

"Crispus will . . . help you," Valerius whispered. "Trust him. You . . . must learn to trust."

"I've got to remove the arrow."

But Valerius shook his head. "Do not wake the Mistress. If they force you . . . the Malice . . . do not wake her."

Praetors were edging closer again. They were relentless, like vultures that wanted their prey.

"Where is the door?" I asked him. "Sir, where is the Malice hidden?"

Another arrow flew through the air, nearly above my head. I ducked as it hit the thigh of the Praetor who had gotten closest to me.

"I have enough arrows for all of you!" Aurelia yelled out. So she was still here, somewhere in the vineyard ahead of me. It must've taken her time to locate another bow. I was never sure how she seemed to find them everywhere when I had yet to find a single weapon simply lying around for the taking.

"I've got help now," I told Valerius. "I'll heal you while she . . ." My voice trailed off. The senator's eyes were closed, and his head had gone limp.

I yanked out the arrow, then pressed my hands to his chest and emptied into it everything I had left. The Divine Star's cold burn was almost as intense as it had been when the Praetors pressed down on it, but this magic wasn't being taken from me. I was giving it to Valerius, all I could.

"Enough of this, Nic," Radulf whispered into my head. "You can't help him now."

"What do you know about help?" I muttered. "Where are you?"

"I am coming. But hold on to your magic for the battle that can be won. It's not with Valerius, not anymore."

Where was Crispus with the unicorn? They should've been here by now. Unless Callistus wasn't there anymore. The Praetors said they had chased him away.

Life was draining from me, and still there wasn't a spark from Valerius, as there should have been. Why not? I was giving him everything. *Everything.*

"Nicolas, I said that's enough!" Radulf's voice came at me so sharp that it snapped me away from Valerius.

I released the senator and looked down at his face, even more lifeless than I felt.

He was gone.

When I looked up again, I saw the flash of white out of the corner of my eye. Livia was in front, but Crispus rode in the saddle behind her.

No, I didn't want Livia in this battle. I stood and ran toward them. But before I could say anything, Crispus dismounted and said, "The unicorn wouldn't ride with me. Not until she came too. How's my father?"

My heart sank. It was hard enough to know what had happened, but having to say it was so much worse. I shook my head. "I'm sorry, Crispus. I did what I could for him."

Crispus nodded and looked away. Livia slid off the unicorn's back and immediately put a hand on his arm for comfort. He pressed his hand over hers, gently and gratefully.

"I'm sorry," I mumbled again. I needed to apologize, not only for failing to save him, but for being the reason he was targeted.

"My father brought this on himself," Crispus said, clearly fighting back tears. "And he'd want us to win this battle. We have to keep fighting."

I nodded, but by then, Livia's eyes had drifted to me. "Nic, your leg!"

She ripped the edge of her tunic for fabric to bind the wound, but I didn't care about that. I started searching Callistus's saddle, checking to be sure the bulla was indeed gone. The rope I had used to knot it was still there, but the bulla was not. It really had disappeared.

Panic swept through me. I had no idea where to begin to search for the bulla, or how I'd do it while this battle was raging.

"Aurelia found Callistus first, then called me over to protect him while she came closer to the battle," Livia said as she bandaged my leg. "We knew he was yours — who else would be riding a unicorn?"

"Was the bulla here when you found him?" I asked.

Livia shook her head while another fire erupted at the far end of the fields, closer to where the fighting between the Praetors and villa guards had moved. There could only be one reason for that.

Radulf had said he was coming to help me. Obviously, he had arrived.

❧ · TWENTY-TWO · ❧

Get my sister to safety," I said to Crispus. "After all that's happened tonight, I know I can't ask this of you, but I need you to keep Livia safe."

Crispus put a hand on my shoulder. "I'm the one who cannot ask anything of you. I'll protect your sister, Nic."

And I knew he would. I trusted him, just as Valerius urged me to do. When they ran off in one direction, I climbed onto Callistus's back, headed toward the fighting, and determined to be strong enough to finish it.

Radulf was somewhere in the middle of it all, sending out balls of fire that he launched at whatever Praetor was irritating him the most. They responded by diving into a small pond not far away to put out any fires that had gotten too close to them. So I put my energy there, using magic to build up the slope of the pond, which became steep and slippery. The men could get into it to douse the fire, but it'd take several more men with ropes to lift them out.

The effort exhausted me, and I leaned forward in the saddle while I recovered. The men who were now stuck in the pond shouted curses at me, but I ignored them. If they didn't stop yelling so loud, I'd send something into that pond to bite them.

While I rested, I turned my attention to Radulf. The fight around him was emptying, and once I got a better look, I saw why. He wasn't really there. It was only a trick of light, similar to what he had done when I fought him outside the baths.

He was here, enough to send magic, and I knew from experience that he could receive the blows of magic as well. But he wouldn't feel the sting from the Praetor swords, and certainly wouldn't be affected by their touch. If only I'd been clever enough to do that tonight. If only I were clever enough to know *how* to do that trick.

A hand touched my injured leg, and I jerked it backward, expecting the worst.

"You kicked me!" Aurelia said. "Ow!"

I slid to the ground where she was turned away from me with a hand on her face.

"I'm sorry," I said. "I didn't know it was you!"

"I need to announce myself before getting anywhere near you."

"Here, let me see it." I gently pushed her hand away and saw a bruise already starting to form. "I'm sorry," I said again. "I can heal it, but I need a few more minutes first."

Truthfully, I needed a week, considering the way I felt. Any magic trickling through me was barely keeping me on my feet.

"Would this help?" Aurelia held up her other hand, with the bulla dangling from it.

"You had it?" Feelings of relief swelled in me, enough that I almost hugged her. Almost. "How long?"

"Since I got here. Why did you think I offered myself to Brutus? To give you the bulla!"

"Why didn't you —"

"When would I have told you? Between your shouting and threatening and making all sorts of stupid deals?"

"I had a plan!"

"Well, I had a better plan," she said. "To get close enough to give you the bulla so you could help your mother and flatten the entire Praetor camp."

"Making yourself a hostage in the middle of the camp is hardly helpful."

"You were supposed to rescue me first. Not honor your deal and tell me to run away."

"My plan involved honoring that deal!" I said.

"And I needed you to break it," Aurelia said. "Sometimes I think we make a terrible team."

I smiled. "Sometimes I think we make a pretty good one." Frankly, it made me happy that she considered us a team at all. I took the bulla from her. "So you found this on Callistus's saddle?"

"I couldn't leave it tied there. That was careless of you, Nic."

"Callistus wouldn't let any enemies near him." Except that Radulf had managed to capture a unicorn once — Callistus's mother — so Aurelia was right once more. It had been a big risk on my part, though I knew the bulla would've been taken from me if I'd brought it into the battle earlier. For one reason or another, every choice I made seemed to be the wrong one.

As soon as I put the bulla on, its strength filled me. I immediately put my fingers on the bruise forming on Aurelia's cheek and let the Divine Star heal it.

Aurelia giggled. "That tickles."

It had already finished healing. I knew that, and yet my fingers were still there, brushing her soft skin. Now it was not just my fingers on her cheek, but my whole hand, and I didn't know how I would ever let her go. Aurelia stared back at me until we had been quiet for too long. Then she stepped back and said, "We'd better get to safety. Where's Livia?"

"With Crispus," I said, finally pulling my head back into the battle. I pointed off to the right. "But let's go this way instead. There's something else I need to do."

We left Radulf to finish the battle behind us, and I had no doubt that he would be successful. There wasn't much the Praetors could do to him, and he was clearly enjoying himself. I wondered if this was how he had become so successful as a general. Maybe he never really attended all those battles he won.

"Can you do that, the magic he's doing?" Aurelia asked.

"I've never tried it," I said. Though now I wanted to. I would practice until it was perfect.

Except for Callistus, who was grazing nearby, the field was empty when we arrived. I pointed in the direction Crispus and

Livia had gone. "Please find them," I said to Aurelia. "And then no matter what, stay out of sight until I tell you it's safe."

"I can help you fight," she said.

"I didn't come back here to fight," I told her. "And I'm not sure what's about to happen. You need to leave."

She nodded, though I knew it wasn't the answer she'd wanted. I asked Callistus to walk with her, and after a brief snort of annoyance, Callistus left his grazing and they walked away.

Once I was alone, I listened again for Atroxia's tears, which rushed at me like raw emotion. I walked the field as I had before, choosing my steps based on the direction in which the crying became louder.

And stopped exactly where I had before, at the ruins of the old temple.

The Mistress was a vestalis. It would make sense for her punishment to take place inside a temple. Though I could not explain why it had been destroyed to rubble since her burial.

I knelt on the ground there, closed my eyes, and waited. It wasn't long before I heard the growl of a wolf. The wolf of Mars.

But I had the bulla now, so I wasn't afraid. Or not *as* afraid as before. I could communicate with the wolf, not force him to obey me. Still, I said to him, "If the temple is here, show me."

Inside my head, above the crying of the Mistress, the wolf answered. Or rather, a voice spoke to me. It had to be Mars, answering through his chosen animal.

"Do you have the key, Nicolas Calva?"

"Yes." I didn't know what the key was, or how I could have it, but Valerius had died to protect my keeping of it and I wouldn't let that be in vain.

"Have you come for the amulet inside?"

My heart pounded. "Yes."

"Are you worthy, Nicolas Calva, to hold a sacred amulet of the gods?"

No. I had the bulla, the first of the three amulets, but I'd stolen it. I couldn't claim worthiness.

So I said, "You must decide that."

Fur brushed up beside me, and when I opened my eyes, I saw the wolf at my side. He used his snout to move my hand over his head, and I smiled. This terrible beast was really only a puppy wanting love. I gave him a scratch, but he hadn't been asking for that.

The wolf looked up, and I followed his gaze. Directly in front of me was an elaborate temple. It was small but grander in workmanship than the Pantheon or Caesar's temple or any temple I'd yet seen in Rome. Only three marble steps led to the base, which was surrounded by marble columns ringed with gold. The blocks of white marble on the walls were fit so carefully together that they almost appeared solid, and the cornice of the arched roof was carved so intricately that my eyes could not find a single flaw. And it was no wonder. No man had constructed this temple.

This temple was built by the gods.

⋈ · TWENTY-THREE · ⋈

Nicolas Calva, we are alone at last."

Startled by the sound of a voice, I turned, hands out. Decimas Brutus wasn't far from me, but the wolf at my side growled, warning Brutus to keep his distance if he hoped to avoid being bitten. Beyond that, the bulla was clearly visible hanging on my chest. And Brutus was alone.

I looked back at the temple, but it was in ruins again and the wolf had retreated into the woods. Brutus said nothing about it, so I was sure he could not see the temple as it really was. That privilege had been given only to me.

"You again," I said completely without enthusiasm. "Don't you ever give up?"

"Don't you?" he asked, arching an eyebrow to show his amusement.

"Not until I win," I said.

He smiled. "Unfortunately, today will not be that day. Dawn will be here soon, and you and I have business to discuss."

"Give up this fight," I told him. "Thanks to General Radulf, few of your men are still standing."

"You saw my army in the woods," Brutus said dismissively. "There are hundreds more of us, even thousands if we measure to the ends of the empire. You have swatted a bee today, but we are a hive, ready to sting."

I was in no mood to debate bee analogies with him. Instead, I said, "Try stinging me now." Then I used the bulla to unwrap some of the unburned vines from their cords and sent them swirling around Brutus's body.

By the time I was finished, only his face was showing and it was nearly as purple as the grapes. I walked forward, picked a grape from about where his elbow would be, and squashed it beneath my fingers. Let him wonder about that analogy for a while.

"How dare you!" he shouted.

"How dare you?" I replied. "You killed Senator Valerius, who did nothing to you and who could give you nothing! I intend to deliver you to the emperor himself, at which point I will tell him every detail of your treason against this empire!"

Brutus started to answer, then his gaze drifted beside me where a light was beginning to form. I had felt the change in the air already and knew what to expect, but I still moved sideways when Radulf faded into view. I didn't know what strange things could happen if he tried to appear right where I was, but I wasn't about to risk suddenly sharing arms and legs with my grandfather.

Radulf was here now, not the trick of light from before, just him. But he looked at me and said, "Is Brutus all that's left?"

"All that's left in this field." I hated to say the next part, but without his help here tonight, I'd have certainly failed. "Thank you . . . sir, for coming."

"I should've come sooner, but your magic was so erratic, I couldn't get a feel for what was happening here."

Brutus arched his neck in defiance. "The only thing happening here is Nicolas and I coming to an arrangement. This doesn't concern you, General Radulf."

Radulf turned back to Brutus. "My grandson always concerns me, Decimas Brutus. When he finds the Malice of Mars, my first act will be to destroy every Praetor in the Roman Empire."

Which was why I could never allow Radulf to get the Malice. Destroying the Praetors was only his first intended act. Radulf hated the empire for what they had done to our homeland, now in service and slavery to Rome. I had never felt the same way. For all its brutality, life was better here than I'd ever known it to be in Gaul. So his plans were clear. After he finished with the Praetors, more destruction would follow.

"I've told Emperor Florian about your plans," Brutus said. "A group of soldiers will bring you to him, by force if necessary."

Radulf chuckled at the word "force." "Those soldiers are loyal to me," he said. "I warned the emperor not to threaten me."

Something about the look in his eye made me nervous. I knew enough about Radulf to believe him. Radulf always meant exactly what he said.

"Nic, is it over?" Aurelia emerged from the path, with Callistus behind her. Crispus and Livia followed behind them.

"Except for this one," I said, pointing to Brutus.

Livia ran up and gave me a warm hug. "Thank the gods you're safe."

"Your sister is beautiful," Brutus said. "So like her mother, wouldn't you agree?"

My heart went cold. "Get behind me," I said to Livia. Brutus wouldn't break free from the vines; I had sealed them with magic. But his tone made me nervous.

Aurelia took her place at my side and murmured, "Don't even talk to him, Nic."

"Talking isn't necessary." Brutus nodded eastward, where the morning sun was beginning to peek over the hills. "The boy knows what will happen now if he does not give me the key."

"He doesn't have it," Radulf said. "If he did, don't you think we'd already have the Malice?"

"Maybe he doesn't know he has it," Brutus said. "And maybe you don't know how to help him find it, but I do. Turn yourself over to me right now, Nicolas, and I will get the key from you. Or if you do not, the men who are holding your mother will execute their orders."

To execute her. I saw her face clearly in my mind, which made it even more impossible to think about losing her forever.

From behind me, Livia put a hand on my arm and whispered, "You must do something."

"He will not go with you!" Radulf said. "I will not allow it."

"Nor will I!" Crispus looked over at me. "I'll be an apprentice to the Senate now. My first loyalty is to Rome, and I can't let you harm the empire, not even to save your mother."

"Listen to them," Aurelia said. "Don't go with the Praetors. I'm so sorry, Nic, but this is how it has to be."

I looked back at Livia, who had put her other hand on Callistus's neck. She was as pure as the unicorn; it was no wonder they looked so right together. Tears rolled down her cheeks, but she only shook her head at me, begging me to think of our family first. I truly didn't know what to do. It was the wrong choice to submit to Brutus, and an equally wrong choice to sacrifice our mother. Livia didn't know I had just come from seeing our mother, and how that tore at me now.

"Give me your decision," Brutus said. "Either you return with me now, or within one hour, your mother will be gone and I will turn my attention to a new target until you cooperate." His eyes drifted to Livia.

"I'm not afraid of him," Livia whispered, though her voice trembled. "Save our mother."

"Nic will not go with you," Radulf said.

"Then his mother will die!" Brutus countered.

"You and I made one bargain!" I shouted above them both. "Let's make another."

"No," Brutus said. "You tricked me."

"But you must make this bargain," I said. "I'm not giving you a choice."

"Oh?" Brutus was amused again. "I'm surprised to hear you taking your mother's life so lightly."

"I am absolutely serious about saving her," I said. "As serious as you are about getting the Malice."

"No, Nic." Radulf stepped toward me, but I turned away from him.

"This is my bargain to make, not yours," I said to Radulf. To the rest I added, "What I'm offering is my decision, and only mine."

"So the slave boy can think for himself after all." Brutus smiled. "Let's hear it, then."

"I do have the key. With it, I will get the Malice of Mars" — I flashed a glare at Radulf — "on my own. I am the only one who knows where it is. The Malice was created by the gods and cannot be destroyed by a human. But something else created by the gods could destroy it." I raised the bulla, and Brutus's smile fell.

He said, "So your bargain is that if I spare your mother, you will spare the Malice. That puts us at an impasse."

It was my turn to smile. "In four days, the Ludi Romani begins, honoring the might of Rome, and also Julius Caesar, who was assassinated by some coward senator you might know, Marcus Brutus."

Decimas Brutus shook his head. "There are no cowards in my family."

My gaze never left his eyes. "If that's true, then the games are the perfect place for you and me to settle our differences."

Brutus chuckled. "You want a chariot race? But you have magic."

"I won't use it, not to help me or to hurt you. This is to be a fair race. Put up any competitor you want, with any team of horses you choose. If I win, you will free my mother and vow never to come after me or my family again. The Praetors will abandon their quest for the Malice."

"And if you lose?"

I refused to look at Radulf, whose glare at me was like the heat of the sun. And there was no way I dared look back at Aurelia. She would be equally angry, though for different reasons. "If I lose, I will give you the Malice, and use it to help you make a Jupiter Stone."

"Creating the Jupiter Stone will probably kill you," Brutus said.

"I know that. Which means our bargain favors you."

"No tricks?"

"No tricks."

Brutus could not have looked more pleased. "All right, Nicolas Calva, we will meet again in four days. I agree to your terms."

⚞·TWENTY-FOUR·⚟

O nce the agreement was settled, I freed Brutus, who quickly left the field before I came to my senses and backed out. Except that I wasn't going to back out. I had just bought myself four days to find the key.

"Arrogant fool of a boy!" Radulf's face was so pinched with anger that I decided to keep my distance from him, even with a shield in place. "You know where the Malice is hidden? How?"

"Valerius told me, before he died." That wasn't entirely true, but it was close enough without giving away to Radulf that he was nearly standing on top of it.

Radulf's argument shifted. "And you are risking all of that on a chariot race? You've only done practices, which are nothing to the real thing, and certainly nothing compared to the Ludi Romani. The Praetors will choose the finest racer in the empire, one who has probably sent a thousand other charioteers to their deaths in the circus."

"I'm a good driver!" I countered.

"The circus spits out good drivers with every bend of the track! You could not have offered him a worse deal."

"Train me," I said. "We have four days. So train me to race."

"It won't be nearly enough time."

"But it's all I have." I was reduced to begging now, which I hated, but I'd be even more pathetic if I denied that I needed his help. "Radulf, I understand better than anyone what happens if I lose. So help me now."

"Tell me this," Radulf said, lowering his voice. "Do you have the key?"

Without looking directly at him, I nodded. I had it, whatever, or wherever it was. But there was nothing more I could say.

"Then I will train you the best that I can. Though in the end, you'll be alone in that chariot."

Finally, I turned to really look at Aurelia and Crispus. His eyes were red, I realized now. He had just lost his father, which surely felt to him like an open wound. And even as he suffered that trauma, I had still begged him to look after my sister, which he did with courage and honor.

I enclosed Crispus in a grateful embrace, patting his back before I let him go. "Valerius was a good man and a good senator," I said. "But when your time comes, you will be even better."

"I have to act for Rome now, in my father's place," he said. "Do you understand that? If you threaten the empire, I must order the guard to come after you."

I smiled. "You can try, but Radulf controls the guard and I have the bulla. Just believe me when I say that I will never be a threat to the empire."

He shook his head. "You already are a threat, Nic, and don't even seem to know it. That's why I had to warn you."

My grin widened, that is, until I looked to Aurelia. The rims of her eyes had reddened, which was hard for me to see. I was used to making her angry, but I didn't like the thought that I could make her sad too. Softly, I asked, "Can we talk in private?"

When she nodded, I took her arm and led her a little distance away. "I know this isn't what you want," I said. "But this bargain gives me a chance. It's the best I could do to save my mother and to keep him from getting the Malice."

"Do you remember in the amphitheater when I said I had a bad feeling about you going in there? You did it anyway, and look at how awful that turned out. You nearly died!"

I faked a smile, hoping it looked to her like confidence. "I survived the amphitheater."

"My father didn't."

The smile felt naïve now, and I let it go. "I'm sorry, Aurelia. I tried to save him."

"I don't blame you for that. But I have a worse feeling this time. Please don't do the race."

"This is different. I had no idea what to expect in the amphitheater, but I do know how chariot races go."

"You're not listening, Nic! I'm telling you something bad will happen if you enter the race!"

"And what happens if I don't? Do you think I offered this bargain because of how good my situation is?"

"We have four days. Four days we can use to find your mother, not train for a chariot race."

"That only solves the problem for a moment. Radulf was right before — I will never be able to run far enough in this empire to get away from the Praetors. They promised to come after everyone I love until I give in. Not only my mother, but Livia, and —" I stopped there, choking on my own breath. Quietly, I added, "Everyone."

Aurelia stared back at me as if all breath had been stolen from her too. Her eyes darted over to Crispus, who was watching us but probably couldn't hear the words that were falling so stupidly from my mouth. I was grateful for at least that much.

"The deal has been made," I whispered.

"Just be careful," she finally said. Her arms slid around my neck as she held me in an embrace. I heard her sniff like she was crying, but I wasn't going to check to be sure. It would embarrass her and weaken my resolve.

When we parted, her eyes were dry, but again, I didn't dare look that closely. Instead, I scuffed my sandal on the ground and said, "Come with me to Radulf's home. You'll be safer there than anywhere. Livia will be there too, and I know she'd love your company."

"So you want me there because of Livia? That's the only reason?"

I shook my head. "No, of course not."

"Then why?"

Because I wanted her there, where I knew she was safe, where I could get her advice and enjoy her friendship. But instead of saying any of that, I panicked. "Er, Radulf has good cheese."

Good cheese? Had I really just said such a ridiculous thing?

Aurelia released me and stepped back. Even the small distance between us felt too far apart now, but nothing I could do would change that.

Aurelia shook her head and looked toward Crispus. "He just lost his father, and his mother will be devastated. Crispus will be expected to immediately begin his apprenticeship with the Senate, and to manage what's left of his father's lands. Livia might want me there, but I'm needed here. I need to stay with Crispus."

A knot formed in my gut, and my tone sounded too bitter considering how much he had lost today. "Crispus has servants to help him."

"Yes, but what he needs are friends," she said. "I'll stay here until his father's burial is over. And I'll be there when you race, as your friend too." She licked her lips. "I'll be there at the end, to celebrate when you claim your victory. Your freedom."

I nodded at her as she started to walk away. Perhaps if I did win my life back, I would be in a position to offer her a bargain of my own.

◄◄ · TWENTY-FIVE · ►►

Once Aurelia and I had finished talking, she and Crispus left to break the terrible news to Crispus's mother. I felt for their family and wished things could've happened differently tonight. I wished everything could be different than it was, in fact. And though the knot in my gut was as tight as ever at seeing her leave with him, I knew Aurelia cared about me too.

Livia came to my side as we walked toward the road back to Radulf's home. She took my arm in hers and gave it a squeeze.

"I haven't seen you race," she said. "But I don't need to. I know you, and that's enough to tell me that you will win."

"I'll do my best," I said.

"No, Nic. You must win. There really is no choice now."

Her nails dug into my flesh, communicating the fear she was trying to hide. But she didn't need to be afraid. I had a plan to ensure my victory, and I would give her the details once we had a chance to be alone. But only her.

Callistus walked along beside her, which was no surprise. He obeyed me, but he was drawn to Livia. As all good things were.

At least three separate times as we walked along the out-skirts of the city, I started to tell Livia about having seen our mother. Back in the sewers, when she found out that I'd had the quick glimpse of our mother in the circus, she was clearly frustrated with me for not telling her. I knew she would want to know now that Mother and I had spoken. That our mother was concerned for Livia's safety and had expressed her love for us.

But Mother had also begged me not to bargain with Brutus, and I had. Mother wanted me to take Livia away from Rome, leaving her behind, which I refused to do.

And if I told Livia about our mother, I'd have to tell her everything. I didn't want her to feel divided about the right choices for us. She shouldn't have to feel the same burn in her chest, warning that what I'd just done might be a big mistake.

Because the longer we walked, the more I wondered if I had done the right thing in making the bargain. Livia was right: There was no choice now but to win the race. Losing it would cost me everything.

On the third time that I started to tell Livia, Radulf began walking beside us, and I clamped my mouth shut. Maybe he knew that I'd spoken with my mother — I wasn't sure if he could sense that through the Divine Star — but if he didn't know, I certainly wouldn't tell him. And I was still keeping myself more than an arm's reach from him. I didn't trust him and understood that I deserved his trust even less. But since I had the bulla, and had just threatened to use it to destroy his life's ambition, I figured I had more reasons than he did to keep my distance.

Radulf glanced sideways at me. "If you thought it was risky to trick Brutus with a fake Malice, then explain how this is a better idea."

I thought about what Valerius had said, that Brutus would sense the absence of magic in a fake Malice. But that still didn't mean this was a better idea. So I only shrugged. My bargain with Brutus was beginning to feel like a terrible mistake.

"Would you really have destroyed the Malice?" he asked. "If Brutus hadn't agreed to your offer?"

"I still intend to destroy it," I said. "Even if it means destroying the bulla too."

"You'd be right in the middle of that explosion," Radulf said. "It would kill you."

"Creating a Jupiter Stone probably will too," I said. "So at least I'll have some say in the reason for my death."

"Maybe it won't," Radulf said. "Your father didn't have the amulets when he attempted to create the Stone. Maybe the amulets will protect you."

Maybe not. I tended to believe that the creation of a Jupiter Stone was meant to kill whoever attempts it, with or without any amulets. It was the gods' way of protecting their magic.

"Besides," Radulf added, "once you feel the magic of the Malice, you won't want to destroy it. You'll never want to give it away."

"I'll be killed for having it." I eyed Radulf. "Or worse."

"Can we please talk about anything else?" Livia released my arm and stood back. "You talk about your death as if it's some theory, some idea that has no consequences. It would be a real thing, Nic, and then I'd lose you. I'd be alone." Her voice let out a small squeak. "What would happen to me then?"

Radulf stepped up beside her and spoke as gently as I'd ever heard him before. "You are my granddaughter and under my protection forever. Whatever happens to Nic, you will be safe. You will never again live in slavery, never again have to suffer or wonder where your next meal will come from."

"Don't think for a minute that my worries have anything to do with my next meal or a life of comfort!" she said, the closest thing to anger that I'd ever heard from her. "I care about my brother. You must help him win that race!"

"Then let's start right away," Radulf said. "It's still very early. If we hurry home, we can get a few hours of sleep and begin at the racetrack after breakfast. Take my arm. My magic will take us there."

Livia obeyed, but I folded my arms and stepped back.

"Do as you're told," Radulf said to me.

"I'll ride Callistus back home," I said. "That's how I'll start practicing."

I had expected him to argue, but he didn't. Radulf only mumbled, "If you wish. Obviously, I cannot force you to do anything." Then he closed his eyes, and without another word, he and Livia vanished.

I stared at the empty space where they had stood, incredulous. It was the closest I'd come in years to feeling free. For the first time in as long as I could remember, I wasn't hiding from anyone, or running, or expecting to be caught. Was this how other Romans felt all the time?

I turned to Callistus, and something about the look in his eye reminded me that while I had some independence, it was not the same as freedom.

"Well, boy, I can tell your opinion of what I've done." I patted Callistus on his neck and continued walking with him. I was glad he couldn't answer me, because I knew what he'd say, and at the moment, it wasn't exactly favorable to either my intelligence or my wisdom.

Four days. I had to be insane to propose that bargain with Brutus. Even now, I was sure I could hear him laughing with the other Praetors at how lucky they would be after the race, hauling me before them on my knees and demanding the key to the Malice.

A key that I had, obviously, but could not use. I hadn't worried as much about the Malice before now. It was easier to believe the key had died along with Horatio. Well, it hadn't. And now, Livia was right: The Malice was no longer a theory, but an amulet, which I would either find and destroy, or which would destroy me as the Praetors forced it from my grip. The consequences of failure were terrible, and very real. I had to recall every word Horatio said to me two months ago, or whether he had done anything that could have given me the key.

I needed that key as much as I needed to draw my next breath. Maybe more.

Finally, I swung into the saddle on Callistus's back. He had the power of forty horses, so I figured testing him to his limits would also stretch mine.

"Run," I whispered.

And he did. He shot forward so quickly that I nearly lost my hold on his saddle. Rather than continuing on toward Radulf's home, he turned around to keep us on the outskirts of Rome. Where the new city wall was not entirely built, Callistus ran into the open land, out to where I had longed to go as a free person.

Wind whipped at my face and dried my eyes to the point that it was necessary to close them at times. Finally, we were in flat, open fields, and I geared up in the saddle and narrowed my eyes enough to give him some direction.

Callistus had the same power in running as I had felt in the griffin as we flew. Yet because Callistus traveled by land, I was more aware of his grace at such high speeds. I leaned in the direction I wanted him to go, and he obeyed my cues.

Only minutes later, a quick glance back told me that the city walls were much farther away than I had expected. Callistus showed no signs of tiring yet, and maybe he would never need to stop and rest. I wondered if he would take me to the farthest limits of Rome, and what I'd find when I got there.

Some of the slaves who had worked with me in the mines had come from lands so far away that little of what they described sounded familiar. There were some men with dark skin who talked of jungles and harsh deserts and survival where water was scarce. Others with fair skin came from the north, with cooler summers than we had in Rome, but winters with snow that could bury a person inside their home for weeks at a time.

I knew nothing of their lives before coming to the mines, or how I'd survive with Livia and my mother if we eventually went into those strange lands. Truly, although it was firm in my mind that I would have to leave Rome if I was ever to find peace, I didn't know where in the world could be any more beautiful.

We had been riding south, I realized, with the scenery passing so quickly that it took me a while to realize where we were headed, and I didn't like it at all.

"Turn around," I said aloud to Callistus. "Let's go back."

But he wouldn't, even after I gripped his reins and tried to turn him. I wouldn't force him with magic; indeed, the last thing I wanted was to put him at risk from anything the bulla could do. But he was clearly willing to risk my safety.

The mines were ahead. The same ones that had taken five years of my life in exchange for filth, starvation, and harsh labor that had all but killed me. My former master, a pig named Sal, was now in charge of the household for Senator Horatio, another reason I doubted Aurelia would return to her home any more often than necessary. But a new master had taken over at the mines, and would likely know my face and the story of how I had run away. I wouldn't go back there ever again. I couldn't.

Fortunately, it wasn't long before we left the road to the mines as Callistus turned us toward the shores of Lake Nemi, the one we miners had called Diana's Mirror because of her temple on the northern shore. But now I understood Diana differently, her powers, her anger and jealousy. Going near the lake was only slightly preferable to the mines, which was only slightly preferable to having my teeth knocked out by wild boars.

That is, until I saw why Callistus had fought me to come. For when we got down to the shoreline, I saw the flutter of a golden wing behind a rock, and recognized it at once.

I leapt off Callistus's back and went running around the rock —

— to the griffin, who nearly sideswiped me with her paw and lovingly curled me into her at the same time.

To Caela, whom I had dearly missed and thought about almost as often as I thought about nearly anything else.

I wrapped my arms around her neck and dug my fingers into the fur there until the lion half of her purred. With the bulla's ability to communicate with animals, I filled her with my love and every memory of how I had missed her these past two months. Then she crouched low, inviting me to ride. It was no accident that Callistus had brought me here, so wherever Caela wanted to go, I would ride with her.

I swung onto her back and told Callistus I would return soon, and before the words were out of my mouth, Caela and I were in the air.

·TWENTY-SIX·

I had forgotten what it was like to fly with Caela. During my last ride on her back, I had been half-dead from Radulf, furious with Crispus and Valerius, and heartbroken from my failure to save Horatio. I barely remembered the ride.

Until now.

Caela soared over Lake Nemi, beneath a moon bright enough to make the water look like black glass, only smoother. The mountains around us were equally dark, but the shadows of their ridges came in the form of tall cypress trees and the outline of Diana's temple, lit from within by candlelight. As we came closer to it, I also noticed a woman standing near the temple, watching me. Waiting for me. Now I was nervous. Caela had not taken me on a pleasure ride.

Caela landed beside the temple, and the woman, a vestalis, walked up to us and stroked the griffin's neck as if they were old friends. She whispered something to Caela, who promptly dumped me off her back by arching it and then shuffling her wings. Then Caela flew away without so much as a glance backward.

I stood and called after her, but the vestalis touched my arm. "Don't worry, Nicolas. She'll return when I call for her."

My eyes narrowed. "You have magic?"

She smiled. "You may have the power of the gods, but I have their ear, and that is enough. Do you remember me?"

Humbly, I nodded. This was the same vestalis who had granted Aurelia and me asylum in Caesar's temple. With her hair nearly as white as her robes, she was old enough to be my grandmother but still as beautiful as I imagined the goddesses to be. There was a kindness in her expression and in the tone of her voice, but a firmness too — she would have little patience for fools.

"I warned you back then not to cause trouble," she said. "You didn't listen."

"I did listen. You should've warned the empire not to cause me trouble."

Her smile was brief. "Perhaps so. I worry that more deaths are coming."

She probably didn't know about Valerius. I had tried to save him. And failed, just as I had failed with Horatio. Every death cut at my heart. If the Praetors struck out against Crispus, or Aurelia, or Livia, or my mother, it would be too much for me to bear. And if I lost the race in four days, all of them would suffer for it.

"You must find a way to stop this," the vestalis said.

I wanted that more than anything right now, more than even my own freedom. "How can I do it?" I asked, absolutely certain that if anyone had the answer to that question, it was her.

She grabbed a torch that was placed against the wall of the temple. "Come with me, Nicolas."

Since the day I had stolen the bulla, my life had felt like a deep hole in the ground. I'd tried everything I could think of to get out of the pit, but instead, it only deepened the hole. If the vestalis had any way to help — even a pebble that might raise me higher, then I would gladly follow her.

As it turns out, it wasn't a pebble exactly. But it was close.

I followed her behind the temple to a large field on a slope that was scattered with loose rocks, each about the size of my fist and all of them as white as Callistus's fur.

"The Jupiter Stone is here," the vestalis said.

I shook my head. "I won't create one of those, not for the Praetors, or Radulf, or even you, my lady."

She closed her eyes and nodded in approval. "You must never create one for the Praetors. They will use it to control the gods. And if you create one for Radulf, he will use it to destroy the gods. And you must not create one for yourself. For it will destroy you."

I looked sideways at her. "What about you?"

She smiled. "I am not asking."

"I don't have the Malice," I replied. "Without it, I can't create a Jupiter Stone, even if I wanted to." And I definitely didn't want to. Creating a Jupiter Stone would require me to challenge a bolt of lightning, and I knew how that encounter would end.

There were whole body parts I'd rather lose before I wanted to create a Jupiter Stone.

"The time hasn't come for you to create the amulet," the vestalis said. "Only to find the stone intended for that purpose." Then she motioned toward the rocks. "*One* of these is the Jupiter Stone. The others are merely rocks. You must learn to tell the difference between them so that when you are returned here — and you will be — you will know which stone *not* to select for your captors."

"My captors?" I asked. "Who will that be?"

"The captors you choose." Then she shrugged. "Though I cannot tell who that will be. You have not chosen them yet."

I wouldn't be choosing anyone — that was the whole point of my bargain with Brutus. I had no intention of letting things get to the point of my capture.

"How do you know all this?" I asked. Because I wanted her to say that she really didn't know, and that she was just good at making guesses.

Her smile dimmed as she motioned again to the rocks. "Find the Jupiter Stone, Nicolas. And bring it to me in the grove."

Then she walked down a hillside, taking the light with her. The only light, I realized, as the air around me became black.

I didn't want to use magic to produce a light. Using the bulla, I'd likely start a fire and burn the temple to the ground. That would hardly endear me to Diana, who probably already hated me enough. And using the Divine Star would alert Radulf to where I was. Above everyone else, except maybe Decimas Brutus, I didn't want Radulf to know I was looking for the Jupiter Stone.

So I worked in darkness, using the moonlight to guide me. The vestalis had given me no hints to know when I had found the Jupiter Stone, but I assumed, like the bulla, it would be one of those know-it-when-you-find-it moments.

There were hundreds of rocks here, none of them any different from the next. I picked up one, waiting for some recognition in my hand, then set it behind me and moved on. I did the same with another, and another, and dozens more. After a couple of hours of this, my back ached from being slouched over, and my hands were as gritty as they'd ever been in the mines. I was exhausted and also beginning to wonder if my method of hoping I recognized the correct rock was foolish. Maybe I'd left the Jupiter Stone behind an hour ago, and if I searched the rest of the year, it would produce nothing but a permanently hunched back and frayed hands.

Enough of this. What good was it to have a bulla hanging from my neck if I couldn't use its power to help me now? I would not search on my knees anymore.

I stood and raised my arms wide and used the bulla to command all the rocks from this field to rise. The mountain quaked beneath me, and for a moment, I thought it would split apart, then I remembered what I had stupidly commanded. No, I did not want *every* rock to rise — that would hollow out the mountain. I only wanted the Jupiter Stone to rise.

The rumble continued beneath me, but different from before. I had no worries for my own safety, or even the temple structure. The rumbling was caused by the stones shifting into new positions. All I could do was step back to avoid their movement.

When the rumbling stopped, I hesitated a moment, because I had commanded the Jupiter Stone to rise, and if a rock was floating in the air, then I could not see it. I needed more light.

Upon my silent command, the rocks sparked, giving off a hot silver light that forced me to shield my eyes. They became as bright as a flash of lightning, but one that does not dim. When I removed my hand and forced myself to look, I saw the rocks had formed into a lightning bolt, as lengthy as what I imagined they must be in the skies, and as bright.

Which was amazing to see, but useless. Because as beautiful and terrifying as the bolt was, that did nothing to get me the Jupiter Stone.

The caw of an eagle overhead caught my attention next, and I looked up, expecting to see Caela there. It wasn't her, however. It was simply an eagle.

No ordinary eagle, that was certain. This one was larger than any I'd seen before, with eyes that reflected the moonlight and pierced me to my core when it looked down at me.

The lightning bolt and the eagle. Jupiter's symbols.

The eagle screeched in a fashion that even Caela would've respected and it seemed to call my name. When the bird was directly over my head, I saw something clutched in its grip. A rock.

I held out my hands to receive it, but instead of delivering it, the eagle crashed into me and took me right over the slope of the mountain. I tumbled end over end, throwing out magic in hopes of finding something to slow my fall, but all that did was create even more falling rocks, an avalanche of magical disaster.

Also, an appropriate symbol for my life, I thought.

Jupiter's eagle was flying beside me, cawing in a way that now sounded more like cackling. As if it was enjoying this. No, as if *Jupiter* was enjoying this.

Well, I hadn't chosen to come here. I didn't want a Jupiter Stone, now or ever, and this certainly wasn't the way I intended to get myself killed.

The rocks sliding below me crashed into a tree, knocking it at an angle. When I came to it, I grabbed at branches until one finally held my weight, then wrapped myself around the trunk as larger rocks continued pushing the tree downward.

My body was bruised and battered, but I still had the bulla's strength, which I used to shimmy up the trunk. As the eagle came toward me again, talons out, I leapt from the tree and grabbed on to its legs.

It screeched in anger and flew higher up the mountain, pecking at me with a beak that tore at my flesh, and trying to shake me off. I didn't enjoy that, but it was still better than falling. The bulla made me stronger, and the Divine Star gave me healing, but neither of them protected me from absolute stupidity.

Which this was, by the way.

I kept one hand holding the eagle's leg and, with my other, wormed my fingers into its talon until the rock it was holding was mine. Then I let go and asked the bulla to find a soft landing for me.

It didn't. The earth was every bit as hard as I remembered. Fortunately, the eagle had tired from my weight, so I was lower to the ground than before and at least I hadn't landed in thorn bushes. It wouldn't have surprised me much if I had.

I rolled a few times on the ground until everything came to a rest, then remained there on my back for several minutes, catching my breath and trying to find a position that didn't hurt.

I shouldn't use the Divine Star — Radulf would know — but I had no choice, and I let it wash through me, carrying away the worst of my pain.

He felt what I was doing, and he was curious, maybe even concerned. I knew he wanted to ask, but he didn't.

The vestalis walked up to me and chuckled lightly. I hadn't even realized the eagle had dropped me so near to her. "Well," she said, surveying my scratches and bruises. "That could have gone better."

I unfolded my fist and looked at the rock caught in my hands. Where the others had been rough and chipped, this was smaller, but perfectly round and as smooth as marble. I detected no magic inside it, but maybe the magic wasn't there . . . yet.

This rock was meant to become the Jupiter Stone. I had just taken it from Jupiter himself.

Another theft.

Another victory.

☙ · TWENTY-SEVEN · ❧

This wasn't really a Jupiter Stone, not yet, since it had no more magic than a dried apple core. But I had it clutched in my fist, the same way I often held the bulla.

I staggered to my feet and followed the vestalis along a path. Diana's temple was above us, and I hoped the path would take us even farther away from anything associated with her.

I knew from my time in the mines that strange rituals took place at this temple, violent ones with screams I sometimes would hear at night. And though I had some protection because of the magic within me, it was still uncomfortable to be here. Surely, Diana knew that I intended to use her magic to stop the Praetor War, not expand it.

The path soon led to a thick grove of trees. Mighty oak trees that were probably as old as the earth itself. The vestalis sat on a marble bench facing one large oak tree that stood apart from the rest.

The moonlight was behind it now and shone brightly through its thick branches. Although we had walked far from

Diana's temple, I felt a reverence here. Maybe that was because we were so far away. Diana was a warrior. The vestalis was not, and certainly I wasn't either.

"Sit beside me, Nicolas."

She didn't ask for the stone, and I didn't offer it. But I did sit, facing the oak tree.

The vestalis was quiet for so long that I began to wonder if she had fallen asleep. And I debated what to do because the truth was, I wouldn't have minded falling asleep too — this horrible day seemed to have no end.

The moonlight was fading now, or more accurately, the sun was rising at our backs. It was early still, and yet those first moments of sunlight touched on the outer branches of the tree as if each had been lit with a flame. It was beautiful in the kind of way I knew I'd never be able to describe to anyone else.

"I can feel your heart," she finally said. "So heavy with fear and sorrow, but it beats for the love that is there too."

"For my mother and my sister," I said.

The vestalis looked over at me. "A mother and sister, yes. But is that all?"

"No." I couldn't lie to her, not even if I was used to lying to myself.

She turned back to the tree. "You want freedom, Nicolas Calva. I feel that in your heart as well. Every decision you make is weighed against the hope of whether it will make you free."

My breath was becoming shallow. "Can you give me freedom? I will trade this stone for it, and the bulla. And the key to the Malice, if I knew how to give that away." Because I knew now, more than ever, that without the amulets I could not gain my freedom. With them, I could not live in freedom.

She smiled softly. "Freedom never comes to those who avoid their problems. To get what you want, you must walk through the fire. And I suspect you will need your magic to survive it."

Then she knew about the bargain I had made with the Praetors. She must, because I figured a chariot race against their strongest competitor was as much fire as anyone could ever walk, or ride, through.

Since first seeing the vestalis again, a question had been stuck like a lump in my throat, and it was time I forced it out. "There's a woman known as Atroxia —"

She cut me off with a heavy sigh. "The vestalis involved in Caesar's death. As punishment, she was buried alive."

"Yes. Can you tell me about her?"

The sacred woman stood and faced into the sun, away from me. "She will test you in a most unexpected way, Nicolas. What you still do not understand about love will become clear through her."

I understood far more than the vestalis seemed to think. I'd sacrificed so much for my loved ones already. I didn't see how life could teach me anything more about the price of caring for another person.

Besides that, I had no intention of being tested by the Mistress, because she was asleep, and I intended to keep her that way. I said, "I'm not supposed to wake her up. I've been told that she's evil."

The vestalis turned back to me, with heavy eyes and shoulders. "Then perhaps you have things to teach her as well."

No, the vestalis was wrong about this. I was certain of it. Or, I hoped for it anyway.

The sun was rising higher now, and whole branches of the tree were visible.

"Do not break those branches, ever," the vestalis said. "Not until the time is right for you."

I stared at her. I had no reason to break any branches of that tree, nor would I cause it any harm. I was tired of only destroying things.

And we sat a little longer until the sun had lit the entire tree. Where the tips had once seemed touched with fire, now the entire tree caught the sunlight like a flame.

The vestalis stood, and I stood with her. "Now it's time," she said. "Place your stone on a branch of that tree, any branch you choose."

I gripped it tighter. "It won't be safe there. Anyone could grab it."

"They won't even see it. Because it's your stone now and will stay in the protection of the tree until you call for it. If you ever choose to call for it."

So I walked forward and reached to the highest branch I could, then rolled the Jupiter Stone onto the limb, near the trunk. I didn't see how anything she said could be possible, and yet the tone of her voice was so certain, I didn't doubt her either.

Once I returned to her side, the vestalis cupped my face in her hands and lifted it so that she could see me better.

"Remember that victory comes in protecting those you love, not destroying those you hate." When I nodded, she said, "You'd better get home now. There are difficult days ahead."

She started to leave but turned when I asked, "*Domina*, will I ever see you again?"

She smiled. "You will, when you need me most."

With those words, Caela appeared overhead with a fierce screech and circled around, looking for a place to land. I called up to her that I would move into a clearing. When I looked for the vestalis again, to offer her some help up the hill, she was gone.

Several minutes later, Caela brought me back to where Callistus was waiting near the lake. He'd had a nice rest and was obviously eager to ride again. Which was fine for him, but I hadn't slept all night and the road back into Rome was far too long. I wished Caela would fly me there while I closed my eyes, but that was clearly not their plan. Before I left Caela, I wrapped my arms around her and whispered, "Do not forget me. For I will never forget you."

She nudged at my side with her beak, a sign of some affection, I thought. Then she flew into the skies and disappeared against the rising sun.

The ride back with Callistus was a somber one. I wasn't sure exactly what had just happened with the vestalis, and she had given me multiple warnings, none of which sounded particularly pleasant. And through my exhaustion, every problem seemed bigger than it had felt before. Although it was still too early to expect many Romans on the street, we had to take extra time to avoid the ones who were already at work. Unicorns were exceptionally rare. Better to keep Callistus a secret.

Radulf was waiting for me in the courtyard when we returned. I knew some of the deeper scratches from my fall and battle with the eagle still hadn't healed. Certainly my torn tunic hinted that something significant had happened. My hair was wild and blown back from my face, which was windburnt on my nose and cheeks. The Divine Star was alive and the bulla was warm, and I was sure he wondered where I had been for the entire night.

But before he could ask, I dismounted from Callistus and strode past Radulf, saying only, "I'm going to sleep. We have practice today."

"It is today already," Radulf said, half grinning.

"Later today," I mumbled. "Unless you want me driving the horses into the wall."

Which, as I thought about it, seemed like a far better alternative than the bargain I'd made with the Praetors.

⊰· TWENTY-EIGHT ·⊱

I was only allowed a couple of hours of sleep before Radulf had me summoned to meet him at the circus. Still struggling to keep my eyes open, I walked with him toward the stables where my horses were kept. Other teams were here to practice, but I was no longer interested in competing against them. Once I raced, it wouldn't be red versus white or blue or green. It was me, riding for my life, and for the future of Rome.

Radulf hadn't asked about last night, though I knew he must be curious. No doubt he would ask soon, but until then, we both knew I had to focus on the coming race.

"Charioteers are drawn at random to choose their starting gate," Radulf told me as we walked toward them. "You want to be one of the last ones chosen so that you can pick the gate farthest away from your toughest competitors. Choose the lowest number possible, though, because once you leave the gates, you must press to the inside track. You want to get ahead and then stay ahead. It's much harder to come from behind."

I understood that, and I had no worry about my courage to

press in to the center. My greater concern was how the Praetor I'd be competing against would try to stop me.

Radulf continued, "For the Ludi Romani, you'll go around the track seven times. The entire race totals about three miles, so you must pace yourself."

"I know all this," I told him. "I've raced before."

"You've practiced before, and you drive too fast too early. You'll wear out your horses if you push them at that speed. Drive just fast enough to stay in the lead."

"How many horses am I allowed in this race?" I asked.

"Four. Though it won't matter since everyone gets the same number. But I am buying us new horses, the finest money can buy."

"I know the other horses better," I said. "The ones I've already practiced with."

"You'll get to know the new ones by the time you race. They'll be here tomorrow."

I wasn't going to argue with that. The horses he'd given me before were strong, but they were older and tired easily. Winning mattered almost as much to him as it did to me, and I had to trust at least some of his decisions.

"Get me one horse," I said, smiling. "So strong that he defeats the other teams and lets me squeeze right between them."

"I'm getting four horses," he said. "So strong that they'll run right over the other teams."

I laughed. "To do that, I'd need at least double that number."

"Too many horses won't help you." Radulf chuckled. "The story is told of that great fool, Emperor Nero, who attempted to race with ten horses, more than twice what the other charioteers were allowed. He was thrown from his chariot before finishing the course, though naturally, he was declared the winner."

I grinned along with him. "I would have liked to see that."

Radulf patted my back. "When I rule the empire, you will see anything you can imagine. With our magic combined, everything will be possible. Even the gods will bow to us."

My smile fell, and I turned my focus back to the circus. "I'm ready to ride now," I said. "I want to get on the track."

"Just the starting gate for today." I started to protest, but Radulf added, "It's the most important part of the race. You need a clean exit from the gate."

Here at the *Circus Maximus*, a building housed the gates that led onto the track. We entered from the stables to the rear, beyond the view of the audience, and then lined up in the building where the race would begin. The twelve gates each had a separate archway with wooden doors that released at the very same moment. The gates were all situated on a slight curve so that every gate had the same distance to the break line, the point at which the competition officially began.

However, the way a charioteer left the gates could make all the difference. That was the reason for today's practice.

My team of four horses was brought to a middle gate, and I climbed into the chariot. I planted my feet on the chariot floor as I started tying the reins around my waist.

"Just hold the reins today," Radulf said.

"Why? When I race —"

"When you race, you won't tie the reins either." Ridges of concern had appeared in Radulf's forehead. "That's how the Praetors will try to win, not in a fair race, but by knocking you from your chariot. You can't be tied in."

"They don't want me killed in a fall. They need me."

"They need to win, just as much as you want the victory. If it looks like they're about to lose, then they'll make sure you fall and that you don't cut yourself free. Those are the stakes. Do not tie yourself to the chariot."

I looked down at the reins in my hand. Maybe I'd made a stupid bargain, but at this point, I needed to race my very best. And that meant I would ride this chariot the way I understood. Like every other charioteer, I would tie myself in with the reins.

Radulf sighed as I wrapped them around my waist and made the knot.

"Very well," he said. "But be aware that I can only help you as much as you are willing to be helped. The rest is up to you."

"In the end, it'll be entirely up to me," I said. "Wasn't that your point last night, that I'll have to do this alone?"

"Yes, Nic," he said somberly. "In the end, you'll be alone on that track."

That was all I could think about as I directed my horses to the gate.

And that was where my practice began. We kept the gate doors open so that I could see Radulf's signal. When he gave it, as quickly as possible, I urged the horses to action and my chariot bolted from the gate. Behind me, Radulf shouted out every error I'd made, but I didn't look back. I kept my concentration on the track, edging as close to the spine as I dared.

When I'd completed one full turn, he motioned me back into the gates.

"You hesitated after the gates opened!" he said.

"For a single second — no more!"

"That single second might cost you the race. When the gates open, your horses must already be in motion."

"If I leave a little behind the others, then I'll get to the spine without competition from their chariots!"

"No. You must be first to the spine and block them. Or else they will block you and it's very difficult to overcome that. Now try again."

So I did. Again. And again. Over and over.

Each time I left the gates, the routine was the same. To leave the gate as quickly as possible and make a full round of the tracks before coming back to start again. The only difference each time was the particular criticism Radulf shouted at me as I rode. However, he was becoming more specific in his attacks on my performance, down to the way I managed the reins and the angle of my feet on the chariot floor. I hoped it meant I was getting better, though each time I returned to the gates, his frustration with me was the same.

"You're acting tired," he said late that afternoon.

"There's a reason for that," I countered.

I was exhausted. Not only from being awake for most of the night, but I'd also been on my feet all day. Even if my mind would be ready in three days, I was beginning to doubt whether my worn body could handle seven rounds of the track. I had stupidly promised not to use magic in the Ludi Romani, though I knew Brutus never would have agreed to the bargain otherwise. Maybe it wouldn't be fair to use magic, but I didn't much care about fairness at the moment.

"Why are you so tired?" he asked. "Perhaps you can tell me where you were all night."

I rolled my eyes. Yes, I had known all along that he would ask. I just wished he hadn't waited until my mind was as tired as my body.

I handed the reins to a nearby stable servant, removed my helmet, and jumped off the chariot. "I don't have to explain anything to you."

"No, that's true, you don't."

Surprised at his response, I turned back to look at him. Respect and understanding were the last things I ever expected from Radulf.

Then he stepped forward and continued, "I can't force you to talk to me. But too often, you make decisions without thinking, ignoring all the danger you are in, until you get into trouble, and then you call me for help. So if you are going to ask for help, I have the right to know where you were!"

"I understand, and you're right," I said, keeping my tone even. "So I won't ask you for help, not anymore."

And I backed away from him into the stands. I wasn't sure why I went there, only that it was someplace to go. I watched the other charioteers manage their horses as they practiced, and compared myself to them. Then I stopped. Mostly because I didn't compare well.

"Look at that man, the one in green." As he spoke, Radulf sat down beside me. Servants accompanied him, carrying some food.

I said nothing, but I did look. I had been watching the green charioteer for some time, trying to figure out how he stayed ahead of the other racers. It didn't even look like he was trying that hard.

Radulf took my silence as an invitation to stay, and maybe it was. I definitely wanted the food, and if I lowered my pride, I also knew that I needed more of his help.

"See how he stands at an angle to the chariot," Radulf said. "It helps him shift his weight when it's time to make the turns."

Then, a few minutes later, Radulf pointed to another man, one with a white tunic. "He's no good. The horses drive him and not the other way around. Let's hope the Praetors choose him to compete against you, eh?"

"They won't choose him," I said grumpily. "His own mother wouldn't bet on him winning."

And I wondered at that, if my mother would bet on me. Then an even more curious question — if I had any money, even a single coin, would I bet it on myself to win? Probably I would, but only because if I failed in the race, losing that coin would be the least of my worries.

"Of all the games of Rome, I've always loved the chariot races the most," Radulf said. "I know all the best drivers in the city. There are perhaps six or seven who are especially good, and who would be happy to race against you, if they were paid well enough. But no amount of gold in their pocket can compare to your reasons for wanting the victory. It's your heart that will win this race, Nic. You must race with passion, above everything else."

Passion was important but so was sleep, and the latter was far more important to me now. I had wanted to think more about the words from the vestalis last night, but thinking about anything at all was difficult. Finally, we decided to return to Radulf's home, where I could bathe and then have the rest of the evening to myself. A man was nailing a curse tablet to the wall as we exited the circus, and when he saw us, he dropped the hammer and tablet and ran.

Radulf went over and picked it up, then used enough magic to crush it to dust in his fist.

"What did it say?" I asked.

"It had your name on it," he said.

Obviously. "But what did it say?" To escape his home, I'd collected plenty of curse tablets, and a few of them had mentioned me, as part of the red faction.

"This was specific," Radulf said. "It calls you a plague to the empire and begs the gods to curse you before you can do them any more harm."

I grinned. "The gods have already cursed me, Radulf. They won't do any worse now."

"Let's hope not," he said. "I'm afraid for what happens to you if things get any worse."

Yes, so was I.

❧ · TWENTY-NINE · ❧

On the second day, I returned to the tracks early. I'd already been awake for hours, trying to learn some of the magic that came so easily to Radulf, and doing more poorly than I wished to admit. So I was glad to leave when Radulf called for me. His new, finer team of horses would be waiting here and he wanted us to begin working together as soon as possible.

But before we reached the tracks, we were met by new curse tablets that had gone up overnight. Dozens of them. I didn't read them all, but every single one I glanced at had my name engraved on it.

Normally this meant the odds had been calculated and people would be betting against me to win. But this time, I thought the tablets meant something else: that the Praetors were nervous. They believed it was possible I might win, and they were begging the gods to side with them.

Their pleas would go unheard. The gods would never help them. If the Praetors won the race, the gods would lose.

Diana alone would be on the side of the Praetors, and I had no doubt that she'd be happy to curse me. Or more correctly, to curse me even more. She needed the Praetors to win if she was to finish her rebellion against the other gods. It was partially for that reason that I would not use the bulla in the race. Diana would surely use her power to sabotage any magic I might attempt.

Radulf seemed more upset by the tablets than I was, though this time we only passed them by. If he tried to destroy all of the ones that had been posted, he'd collapse half the stands.

Once we got back to the stables, Radulf was presented with his new horses, which looked as fine as any I'd ever seen. The four horses were tall with broad chests, bright fur coats, and eyes that seemed every bit as alert as Callistus's were when he looked at me.

"They have been tested in other races and performed well," Radulf told me as he ran a hand over the mane of the tallest horse, a muscular black male with a white star on his forehead. "With them, you'll be faster than ever before."

I patted the horse, and whispered to him my excitement to test Radulf's words. I knew he was right.

Today, our plan was to work on managing the curves around the spine. The spine itself was the narrow center of the track that kept racers from crossing into oncoming drivers. It was built of brick and stood off the ground about four feet. A large obelisk rose up in the center of it, looted from Egypt after

Rome's victories there. At either end, three tall poles were stationed to protect the spine from any chariot crashes. The turns there were so sharp that few races were ever completed without at least one charioteer losing his balance. For that reason, the more cautious charioteers made wider turns on the outer rim of the track. Maybe they'd survive the race, but cautious drivers never won. As a rule, I was rarely cautious, and besides, I had no choice but to win. I needed to practice those curves.

With the Ludi Romani being so close, at least twenty teams were already on the track today. Many of them were doing full races, hoping to be chosen for their faction.

"We'll come back tonight." Radulf's tone was tense, and he spoke in a low voice so that we wouldn't be overheard. He was worried, that much was obvious. But I doubted it was for my safety. More likely, he thought I would expose my inexperience to the other charioteers and look even worse by comparison.

But I was already hooking up my chariot to the new team of horses. "No," I said eagerly. "I'm riding."

I used the first few laps to test the new horses. They were far stronger than my original team, so much that I knew I was borrowing strength from the bulla just to keep them from pulling too hard on their reins. They were faster too. I nearly lost my balance on our third lap.

These were winning horses, certainly. Radulf had chosen them well, and he was right to insist I use them. I nodded my thanks to him as I rounded the track. He shouted back something at me, a criticism of my performance, of course, but I didn't care. I'd rarely felt happier in my life. My hopes to win the race were growing.

I spoke to the horses as we rode, freely using the bulla to tell them what I wanted and expected of them. The horse farthest to my right was the fastest; because he was on the outside, he would run more distance than the others. But the horse on the inside had to be the strongest. I needed him to keep the entire team together as we rounded each turn. I told them these things and hoped to understand what they expected from me as well. Though I wasn't competing against the other teams on the track, it was a successful morning. When I gave them a midday break, along with a fat apple and a pat on their backs, I thanked each horse personally for his strength and speed.

Radulf and I were eating lunch again in the stands when a charioteer in a green toga approached us.

"You drive well, although I think you are far too young to race," he said to me.

I glared back. "And you drive well for someone far too old to race."

Radulf lightly swatted my leg, then said to the charioteer. "Is there something you wanted?"

He nodded at Radulf. "The grandson of Rome's finest general is on the tracks. It would be an honor to race against Nicolas Calva."

Radulf shook his head. "Today is a practice for the Ludi Romani. If you qualify, you may race him then."

The charioteer motioned toward the tracks, where several of the horse teams had stopped to watch us. "Actually, we all want to race the boy. We've seen the curse tablets and wondered, why are all of them in his name? Is it because he's so bad" — he arched an eyebrow and stared directly at me — "or so good?"

I started to answer but Radulf spoke over me. "He's a fair driver. Not worth your trouble."

"What a pity." The charioteer was still looking at me. "I saw you in the amphitheater. I know the things you can do with a wave of your hand. I suppose what the people say is true, that without that bulla around your neck, you are helpless."

I stood. "I don't need the bulla to race."

"Nic —" Radulf began, but this time I ran over his words.

"I accept your offer," I said, putting the knife back in my belt. When I finished, I reached for my helmet.

"Perhaps the loser will muck out the stables of all the winners," the charioteer said, smiling.

"If you think you can spare the time for all that work." I made sure my smile was just as wide as his.

He nodded, and I started to follow him down the steps toward the track.

"You'd be easier to control if you didn't insist on such foolish agreements all the time," Radulf called down to me.

I stopped long enough to grin at him. "Yes, Radulf, that is my plan. I will not be controlled."

He wasn't smiling back. "Then I am sad to say that you will have to learn the hard way."

⊰ · THIRTY · ⊱

Several minutes later, I and nearly twenty other chariot teams were in two rows at the break line of the track. There was no room for all of us from the gates, and out here, we drew for positions by the length of sticks in one of the players' hands. I pulled a middle length, meaning I was in the front row but nearer to the outside. It could've been worse.

It also could've been better. Namely, that I just might be the sort of person who was determined to learn everything in the hardest possible way. Radulf was right about that.

Up in the stands, money was already changing hands as people realized an unofficial race was about to begin. The empire might pretend not to see any gambling on game days, but they'd be less tolerant today. I noticed Radulf shaking hands with a couple of men and handing them a small sack of money. I wasn't sure how much he was gambling, and especially wasn't sure whether he was betting in my favor. I wanted to think he was on my side, but I also knew he wasn't a fool. Some of the drivers here seemed to know what they were doing, far more than I.

A man was chosen to drop the white cloth that signaled the start of the race, and as he raised it, I recalled what I had learned from Radulf so far. By the time the cloth fell, I was already in motion.

My chariot was the first to launch from its position, which gave me a small advantage. Although I'd made no official agreement to withhold magic, I still wouldn't use it. Today was a test of how the Ludi Romani race would go in only two days.

By the first turn, I had cut midway into the center, which gave me an easy angle around the spine. The horses of two teams ahead of me collided in the turn and fell in a tangled mess. Their drivers cut free, and it looked like they were about to start a fistfight, when the oddest thing happened: Two other drivers slowed enough to pick them up.

That made no sense to me. A second driver weighed down their chariot while giving them no advantage, and the time they'd lost would surely cost them the race.

But I also couldn't worry about any of that. I was quickly headed for the second turn, which would complete the first lap of seven, and I was determined to be inside by then.

Three chariots were ahead of me, each of them riding so close together that it almost looked like they were one wide chariot with three drivers and a team of twelve horses. I thought about the story Radulf had told me of Nero's ten-horse chariot. It had sunk him, and it would hurt these teams as well.

Another charioteer to my left was doing his best to edge me out, but my horses were strong and I wasn't about to give him any room. When we took the corner, I leaned my weight hard to encourage the horses farther inside and it forced that chariot to back off or be crushed against the columns.

The stands around us had come alive with cheers and shouts. Radulf was on the other side, opposite from me, so I didn't bother looking for him, or at anyone else, but I did hear the crowd. As always, the green and blue factions were the most popular, and they were receiving their encouragement, though I also heard a few calls for white. My faction, the red team, only had a couple of other charioteers amongst them, and both were behind me. So most of what I heard for the red was hope that we lost.

The second lap went well. The three chariots were still ahead, still locking me out of position, but everyone else had fallen behind. I'd never keep up if I tried overtaking them from the outside, and they were riding so close together that my horses had no way of pushing between theirs. My only chance was to beat them on the inside. It would require an extremely sharp turn at the spine, but I figured it was better to test my team of horses today than at the Ludi Romani.

I got into position and pushed so near the center that I could've touched the columns if I held out my hand. When it was time to turn, the other teams made the usual wide arc with their horses, but I pulled hard on one rein and then counterbalanced with my weight. My chariot bumped into the first column when we turned and I nearly fell, but I grabbed the side of the chariot long enough to reset my feet and saw all the other chariots slide into place behind me.

Although five laps remained, I could already taste victory in my mouth, like the sweetest fruit at perfect ripeness. I cared nothing for the win itself — no emperor was here to place a laurel wreath on my head, none of the gambling money would come to me, and from the chants in the stands, nobody here would be particularly happy if I won. But at least I would know that I had crossed the finish line first and, more important, that I could do it again in two days.

With half the race still to complete, I was the clear leader, and as Radulf said, it was much harder to get ahead than to stay ahead. All I had to do was keep my place on the inner track, and I would win.

And then I looked behind me, to the three chariots that had been riding in such a tight formation. They clearly weren't happy that I'd passed them, and they were motioning to other chariots still racing.

That didn't bother me. Or didn't bother me too much until I realized the other chariots had slowed to near crawls. Why would they? There was still plenty of time for any of them to pull into the lead, or to attempt it anyway. But at this pace, I'd be finished and back at Radulf's home sipping a hot tea before they started their final lap.

The two teams who had picked up the fallen charioteers had no hope of winning now; at best they were still a full lap behind me. They rode evenly but were spread apart at about the length of a horse team. It was risky to drive between them, but it was the only choice if I wanted to keep my lead.

The instant I committed myself to this route, the extra charioteer to my left tossed one end of his whip to the man on the right, who caught it, and then together they pulled it tight.

There was no time to react. At the speed I was going, I would run directly into the whip. If I ducked too low to avoid it, then I'd pull on the reins tied at my waist and lose control of my horses. And if I didn't duck low enough, the whip would catch me across my neck. It'd create an entirely new definition of the phrase "sore throat."

As it was, I pulled the knife from my waist and began to cut free of my reins, but I'd only sliced through one when the whip connected at my chest, stripping me off the chariot. With one rein still pulling me forward, my whole body fell to the ground and was dragged through the dirt while I tried to get free. The sand on the track covered a hard dirt surface, one without forgiveness. Every one of the small rocks kicked up by the horses found my arms, legs, and my side. The knife was still in my hand, but I was being dragged at such a high speed, it was difficult to get the knife against the knot. A chariot was also coming up directly behind me, ready to run me over if I didn't get out of his way. And perhaps he had already decided that I wouldn't get out of his way.

Finally, I sacrificed my shoulder enough to raise my other hand and cut the rein. Then I immediately rolled toward the spine, out of the way of the chariot directly behind me. It still wasn't safe on this part of the track, particularly from the other horses. To be safe, I needed to climb onto the spine itself. Better yet, get to the outer track where I could reach the stands, but I'd never make it that far alive, especially not the way I was feeling. My shoulder was shredded and raw, and my arms weren't much better. But more than any pain in my body was the heat in my chest. I was furious.

I hadn't used magic for the race, though considering what they'd just done, I would have been more than justified in doing so. But I did use it now, letting the Divine Star work through me to heal the skin and repair the muscles.

While I healed, I forced myself to climb onto the small platform to rest. The farthest I could go was to the tall obelisk in the center, where I leaned back facing a statue of Apollo with his chariot being pulled by a griffin. Pulled by Caela, I supposed. The expression carved into Apollo's marble face mocked me, now that I had to race with horses instead of his noble animal.

A few slaves assigned to the circus were there with me, but they left me alone. My team of horses had been safely led off the track, though I intended to check on them as soon as possible. I was still sitting there as the charioteer who challenged me finished his final lap. Every other chariot came in behind him, including the two teams with a second man. Technically, they had finished the race too.

I was the loser, of the race, and of our bet.

My shoulder was healed now, or close enough for me to run up to the winning charioteer, who was climbing off his chariot.

"You cheated!" I shouted.

"We gave ourselves an even chance!" he shouted back. "You had magic!"

Yes, and I certainly wanted to use it now. My fists were curled up tight, but not to hold the magic in. If he took a swing at me, I'd have something much bigger waiting for him.

I only stood as tall as his shoulders, and he used the advantage of height to get close to me and look down.

"I know all about you," he sneered. "You dress like the patricians and walk amongst them, but you're not one of them and never will be. You're nothing but a runaway slave who should have been whipped, branded, and sent back to the mines where you belong. If it hadn't been for your grandfather, the emperor would've executed you by now, instead of allowing you to race in the finest circus of Rome. You don't belong here, Nicolas Calva."

Magic was gathering in my hands, so much that I could barely keep my fists clenched. If he understood how much power was in even the tips of my fingers, he never would've spoken that way to me. But that was the exact reason I needed to control myself now. Because I had powers he couldn't begin to comprehend. And the will to control them.

I knew I could call in a storm — though lightning made me nervous, it was a good way to use the excess magic without causing any destruction. And if I focused it into the smallest possible storm . . . well, that could be fun.

I looked up as a small and very dark rain cloud formed overhead. "Celebrate your win," I said with a grin. "You have my congratulations. Now if you'll excuse me, I have some stables to muck out."

And I turned on my heel as thunder cracked overhead. Well, over *his* head. Mine was fine.

A rainstorm was pouring down on him right now, only him, and would last until the cloud I'd called in had given up all its water. Whenever that was.

I whistled happily as I headed toward the stables.

⊰ · THIRTY-ONE · ⊱

I was on my third stall by the time Radulf showed up. He was holding a small bag that jingled when he shook it at me. The money he had won.

"You bet on my losing?" I asked.

"I saw the way they talked before you were challenged to race. They were huddled together and pointing to one another. I'm a military man, Nic — it's not hard to see when trouble is coming. I knew they had a plan."

"You might've told me."

"So you're listening to me now? Respecting anything I have to say?" When I only growled and went back to work, he leaned against one of the stalls and frowned down at me. "You never should've accepted that challenge. You deserved what came to you."

Yes, I knew that. They had intended that exact trick from the beginning, and used my foolish pride against me.

"Do you think there weren't Praetors who saw that?" he asked. "Who don't know that all they must do is taunt you a little and you'll play into their hands every time?"

"I didn't play into their hands, Radulf. I was winning that race."

"Yes, you raced exceptionally well, better than I would have expected, in fact. In a fair world, you'd be celebrating a win right now. But you can't possibly believe the Praetors are going to be fair with you, not when the stakes are so high. If you want to win, then two days from now, you must give yourself every advantage." His eye fell to the bulla around my neck.

I grabbed the bulla and shoved it beneath my tunic. "I don't expect fairness, but I won't cheat either. When I win, it'll be a victory that I earned, one that belongs to me."

"Then you have a difficult job ahead." Radulf's tone showed his growing impatience. "Enough of this. You know a faster way to finish this work."

I did and I'd already thought about that, but I continued pulling out the old hay. "I earned this loss. I'll clean them myself."

"Then there is only so much I can do to help you." I knew what he meant, and it involved far more than these stables. He left without another word.

By the tenth stall, I was feeling less stubborn than before. Yes, it was my fault for being goaded into the race, but I had already paid for that by being dragged through the dirt. I didn't need to clean any further.

I removed the bulla and set it at my feet before continuing. With too much magic, I risked exploding the stables — highly undesirable — and besides, I wanted to practice with the Divine

Star. Then I stood back from the stables, raised my arms out wide, and sent magic to every stall for which I was responsible. They spewed out their waste and old hay like vomit, and it was no small thing to avoid being hit.

It tired me, but less than before. My strength for performing magic was returning again. It was better than ever, though, because I was less dependent on the bulla than when I'd first taken it.

I stood back to admire my handiwork and felt only a twinge of regret that I hadn't done this earlier. Or admittedly, I felt a lot of regret. This hadn't been the best use of my time. Not when so much was required of me over the next couple of days.

With my remaining magic, I attempted another trick of light, similar to what Radulf could do. Back when he and I had fought outside the catacombs, he had tricked me by making me believe Livia was there too. He claimed it wasn't difficult magic, though I'd always felt he only said that to insult me. Nevertheless, I needed to be able to do it.

I chose to practice with Aurelia's image. Not only because it was easy to picture her, but because if I made a mistake and actually brought her here, that wouldn't be such a bad thing.

I raised my hands and let everything fade around me except for the empty space of air where I wanted her to be. I saw Aurelia in my mind as clearly as if she was right in front of me. I pictured her chestnut hair, not the fancy braids given to her by the servants in her father's house, but the simpler look of wearing it straight down her back. Next came her eyes, constantly on fire for whatever I'd done lately to irritate her, and the compassion and caring that lay deeper within them. I saw her smile whenever she was truly happy. If there was magic in the mark on my shoulder, then there was magic in her smile as well. It was different, but in many ways far more powerful.

Slowly she faded into view, almost. It wasn't her, but it was very close, and if a person didn't look too carefully —

Footsteps sounded behind me, and I leapt for the bulla and quickly put it on again. I glanced back at where the image of Aurelia had stood, but nothing remained. An instinctive rush of magic passed through me, but it wasn't necessary. A few of the red faction charioteers had come. We were all on the same side of any race. Or at least, we had been until now. They didn't look particularly happy.

The strongest of our drivers was Theon, a Greek who fought whenever Radulf called him into battle and who had allowed me to ride with the red faction. He let me race with them, but that didn't mean Theon liked me.

"I've just been told that Radulf has entered you in the first race for the Ludi Romani," Theon said.

I didn't like the tone of his voice, but still I nodded.

Theon exchanged unfriendly looks with the other charioteers. There were many races throughout the year, but the first race of the Ludi Romani was considered prestigious. If Emperor Florian had been in Rome, he would've presided here, along with attendance from foreign guests, high officials, and a quarter million other Romans who'd been waiting all year for this event. Every charioteer wanted to ride it, and Radulf had just given me one of the three slots our faction was allowed.

"If General Radulf wants you to race, then there isn't much I can do about that," Theon said. "But you won't ride with a red tunic."

"I have to!" I protested. Ultimately, each charioteer raced for himself, and he alone took the winnings of his race. But the factions were also there to help one another and to protect against abuses of the rules, such as what had just happened to me with the whip in the practice race. Whoever the Praetors chose as my opponent, he would have a faction determined to stop me. For my own protection, I needed to ride with a faction too.

"You race for yourself, and for yourself alone." Theon's eyes narrowed. "From what I'm told, you'll be racing for your life."

"I race for Rome," I said. "Because if I lose, then everyone loses."

Theon chuckled and stepped toward me again. "Why is that, magic boy? You wave your hand and destroy whatever you want, then look around for people to cheer you for it, as if you've served this empire."

I wanted to wave magic toward him right now, that was certain. But I held it in, and held my place.

"Let me ride with a red tunic," I said. "When I win, the red faction can take my earnings. I don't want them."

Theon scowled, then rushed forward and shoved me against a stall door with his forearm butted against my neck. I gasped for air and grabbed his arm to buy some breath, but I wouldn't do anything more. These were my own teammates, or were supposed to be.

"Do you think we care about the earnings?" Theon asked. "We care about *our* lives, Nic. You have some powerful enemies, and it's not worth their threats to keep you in our faction."

"Who threatened you?" I asked, though I already knew the answer. Brutus was obviously behind this.

"It doesn't matter; you're not one of us anymore," Theon said. "If you show up at the circus with so much as a red thread woven into your cloak, I will make it my purpose to end your race on the first lap. What happened to you earlier today will be nothing compared to what I'll do."

I needed air, so I kicked him, and though he released me, he also swung back and connected his fist to my eye. I reeled backward while stars appeared in my vision, and shook my hands to release some of the pressure of the magic.

The rest of the team took that as a sign I was intending to fight and rushed at me. I raised a shield long enough to say, "I'm sorry they threatened you. I'm truly sorry for that."

Then I closed my eyes and pictured Radulf's home, though in the moment all I could see was the small pool in his atrium. I let the magic grow in me until I could feel the pool's water, and my feet on the tile floor, and the smell of the sweetbreads Radulf was so fond of eating.

The fire light for the stables dimmed in my vision.

"What's he doing?" Theon asked.

I never heard their answer. For only seconds later, I opened my eyes inside Radulf's atrium. It was the first time I'd successfully accomplished this trick, and Radulf was right. It was easier than I had thought.

Livia must've been nearby at the time and hurried over to me. "Nic?" When I turned to her, she gasped. "Your eye!"

I touched it gingerly, though I already knew it was beginning to swell. "Don't tell Radulf," I whispered. "I can heal it."

"Don't tell me what?" Radulf said behind me.

I remained facing away from him and said, "I learned to disappear. That's how I got here just now."

"You should've known that trick the day you got the mark. What do you not want to tell me?" He was in front of me now. "Look at me when I'm speaking!"

I looked up, and he grabbed my face to see my eye better. "What happened? Was it the Praetors?"

"No."

"Then who?"

I stared back at him. "It was nothing."

He grinned. "Well, if someone did that to you, I can only imagine how they looked once you gave them a taste of magic."

"I didn't do anything to them. I disappeared here instead."

"You left the fight?" Radulf's disappointment was evident. "Why? With all you can do —"

"I left *because* of all I can do!"

"The grandson of a general would never abandon a fight. He would finish it and leave his opponents begging for mercy."

"Then don't consider me your grandson anymore," I said. "Our magic should build Rome, not destroy it. Otherwise, it's just a curse."

Radulf grabbed my arm. "This empire was cursed long before you set foot in it. Do not forget what the Romans did to our family. Your father would still be alive if it weren't for them. Destroying the empire is the only way to remove the curse. And for that, you will use your magic to help me bring down this empire."

"And what must I face if this empire falls? You?" I yanked my arm from his grasp and began leading Livia away with me. "I will not use magic for you!" I shouted as we left.

And that should've been the end of it, but in the quiet that followed my shouting, I heard him say, "Yes, Nic, you will."

❧ · THIRTY-TWO · ❧

I did another practice race the following morning, though it wasn't organized with any other competitors. They went at whatever pace they wanted, and I went a bit faster. My goal was to become more comfortable with Radulf's horses and to build up speed with them. For the most part, I was succeeding. They were the finest team of stallions that money could buy; no one could doubt that. And despite my relative lack of experience as a charioteer, I was becoming confident that I had at least some chance of winning tomorrow.

That is, until I sat in the stands at lunch — alone this time — and watched another competitor, one who regularly rode for the green faction. Gamblers around me were discussing the number of racing records he had won and which records he was expected to beat. Also, *who* he was expected to beat. I heard my name mentioned more than once. Or rather, they talked about "that runaway slave the empire won't execute like they should." I figured it was safe to assume they meant me.

"That green charioteer is not even the best we'll see," Radulf said a few minutes later as he came to sit beside me. I hadn't known he was here and definitely hadn't expected him. He brought some bread and a cup of ale that he knew I liked. It was his form of an apology perhaps. But taking the food wasn't my way of accepting his apology. I was just hungry.

Radulf gestured to the charioteer. "His faction will probably choose him for the first race tomorrow, and he'll do well. But the finest charioteers aren't here to practice this week. They don't need to."

I set my jaw forward. "Why are you here, Radulf?"

"I raised my son to be a warrior. How did he give me a grandson who speaks of compassion and service to an empire that wants to destroy him?"

"Stop calling me your grandson. I don't want your help."

"No, but you need it. You rode well this morning. I liked your confidence on the track."

I wished I were still feeling it now. Maybe I was better on the track than before, but if Radulf was right, then I'd only done well enough to come in ahead of charioteers who probably wouldn't qualify for tomorrow's race anyway.

"Your horses are strong and experienced," Radulf said. "Trust them. And I will speak to Theon and the other members of the red faction who'll race with you tomorrow. They'll help you."

No, they wouldn't. I didn't know how the Praetors had threatened them, but they were frightened last night. Radulf didn't know that.

He said, "With enough gold in their pockets, your faction will take care of your competition."

"Just as those charioteers took care of me in yesterday's race?" I asked. "You'd have me win by cheating?"

"I'd have you win any way you can!"

I stood and threw down the rest of my lunch. "If it's not an honest win, then it's a loss. I won't cheat, even for this."

"If you lose —"

"Then we both lose, I know." I sighed, but continued staring directly into his eyes. "Did you only care about my father for the way you could use him too?"

Radulf recoiled as if my words had hit him. "Your father was everything to me!"

I shrugged, feeling almost numb. "And my family was everything to him." Then I turned on my heel to leave.

"Where are you going?"

I didn't know. The pressure on my chest felt like thousands of weights had dropped on me, and everything Radulf said made it worse. Once I found a place to be alone, I made myself disappear back to Radulf's home.

Livia was there, as she usually was, this time with Callistus as he ran in circles around her in the small courtyard.

"What are you doing back here so early?" she asked. Though she was still looking at Callistus, I saw her brows press together. "Is everything all right?"

I faked a smile. "Of course." Livia glanced at me. She looked as tired as I felt, so I knew she wasn't sleeping well. I didn't want to make her worries any worse than they already were.

She turned her attention back to Callistus, who had come to rest at her side. "Just before you came, I was thinking how much I'm like this unicorn," she said.

I smiled back at her. "Pure?" I said.

"Trapped." She turned my way but didn't really seem to see me. I got the feeling she was avoiding my eyes. "If you lose the race tomorrow, what happens to me? I don't want to stay here."

I picked up the saddle from the fence post and placed it on Callistus's back. "We're going to be fine," I said. "I have a plan, remember?"

Once Callistus was saddled, I whispered to him, and then with a nod of his head, I helped Livia get on his back and climbed up behind her on the saddle.

Radulf had begun repairs to the hole I had torn in his courtyard wall, but I blew it open again. If he truly wanted me to use my magic for destruction, then I wouldn't feel any guilt about testing that idea on his new wall.

We rode to Crispus's home with all the speed and fury only a unicorn could provide. Like before, I arrived at the rear of his property where I could more easily hide Callistus.

The crying woman — the Mistress — instantly flooded my head again. In only a few days, I had forgotten the torment of hearing her, or perhaps I had convinced myself that no sound on earth could be so desperately sad and afraid and alone. It took only seconds to remember what it was like to have those cries press against my every thought.

"We shouldn't be here," Livia whispered. "If the Praetors weren't watching this land before, surely they are now."

"They're not here." I had already asked Callistus to tell me if he sensed anyone else on this property. If we were still here, then I trusted his instincts. "Besides, the Praetors have a big race tomorrow. They're preparing for that."

"*You* have a big race too. Why did we come?"

I helped her off Callistus's back, then led her toward the temple ruins. As before, I knelt in front of them, motioning for her to do the same. "I need you to see this," I said.

"See what?"

"This." I closed my eyes and placed a hand flat on the ground. It rumbled beneath my touch, but I didn't move. I trusted the magic as it flowed into the earth.

"Nic?" Her voice was shaking, but she didn't need to be afraid.

"It's all right," I whispered. "It's me doing that."

"No, look. There's a wolf behind us."

I turned and saw the same wolf who had shown me the temple before. I gave Mars's wolf my nod of respect and said to him, "She needs to see it too."

When I looked back at the ruins, the same temple as I'd seen before was there instead. It was small and square and as impressive to me as the first time I'd seen it.

Beside me, Livia was still more concerned about the wolf, understandably. She wasn't looking at the temple at all.

"Sit," I said to the wolf, who did as I asked. Knowing he would obey me seemed to ease her concerns a little. But she scooted in closer anyway.

I directed her attention to the temple and asked, "Do you see it?"

She shook her head. "See what? The rubble?"

I put my hand on the temple, then took hers and placed it next to mine. Her palm landed flat on the marble wall, just as mine did, so I knew she felt it.

"I see it now!" Livia's eyes widened. "It's so beautiful — how could it only look as rubble before?"

"It's a protection put in place by the gods."

"Protecting what? What is this place?"

"There's a woman inside named Atroxia. She was a vesta-lis, though now they call her the Mistress." I hesitated a moment and listened for her. "Can you hear her crying?"

Livia shook her head, but I could tell from the sympathy in her eyes that just knowing someone inside was crying bothered her as much as it did me. It was a good thing for her sake that she couldn't hear the woman. Livia's gentle heart would be tortured by it.

"Somewhere here is a lock," I said. "Help me find it."

We started together on one wall and then moved around the temple. We searched high and low for anything that might fit a key. But not only did we fail to find a lock, we also could not find a door. This temple was only made of marble walls, as if they had been built up around the doomed vestalis who had cried herself to sleep.

There was no way to get inside.

⊲· THIRTY-THREE ·⊳

Nic? What are you doing here?"

Crispus was walking down the path from his home. His eyes had heavy bags beneath them, and his back was hunched, like he'd spent too long holding himself tall. It was to be expected considering his past few days probably had been far worse than mine. He wore an all-red toga with purple trim, evidence of his mourning for someone who had been important to Rome.

I knew he couldn't see the temple — to him, it was still only a pile of rubble — but I moved my body to block the temple walls, as did Livia. We stood there as if we had come to commit some sort of crime. And perhaps we had.

Rather than answer, I asked, "How are you?"

He shrugged. "It's been a bad time. My father wanted his burial done quickly so that his soul could hurry on to the Elysian Fields. So we held the funeral procession yesterday — Aurelia was very helpful with that because she went through the same thing with her father." He narrowed his eyes. "You weren't there, Nic. You didn't come."

I felt awkward and stupid and selfish to my core. No, I hadn't come, even though I'd known about it, just as I had known about Horatio's elaborate funeral procession. It had been one of the rare times when I was grateful to have the excuse of being locked up in Radulf's home. But that wasn't the case now. I couldn't tell Crispus that I felt at least partially responsible for Horatio's death and even more responsible for Valerius's. If I had been stronger in my magic, or better still, if I didn't draw enemies to me like bears to honey, then they would both be alive. I didn't cause their deaths, but I had not been able to stop them either.

And because I couldn't say any of that to him, instead he was left to believe even worse things about me, that I had missed his father's funeral procession because I cared more about racing chariots. It wasn't that at all. The guilt for being too weak with my magic was overwhelming.

I scuffed my sandal against the ground, something I'd done so often lately it was beginning to wear on the sole. "I'm sorry, Crispus. You're right, I should have been there."

Crispus sniffed and his moist eyes darted away. In response, Livia walked forward with open arms and wrapped them over his shoulders, closing him into an embrace just as my mother used to do when I was young and upset. Crispus responded, folding his arms around her as if he had needed that very thing. I should have been the one to offer him comfort, even if just to have the right words to say. Livia barely knew him. But then, she was so much better at things like this than I ever was.

When they parted, Livia whispered something to him that I couldn't hear even from where I stood. But he smiled a little, so whatever it had been, she had obviously said the words I should have already spoken.

Once Livia had returned to my side, Crispus turned around the cleared field. "I suppose all of this is mine now."

"You have your father's wealth, and one day you'll have his title as well."

Crispus's chuckle was bitter. "No, I won't. I told you before: I am not a politician. I don't enjoy it, and I'm not good at it. In my father's last speech before the Senate, he asked them to take me on as an apprentice, should anything happen to him. After the news of his death was released, it took the senators exactly three hours and twenty-two minutes to convene and vote to reject my father's wishes."

My jaw dropped open. "How can they do that? You're a senator's son! That must entitle you to some respect."

"Oh, it does. They gave me a position that is supposed to carry some authority, just not enough for me to do any harm. I'll be trained to become a judge in the courts. Eventually, I may work my way up to senator, but probably not. I don't like the law any more than I enjoy politics."

"Do you have to accept that position?" I asked.

He shrugged. "No, but what else can I do?"

"What would you do?" Livia asked. "If you had the choice."

"First, I would travel the empire, or even beyond." Obviously, Crispus had already put thought into this. "Did you know Egypt has pyramids that are over two thousand years old? How could their slaves have built them with none of the tools or techniques we have today? In the eastern part of the empire is a palace built to resemble a mountain, with gardens that grow from every ledge. And I'm sure if I went beyond the empire's borders, even greater things could be found in the world."

I smiled back at him. Crispus had been so confined by his duty to his father and the expectations for his future, that I'd never even dreamed he had such ideas.

And Crispus wasn't finished. "When I've seen the world from end to end," he said, "then I would return to Rome and build the greatest monument to the empire the world has ever seen. It would put the amphitheater to shame, or the Pantheon, or the emperor's palace."

"You should do that now," Livia said. "Don't become a judge. Not if you don't want that."

His eyes had lit so much in speaking that they became even sadder now. He sat on a rock and shrugged. "I must honor my father's wishes. I'll become a judge and hope to one day be elected senator."

"Does Aurelia know about this?" I asked. "What did she have to say?"

The one thing I knew about Aurelia was that she *always* had something to say about everything. The emperor himself could not possibly have as many opinions as Aurelia did.

Crispus threw up his hands in frustration. "She was angry,

as you might've guessed. She had the same idea as Livia, that I should do what I want with my life."

"Let's go up to your home and see her," I said. Not only would she help me convince Crispus to live a life of his choosing, but I also genuinely wanted to see her again.

When the vestalis had spoken to me in Diana's grove, she had said some things that bothered me, things I very much wanted to discuss with Aurelia. The vestalis said the Mistress would teach me about love, and that I would teach the Mistress as well. I could not think of how I had anything more to learn about such a basic concept. Even if I did, I was no teacher. But Aurelia would know what to do.

Crispus frowned. "Aurelia's not here anymore."

"Where did she go?"

"Whoever knows where she goes?" he said. "We had a fight this morning about this very subject. She said that once you got your mother back, you would take your family and leave Rome, and that she intended to go with you."

My ears perked up. Aurelia had said that?

"She wants me to leave with you as well."

And as quickly as it had risen, my heart fell again. I had constantly searched my friendship with Aurelia for any chance of finding something more between us. But for every weak possibility I found, there were a dozen more reminders that hope was a futile thing. My friendship was important to Aurelia, but so was her friendship with Crispus. It was time to give up hoping for her.

"Are you coming to the race tomorrow?" Livia asked.

Crispus shook his head. "I can't sit with the other senators, and I don't want to sit alone." His eyes drifted to Livia. "Perhaps you'd sit with me and Aurelia, if she comes back."

"Perhaps," Livia said quietly. It was a significant offer — the circus was one of the rare public places men and women could sit together.

I had another suggestion. "Come with me," I said to Crispus. "Help me get started in the race."

His expression brightened. "Won't your grandfather be with you?"

"He'll be watching the race," I said. "Please come. I really could use somebody on my side at the gates."

Crispus smiled. "I'll be there, then. But it won't only be me, Nic. *A caelo usque ad centrum.* Have you heard that phrase before?"

From heaven to the center of earth. Yes, I had heard it. But only once before.

When I nodded, he continued, "If spirits are allowed to wander from the heavens, then my father will be watching you race. He would want you to win tomorrow."

I risked a glance over to the temple, which I could still see perfectly well, even if Crispus could not. But I did not risk smiling — that was too much — and quickly looked away. At last I understood how to use the key on a temple without a door. Better yet, I knew what the key was, and that what everyone suspected was true: I'd had it all along.

The crying woman had quieted in my head while Crispus had been talking, but even as her pleas for help filled my thoughts again, one thought still emerged, one which I hope she could hear.

Tomorrow, I would answer her call.

I would open the temple and get the Malice. And claim my freedom at last.

❈·THIRTY-FOUR·❈

We spent much of that afternoon and evening with Crispus. My reasons were more selfish than I wanted to admit. Certainly, I had forgiven him and Valerius for what they'd done in the amphitheater — Valerius had more than paid the price for any harm that had come to me as a result of his actions, and Crispus had probably never known of his plans until it was too late. Besides that, the better I understood Crispus, the more I liked him.

He felt bound by duty to his father and remained loyal to Rome, despite all the harm it had done to him. The same could be said of me. At least when Crispus did his duty, whole streets weren't torn to shreds or flooded beneath several feet of water.

And I liked knowing that Crispus had his own dreams, just as I did too. Maybe he and I weren't so different after all.

But that wasn't why I accepted his invitation to stay. The selfish truth was that I had hoped Aurelia would come back. I still wanted to speak with her, more than ever, in fact. Yet suppertime passed and into the evening, she still hadn't returned.

"Your fight was about whether you should become a judge or a builder?" I asked Crispus. "That's all?" Aurelia's temper wasn't *this* unreasonable.

He hesitated before mumbling, "No, that wasn't all."

"Then what?" Livia asked. Though Livia rarely involved herself in any conversation, she had shown an unusual interest in Aurelia.

Crispus looked at me, then quickly turned away, as if he hadn't intended to look at me in the first place. "We fought about a lot of different things."

No, I doubted that. From Crispus's reaction, I was certain they had only fought over one thing, and that it involved me, though he clearly wasn't going to give any more details.

Once it became too late to hold out any further hope for Aurelia coming, Livia and I stood and thanked Crispus for allowing us to stay.

"I'm glad you did," he replied. "Really, I am. This place feels too big right now."

"Where's your mother?" I asked.

"She's spending her mourning period in bed," Crispus said. "I understand that, but I can't sit beside her hour after hour. It's depressing. That's not what my father would've wanted."

"I hope she feels better soon," Livia said.

So did I. Mostly because I was still holding on to the guilt for his death, and it didn't help to hear things like that.

We nodded to one another and started out the door, then Crispus put a hand on my shoulder and I turned.

"The fight Aurelia and I had isn't what you think." Crispus spoke quickly, as if the words were forcing themselves out. "It wasn't really even a fight."

"Oh?"

"I explained why you can't offer her marriage. Not now, when things are so dangerous."

I licked my lips, hardly daring to ask. "What did she say?"

"That she isn't afraid of the danger. And she doesn't want you to be afraid either."

Hope leapt inside me, one of the few times in weeks I'd allowed myself to feel this way. "If she waited until this is over —"

"Well, that's the problem. She can't wait. Your old master, Sal, has gone to the courts. His argument is that as the head of the household when Horatio died, he should have the inheritance. Aurelia cannot change her father's will. The courts must rule in Sal's favor. Even if they wanted to help her, the law is clear, and they won't have any choice. Sal will take everything from her, and she'll be back out on the streets."

My fists clenched, and beside me, Livia huffed with anger. This time she hadn't even pretended not to be listening.

"I told her I would marry her, just as a favor, and she said no." Crispus pressed his brows together. "Do you care about Aurelia, Nic?"

"Of course I do!"

"Then offer her marriage."

I would have done it a hundred times already, yet I felt panicked at the idea of making her a part of my future when it wasn't at all clear that I had a future. I shook my head. "My life isn't —"

"Whose life is safe? There are no guarantees for any of us, but we have to continue living while the gods allow it."

"That's my point," I said. "I doubt the gods are very happy with me right now."

Crispus stepped closer. "Listen, you'll win the race tomorrow. I'll help you in any way I can — I owe you that. With that victory, you'll win your life back and then you can repay Aurelia for everything you owe to her."

Though I knew it would never be as easy as he made it sound, I still nodded. My decision was made. First chance I got, I'd speak to Aurelia.

Minutes later, Livia and I walked back down the path toward the open field where Callistus would be waiting. She took my arm and said, "Are you still thinking about Aurelia?"

"I should be thinking about the race tomorrow," I said, which wasn't exactly an answer to Livia's question. "If I don't win, nothing else matters."

"How can I help?" she asked. "Radulf will be in the spine to monitor the race, and Crispus will be at the gates. It seems ridiculous that I'm only in the stands, sitting by uselessly."

We reached Callistus. I helped Livia into the saddle and then followed behind her again. As we rode away, I said, "It's too dangerous to help me, Livia. I can't protect you and drive the chariot too."

"Do you remember when Mother was with us in the mines?"

"She wasn't there for long, I remember." Though I now understood why. She knew she'd be identified with my father, which meant the empire could find me. And although I didn't have magic at the time she left, I'd also learned that magic is drawn to some families more than others. If they had known who I was, the empire would've executed me at once. They still would do it, if Radulf allowed it or if they ever got to me without my magic.

"The night before she left, Mother pulled me aside and told me the empire would try to find you, that it was my job to keep you hidden. I did everything I could for you at the mines, but since we've come to Pater's home, I've been useless. I wander his halls, swim in the baths, and let the servants do my hair — a job I wouldn't have even been allowed to do for someone else two months ago. The day we escaped, using those lead tablets, I thought this was a chance for me to matter. We'd leave Rome and I would help you, not be a burden that you have to worry about. But now we're back in his home again, and I'm miserable."

"I'm sorry." I'd been so wrapped up in my own rebellion and troubles that I hadn't taken the time to consider that she had troubles too, in some ways worse than mine. "I didn't know."

"Let me help you in the race tomorrow."

I looked around the area, even though it was late at night and we were still far from the main roads.

"All right, I said. "I have an idea, but give me a few hours to work on it."

And from there, she let me have my silence to begin thinking. Once we got into town, I asked if we could stop by the stables at the circus to check on Radulf's new horses, just to make sure they'd been bedded down properly for the night. Normally they'd be corralled at Radulf's home, but they had to be here for the first race in the morning and I wouldn't leave their care to some indifferent servant, or worse, a servant who preferred to see someone else win tomorrow.

Livia agreed, and we made our way there. But from the moment that we entered the stables, I knew something was wrong. The stall doors for Radulf's horses were wide open.

I leapt off Callistus's back and ran to them. Curse tablets had been nailed to every spare inch of the doors, and most horrifying of all, the stables were empty. The horses had escaped.

No, they didn't leave on their own. My horses had been stolen.

⊰ · THIRTY-FIVE · ⊱

urious, I kicked at a nearby water bucket. Magic went with it, sending the bucket much farther than it ever should've gone. If I wanted to see the ends of the Roman Empire, all I had to do was follow that bucket.

Instantly, Livia was beside me with a hand on my arm, though I wasn't sure if she was giving comfort or hoping to receive it. I didn't want her to see the curse tablets with my name scrawled into the lead, because she already worried too much. But my thoughts were flying apart, and it didn't matter now. Anyone could look at me and know the curses had done their job.

"Who did this?" She didn't speak with worry, or fear. Livia was angry. "Nic, who took your horses?"

I didn't know. It was no accident — the curse tablets made that clear. It might've been one of the other factions, or for that matter, it might've been my own faction, ensuring I did not race with them tomorrow. Or most likely, it was the Praetors. If I forfeited the race for any reason, that would be counted as a loss.

"It makes no difference," I said, already feeling defeated. "They're gone."

"What about the horses you rode before? Radulf still has them, I think."

"He does, though they've got no chance to win. They're fast enough for an ordinary race, maybe, but not for what's coming tomorrow."

"They'll have to be enough," Livia said.

I walked her back to Callistus. "Take him home and tell Radulf what's happened. He'll have his servants bring the old horses here by morning."

"What are you going to do?"

"I'll try to find the ones that were lost." Though I already knew it was futile. The horses had not wandered off and would not be left within miles of this place, or anywhere I might find them.

Once she was in the saddle, I whispered instructions to Callistus to get my sister home safely. After they rode away, I checked every other stall in the stables, just in case there had been some mistake. I knew there wasn't. Nobody accidentally nailed those tablets to the stable door, just as my horses had not accidentally released themselves.

But the fact was, I had no idea what else to do. And when I failed to find my horses in the stables, I merely walked back to the stall where they should have been and slid against one post down to the ground. If magic was strong enough to solve this problem, I couldn't figure out how, and certainly my mind was even weaker for coming up with any solution.

Radulf would send his old team of horses, just as I had asked. But they hadn't been run for two days, and even in their best condition, they wouldn't bring me across the finish line first.

After a while, I gave up any hope for tomorrow's race or of finding the horses, and shifted my thinking to Livia's request to help me. She'd be talking to Radulf by now, and that certainly was helpful, but that wasn't the kind of help she had meant. She wanted to make a difference tomorrow. And no matter how much practice I had put in since bargaining with the Praetors, the reality was that my hopes of winning were not as good as they had seemed even an hour ago.

But though I had promised not to use magic to help me win the race, I had never promised not to use magic to get the Malice. It would have to be stolen from Atroxia's cold grip, if necessary. And it'd have to happen before I completed the race, just in case things went badly.

I didn't want to return to Radulf's house, or to stay with Crispus. So I remained in the stables and eventually fell asleep in the stalls where my horses should have been. I was awoken that morning with a kick to my legs.

Theon stood before me, the red faction leader who had given me the black eye earlier. Considering that, I was lucky he hadn't kicked any harder than he did.

"So the general's grandson spent his night like a slave," Theon said. "How appropriate."

"We have nothing to discuss," I said grumpily. "I'm not riding with the reds anymore."

He peeked in the empty stall behind me. "It looks like you're not riding at all."

"They're at the baths, getting massages. I'm sure they'll return soon." I glanced around. "You've come with no horses either. Aren't you riding?"

Theon licked his lips. "My position was bought out. Every faction had their positions bought out. Except for you."

My eyes narrowed. "Who bought them?"

He grinned. "Faster charioteers than you, I'm certain. I'd wish you luck in the race, but somehow, I don't think that will help."

He left in one direction, and I went in the other. Radulf's men would be here soon with my original team of horses. A team that could never give me a victory.

Once I came to a clearing, I put out a silent call for help. But I was interrupted by Livia calling my name from back at the stables. I ran that way and saw her there with Radulf, two of his servants, and the older team of horses.

Radulf didn't scold me, either for being gone all night or for the loss of his prize horses, both of which I had expected. He only walked up to me and said, "Are you ready for this?"

Of course I wasn't, and he knew that.

He nodded toward the stables. "The Praetors stole them."

"I know."

"They're willing to cheat to win. I'll tell you one more time, Nic. You must cheat too. It's your only choice now."

"I won't."

"Your life is at stake!"

"That's why I can't cheat!" I sighed and took a few steps back. "If I don't earn this win fairly, then they won't respect our terms and we'll be right back where we were before."

"You won't be back where you were before, because you won't win." Radulf motioned toward the horses. "This team is fast, but not fast enough."

"Have your men strip down the chariot to as little as possible. I don't want to carry any more weight than is necessary."

"That chariot protects you in the race."

My smile was grim. "No chariot can protect me today. Strip it down."

When Radulf left to put his servants to work on the chariot, Livia came forward and unfolded a new tunic, one with such a deep yellow color that it almost looked woven in gold. The edges were stitched with symbols of the gods: Jupiter's lightning bolt, Neptune's trident, the spear of Mars, and Minerva's shield. Diana's bow was missing from the symbols.

"Where did you get this?" I asked. The tunic's weave was so fine, I hardly dared touch it, much less to breathe on it.

"Since you're not with the red faction anymore, Radulf had this made for you last night. He wanted you to appear on the track as your own faction, with your own color."

I glanced over at Radulf, who had been watching Livia and me. I held up the tunic and nodded gratefully to him. It was the first respectful nod I'd ever given him, and I admit that it was good to feel like he and I were truly on the same side.

"Nic! There you are!" Crispus came running over. His eyes widened when he saw the tunic. "Where did you get that?"

"From our grandfather," Livia said. "The pads for his knees and wrists match the colors, though we didn't have time to get a new helmet."

"I've never seen its equal." Crispus smiled as he brushed a hand across the cloth. "If that tunic is any sign of things to come, it's going to be a good day."

My smile at him was even more hopeless than before. Fine as the tunic was, I doubted it could be taken as a sign of anything more than Radulf's willingness to spend a great deal of money on me. Maybe his generosity was its own form of luck, I supposed.

Livia said, "Maybe you'll feel better when properly dressed. Wearing the clothes of a victor."

I nodded and walked around to the back of the stables, then changed into the new tunic. The weave was strong, and the stitching seemed flawless. The bulla against the cloth was such a close match that they practically blended together. If it weren't for the bulla's strap, from a distance, no one would know I had it. Livia was right: I did feel better wearing this.

And I would have continued feeling better if I hadn't

walked out in time to see Decimas Brutus and at least another dozen Praetors coming into the stables.

"Nicolas Calva!" Brutus boomed. "Look at you this fine morning. Didn't anyone tell you that dressing like a winner doesn't make you one?"

"It seems to work for you dressing like a loser," I said. From the corner of my eye, Radulf grimaced. Or perhaps he smiled a little. I could've sworn he did.

Brutus brushed off my insult with an annoyed glare. "They told me I could find you here. Has it been four days already?"

Radulf stepped in front of me. "He owes you a race, not a conversation."

Brutus pushed past him. "I didn't come here to start a fight, General Radulf, and don't expect one from your grandson. I simply want to verify the terms of this race."

I walked forward, flanked by Crispus on one side and Livia on the other. I wished Aurelia could be here too. This didn't feel right without her.

I said, "The terms have not changed. If I win this race, you will release my mother and give up any bid for me. You and I will never speak again."

He smiled. "And if I win, then you will turn over the key to the Malice, and put yourself and your magic under my control."

"Seven laps," I said. "You choose your horses, and I'll choose mine."

He glanced at my horses and laughed. "Them? They're your choice?"

"Not at all." I grinned, and enjoyed watching the smile fade on his face. Radulf looked equally confused, but I hadn't wanted to say anything to him until my silent request was answered. And at hearing the sound approaching from a distance, I knew my answer had arrived. Callistus entered the stables, brushing roughly against Brutus as he passed him and then came to stand beside me.

Callistus. I intended to race with a unicorn.

❧· THIRTY-SIX ·❧

After he got over the initial shock of seeing an animal of the gods, it took Brutus's face less than a second to go completely purple with rage. "This is not a horse!"

"A unicorn is one of many breeds of horses," I said. "The favored breed of the gods, I would guess."

"No one can race chariots with a unicorn," Brutus sputtered. "It's not allowed."

Radulf smiled over at me, as proud as I'd ever seen him. "Which rule forbids a charioteer to use a unicorn?"

"Every charioteer has a team of four horses —"

"*Up to* four," Radulf said. "Nothing forbids Nic from riding with fewer."

Brutus excused himself, and the Praetors closed into a tight circle for a discussion that was loudly punctuated by more than a few curses against both me and Radulf. We only smiled at each other. I knew this was as irritating to them as an outbreak of lice, but in the end, they would not be able to challenge it.

Callistus was qualified to race, and even if they went to the emperor himself, they would not be able to stop me.

Finally, Brutus separated from the other Praetors and walked back over to me. "Your unicorn will race, then. But when my charioteers come at you on the track, and trust me, they will, it will not be my fault if your . . . horse . . . is injured beyond saving."

"Charioteers?" Radulf asked. "You are allowed only one competitor against Nic. Whichever of the two crosses the finish line first is the victor."

"Yes, I know that, but in the Ludi Romani, there are twelve teams who race." Brutus nodded to the Praetors. "Have the charioteers brought in."

Radulf pulled me aside. "They're going to bring in the strongest racers they can find, but there's only one that you must defeat. The rest are simply meant to intimidate or scare you. Don't let them."

"I won't," I said, which wasn't exactly true. Even with Callistus for my team, I was already plenty scared.

And just as Radulf had warned, the charioteers who came to the stables looked like monuments of muscle and cruelty. Some were quite large — they'd weigh down their chariots like boulders, but their purpose obviously wasn't winning. They were to make sure I didn't. Some of them were lighter on their feet, but every cut of their body was chiseled in strength. Based on appearances alone, any of them had a chance of coming in ahead of me.

"These are none of Rome's usual charioteers," Radulf said. "Where did you find them?"

"They are slaves, all of them," Brutus said. "Some were collected from the rowboats, others are builders, and others are charioteers who have won great victories elsewhere in the empire."

My heart pounded. If he had chosen slaves, then I could already guess at their agreement. Anyone who knocked me off my chariot would be given his freedom. Anyone who failed would be given death. Their motives to win were just as desperate as mine.

"This is a waste of time," Radulf said. "Nic does not have to defeat them all, only the one you have chosen. Which one is that?"

I counted them. Ten charioteers. I was the eleventh. Who was the twelfth?

Near me, Crispus had been doing the same. He stepped forward. "You're missing one."

"Am I?" Brutus looked back at his men as if surprised, though he obviously wasn't. "Well, before I bring out my final charioteer, I want to finalize the last term of our agreement." His eyes fell upon my bulla.

"I won't use magic," I said. "I'll keep my promise."

"How will I know that?"

"The magic I do is never subtle," I said. "If I use magic, you'll know it."

Brutus stepped closer to me. "If you use magic, if even a scent of it is released in that race, it will be an automatic loss."

I glanced at Radulf, whose mouth was pressed in a tight line. I knew he wanted to dispute this rule, but I didn't see how we had any chance of winning the argument. With magic, my victory would be assured from the beginning, meaning there was no reason for the Praetors to compete.

"No magic," I promised. "Now, let me see the Praetor I have to defeat. Because so far, you've shown me no one who's any threat. They're too big to even catch the dust from my wheels."

I didn't mean any of that. The truth was that any of these men was a significant threat to me, both to my safety and my chances of winning. And if these were the ones that Brutus didn't want to use, then I worried about the person he had chosen.

Brutus smiled. "The twelfth charioteer is no Praetor and, in fact, isn't really a charioteer at all. But my racer is highly motivated to win. If she fails, then she will die."

My heart sank. "She?"

Two more Praetors rounded the corner, and between them was Aurelia. Her hands were chained, and her eyes were wild with fury as she resisted their pushing her forward. That is, until she saw me, and then a tear rolled down her cheek and she shook her head as an apology.

Aurelia had been chosen for the race, perhaps the only competitor who could have sent my head spinning. Because now, I genuinely had no idea what to do. I had to win, or else the empire would collapse, and a war would be launched between the gods. I would lose everything.

But she had to win, or she would be dead. And then I would lose even more.

❧ · THIRTY-SEVEN · ❧

I rushed forward, my entire body filled with magic. "No!" I yelled at Brutus. "This is not what we agreed!"

Radulf caught me and pressed me back. "We can't fight here, Nic."

"I won't race against her!"

"There's no choice." Radulf shook me to get my attention. "They're within the terms of their bargain."

"I never agreed to this." Panic swelled inside me. "Not to this!"

"I'm sorry, Nic," Aurelia said.

The Praetor beside her put his sword to her chest. "You were warned not to talk, girl."

When he swung it back, without even thinking, I sent a burst of magic to him, dropping him to the ground like a swatted fly. Maybe it was only a threat, but I didn't care. In response, every other Praetor withdrew their weapons, half of them aimed at Aurelia. I couldn't even focus on where the others were aimed.

"Lower your swords," Radulf said. "Brutus, this girl is a

Roman citizen. You cannot force her to race, or punish her if she fails."

"I am a judge in Rome," he said. "She is a criminal accused of helping your grandson escape his master two months ago. I believe my fellow Praetors will support my interpretation of the law."

"No!" I shouted. "You cannot get away with this!"

"Test me." Brutus's coal eyes became even darker. "I dare you to test me, Nicolas."

"Not here, not now," Radulf said. "We accept the terms!"

I looked at him, angry enough to send magic his way too, but he shook his head, warning me to back down.

"They have her, and they have your mother," Radulf said. "If this is the number of Praetors that we can see, then you can bet half the stands are filled with more of them. There will not be another chance to bargain with them. If you want to save your mother, you must race."

I shook my head, begging him to give me another solution, but it was clear that he didn't have one. Brutus gave us a deep mocking bow and said he would be waiting to meet me again at the finish line. Aurelia was dragged away without being allowed to say even a word.

Once they had gone, I turned to Radulf, but before I could speak, he said, "I warned you not to expect fairness. I warned you, Nic!"

"I expected all of this," I said, almost under my breath. "Just not Aurelia."

Crispus had come beside me again and was so upset he could barely talk. "If I hadn't let her leave my home —"

"I made the bargain. I even set the terms," I said. That was most horrifying of all, realizing this was my fault.

"What will you do?" Livia asked.

I turned to her. "Radulf's horses can't remain here in the stables, and I don't want them stolen too. Someone needs to take them home."

"Those old horses are the least of my concerns right now," Radulf said.

"Well, it's the greatest of mine!" I shouted. "I don't want my sister to watch this race!"

I pulled her aside, just the two of us, and explained everything. What I now understood about the key to the Malice, why she couldn't be here at the race today, and what needed to happen if I was to succeed. It was hard to say, even though she had asked to be a part of it. I knew she was afraid for me. Worse still, I knew that she didn't like what I was asking of her, and I could only hope she would do it anyway. When we came back to Radulf, she said with tears in her eyes, "I'll take the horses to your home. But when I come back, I'm going to watch Nic race. I have to."

I nodded at her, though my heart was pounding too loudly for words.

Radulf sent one of his servants to accompany her home while the other began hitching up my chariot to Callistus.

While they did, I went to his side and whispered an apology to him.

"You aren't meant for such a task," I said. "But I've had to ask it of you anyway. The race will be difficult. You must stay ahead of the other chariots; that is the only way to protect yourself."

Callistus tossed his head, and I hugged him with full gratitude.

"Can I speak to you alone?" Radulf asked me.

Radulf was the last person I wanted to speak to privately. I didn't need his scolding, his reminders of all the times I'd failed, or his threats or curses of my stupidity. I knew all that without him telling me so. And my expression showed it.

"Nic, I will speak to you." Radulf's tone was firmer than before. "Now."

"I'll make sure the chariot is hooked up properly," Crispus offered.

So with obvious reluctance, I followed Radulf to a quiet area behind the stables. He stood facing me, but not as he usually did — as a proud general who tried to control everyone and everything around him. No, this time, he looked as uncomfortable as I felt, as if he had never been in this situation before.

"Don't tie yourself to the chariot," he said. "You ignored that advice before. Will you listen to me now?"

I didn't answer. Mostly because I still doubted the wisdom

of ever listening to his advice. I wanted to hear what he had to say first.

"You have to win today," Radulf said. "Even if it means Aurelia loses, you must win. I hope you can understand that."

My jaw clenched. "I won't let her lose."

"Listen to me," he said. "You have a responsibility to the magic within you. The gods have trusted you with these powers, and this race has put that at stake. If you lose, the Praetors will take the Malice, they will awaken the Mistress, and they will force you to make a Jupiter Stone. With it, they will control the heavens and destroy even the dust beneath your feet."

"I know what's at stake, sir. More than anyone."

"Aurelia will understand why you have to win."

"I will not ask her to understand! I will not do that to her, especially not for your reasons!" I bit into the words. He didn't care for Aurelia, no more than he cared about me or Livia or anything other than his own personal power.

I started to walk away, but he grabbed my arm and turned me again to face him. But instead of speaking, he only stared at me as if the thoughts were clear in his heart but hadn't yet become words in his head. As if he didn't even know the right words for what he was feeling. Well, if his feelings were anywhere near mine, I could suggest a few choice words, but he wouldn't like them.

"Let me go," I said, pulling free. "I need to prepare for the race."

"I don't want you to lose," he finally mumbled, then

swallowed hard and tried again. "That's not the right way to say it. What I mean, Nic, is that I don't want to lose *you*."

I stared back at him, not entirely sure of what he meant. If those words had come from nearly anyone else in my life, they would've made sense. But this was Radulf, who had been my enemy and captor, who had all but killed me in the amphitheater, and who had made it clear on more than one occasion that the only reason he never finished the job was because he intended to use me to create a Jupiter Stone.

Surely nothing had changed between us. Or had it? Perhaps sometime in recent days, he had changed.

Radulf shifted his weight, even more uncomfortable than before, if that was possible. "I am your grandfather."

"Don't say that."

"I loved your father more than I thought it was possible to love a person. He was a better son than I could've hoped for, better than I ever deserved. When the Romans invaded Gaul — on one of their many invasions — I was taken from him and forced to become a gladiator. At the time, he was just a little younger than you are now. At first I fought for the Romans because I believed if I did well enough, then I could earn enough money for my freedom so that I could get back home to your father. Perhaps you can understand a little of how I felt in those early days."

I understood that perfectly. Finding a way to free my mother and sister had obsessed my thoughts every day I worked in the mines.

"The more I fought, the more the people cheered for me. And after a while, I was no longer fighting for freedom, I was fighting for the people's love, while never loving them in return. Too much praise will do that to you. If you desire praise too much, it becomes your master. Then the Romans made me a soldier and asked me to fight for victory and honor." Radulf's faced softened. "I forgot, Nic. I forgot how to fight for my son, for those I care about. But I remember now."

"My father's gone," I said stiffly.

"I know that." Now Radulf's tone matched his expression. "But he's here again, in you."

I stepped farther back. "I don't remember much about him anymore."

Radulf's eyes moistened, something I hadn't thought was even possible for him. "I remember everything, whenever I look at you," he mumbled. "I already lost your father. And I don't think I could bear it if I lost you in the race today."

Crispus peeked into the clearing where Radulf and I stood. "Nic, they're calling for the racers. We need to go."

"You are my grandson, Nic, and one day I hope to earn the right for you to call me grandfather, willingly. Please do not lose this race."

I stared at Radulf for only a moment, before I nodded at him and then walked away with Crispus. As we passed the stables, I shook my hands to clear the excess magic in them, and the curse tablets that had been nailed to the stables all fell to the ground. With another toss of my hand, they melted into a lead floor. So much for the curses.

"You seem unsteady," Crispus said. "What did Radulf say to you?"

I glanced back in the direction from which we had come. "I'm honestly not sure. I'm beginning to think Radulf might actually care about me. Maybe."

Crispus raised an eyebrow. "Really?"

"I don't know." My heart began pounding again. "I don't know about anything right now."

"You can sort it out with Radulf after the race."

"No, that's what I mean, Crispus. I don't know how to finish the race. I don't know what I should do next."

He smiled over at me. It wasn't a real smile, but it was nice to see anyway. "You will find a way," he said. "I believe in you."

❈· THIRTY-EIGHT ·❈

Though I hadn't seen the crowds for myself this morning, Crispus had described the heavy flow of people into the circus, beyond seating capacity. The extras stood along the top rows and pressed into every arched entrance. Certainly the start of the Ludi Romani was exciting, but there was more to the games this time. The people had heard that the runaway slave with magic would be racing, and they expected a show similar to what they had seen in the amphitheater two months ago.

Well, I wouldn't give that to them. The bulla was already warm and swelling with magic, but I pushed the feelings away. I would not use it now, especially not when Aurelia would be on the track with me.

Crispus and I walked upstairs to the roof of the building that housed the starting gates. Here, in full view of the audience, we would draw our lots for the race. The crowd was already making noise for the other charioteers, but when I came up, we heard a swell of both cheers and jeers. The other charioteers looked at me like I was a meal to be devoured. I glared back at them, but it did nothing to remove the look of hunger in their eyes. Slaves had prepared our horses and were attending to them down below, but no one would go to the gates yet. Not until we drew for our positions. Radulf had hoped my name would be one of the last ones called, so that I could choose a racing position as far from any enemies as possible. Looking around me, I saw what a useless strategy that was — everyone up here was against me. The only chance I had of avoiding all my enemies was to choose an empty track on the farthest corner of the earth. And maybe even that would not be enough.

I looked for Aurelia, but she wasn't here. One of the Praetors was probably drawing a number for her.

"She's all right," Crispus whispered when he saw me looking. "They want her to win, so they won't hurt her."

No, not yet, and not if she won. Not if I lost.

In the absence of Emperor Florian, the sponsor of today's games was supposed to have been the presiding magistrate of the Senate, Valerius. But he was gone and another senator might not have been chosen to replace him yet. Still, I expected it would be at least one of the senators, so I was surprised when the sponsor was announced to the people, and the cheers went up for Decimas Brutus as he climbed the stairs. It wasn't unheard of for a Praetor to preside over the games, but I had hoped it would be anyone else. Brutus accepted the applause of the crowd as if he were the emperor himself, then walked back to address us.

"Welcome to the first chariot race of the Ludi Romani," he said. "As you all know, we race in honor of the gods and for the glory of Rome." Then his eye fell on me. "But then, you also know that there is much at stake for your own futures. Unless you are the victor, it's probably not worth your trouble to survive all seven laps. Except for you, Nicolas Calva. They will bring you to me alive. I will see you immediately after the race . . . or sooner."

I arched an eyebrow, but he gave no further explanation for those strange words.

A large vase was in the center of the staging area, taller than the biggest man here. It had already been loaded with balls that had been carved with our names. Usually, the balls were simply painted with each faction's color, but there were no factions today, not unless there were only two: me, and then everyone else. And Aurelia was a third faction, perhaps. Brutus turned a bar until a ball dropped out from below the vase. He picked up the ball, rotated it to see the name etched on its face, and shouted out to the crowd, "Kaeso!"

A chunky man stomped forward, the only way I assumed he knew how to walk. He shouted out, "I will have the second gate!"

He glared at me as he walked back, and I immediately determined not to choose the gates on either side of him.

A second man was called, who chose the twelfth gate, likely hoping it would keep him as far from the danger as possible. It wouldn't be so bad to ride next to him, but then the third man to be called up chose the eleventh, and I definitely wanted to avoid him. He looked like a bull and was probably just as mean.

As it turned out, I was the last to be chosen, and when the ball with my name on it was released, I saw why. It had been made much larger than the rest, so it would only fall out when nothing smaller remained inside the vase.

Brutus held up the ball and called out to the crowd, "Nicolas Calva, which stall will you have?"

The only one that was left, so I didn't bother to answer him. I'd be in the third position, which wasn't bad but wasn't the best I could've done either. Other than the man leaving from the eleventh gate, the cruelest-looking competitors had taken the lower numbers.

"The runaway slave will have the third gate!" Brutus called to the crowd, then turned to me and grinned wickedly. "Congratulations, my boy."

Heat filled me. I was not his boy. I was no one's boy.

"Come on," I said to Crispus, already marching away while the other competitors remained upstairs to receive their applause from the crowd.

"Third gate puts you close to the spine," Crispus said. "So at least two chariots won't try to take your place."

"Those racers are not ordered to take my place," I said. "They are ordered to remove me from it. Now, please have the unicorn brought to the gates as quickly as possible. I'll meet you there."

Since most of the other charioteers went directly to their horses out back, I was the first to arrive at the gates. No, I was the second.

Aurelia was already there, chained into a pathetic chariot that had probably been around since Nero's time. The option of leaving the race was not given to her. She was already set in the tenth position, where she'd race directly beside the man I had thought looked so cruel. He would run right over the limp team of horses Brutus had given her for the race.

She leaned my way when she saw me coming. "There isn't much time, so listen carefully. I won't win, so don't waste your strength trying to change that."

"You have to win," I said.

Her face tightened. "I've never driven a chariot, and I'm not good with horses."

"Exactly why you have to win. I can catch up to you, but you'll never catch up to me. Not with this team."

"You're not making sense! And more than that, I know what happens if you lose. Do not make me responsible for the consequences of you losing!"

The corner of my mouth turned up. "Well, here's the problem. You're chained to that chariot, so there's not much you can do to stop me."

Her eyes narrowed. Hardly the first time she'd been angry with my choices. "If you're thinking of —"

"Yes, Aurelia, I am." Under my breath, I mumbled, "I am thinking of you."

Crispus was approaching with Callistus already harnessed to my chariot. I motioned them over and said, "Quickly now, unhitch that while I unhitch Aurelia's."

"Nic, don't you dare!" she said. "I'll scream."

"Save that for later," I said, grinning, "when you yell at me for this." Which she would. There was no doubt of that.

I had done this often enough that I unhitched Aurelia's team quickly and, with her continuing protests, rolled her chariot backward and out of the tenth gate. And since Crispus only had to unhook Callistus from my chariot, he finished at nearly the same time. Other teams were arriving by then, and we got plenty of strange looks, but no one attempted to stop us. Even those who realized what I was doing must've figured it wasn't helping my chances of winning, so ignoring me worked in their favor.

I returned Aurelia's chariot to the gate where it belonged, but this time, with Callistus at the head.

"Please don't do this," she said.

"Listen carefully," I told her. "It doesn't matter if you know about horses or know how to race. You're chained in there so you won't fall out, and Callistus won't crash. You let him do the work, trust him, and he will get you over that finish line."

She shook her head while tears rolled from her eyes. "No. I don't want this."

"And I don't want it any other way." I put my hand over hers. "When we were in the sewers together, you asked me for a favor: to save your inheritance. I'm your friend, so I should've offered my help then."

"Don't help me because of the inheritance." She wouldn't look at me, but she did turn her hand and lock her fingers with mine. "It has to be a better reason than that."

"Nic!" Crispus called.

I had to go before we ran out of time. I said to Aurelia, "I will see you soon. Then we'll talk."

"I'm afraid, Nic."

I gave her hand a quick squeeze. "It's all right. Trust me."

Then I released her hand and walked back to the third gate, where Crispus was finishing attaching my chariot to Aurelia's team of horses. They were sturdy but didn't seem to be even half as strong as any other team here.

I gave each horse a greeting, explaining that I would do my best for them if they did the same for me. I didn't use the bulla to speak to them, so I had no idea if they could understand me. But at least I had tried.

Crispus was somber as I climbed into my chariot. Like the others, it was only made of wicker bound together with leather straps, not much different from riding in a bread basket. But my carriage was even lighter now. There was nothing on the floor of the chariot but a single board — the axis of the cart. If I slipped, my feet would go straight through to the ground. *I* would go straight through, beneath the wheels.

Crispus handed me the reins and climbed up behind me to tie them around my waist.

"Don't," I said.

"These horses will expect that," he said. "That's how they're used to racing. And it's the only way you've ever raced."

"I won't be tied in." Radulf had always been right about this. For the kind of race ahead of me, I needed to control the horses with my hands.

"It'll protect you. If you slip, this will keep you in the chariot."

"Get down, Crispus, please."

He sighed, but obeyed and stepped back. "I will see you in seven laps, my friend."

There were words in my head, thoughts that I wanted to say. Such as apologies and explanations, and pleas for him to watch after Livia if anything went wrong. But when I opened my mouth to respond, nothing came out. So I gave up and let him go with only a nod.

❧·THIRTY-NINE·❧

While some chariot races began straight out of the gate, because this was the first race of the Ludi Romani, we were to have a procession first. Since the emperor was not in attendance, today's procession would be more simple than usual — a single lap at trotting speed. Because I was on an outside track, my horses would have to go faster at the curves to keep our processional line even, tiring them faster.

Roman soldiers on horseback and carrying the banners of Rome came into the building. Several of them looked back and nodded at me. These were Radulf's men today, and though they could do nothing for me, it helped to see their good wishes. The trumpets blared, warning the crowd that we were about to come out. They would play twice more — at the start of the race when the white cloth was dropped and then at the start of the final lap.

The soldiers rode out first, to the swell of noise from the crowd, nearly five times the numbers who had deafened me in the amphitheater. Radulf had told me that by some estimates, almost one person out of every four in the city of Rome could fit inside this circus. I didn't know if that was true, but looking at the crowd, I certainly believed it. The trumpets continued to sing, and once we rode out, the noise exploded. It filled my head and swarmed my thoughts.

But one detail demanded my attention, which was finding the seat that had been reserved for Livia. Although Radulf would be in the spine, she was the general's granddaughter and would be given a seat of honor.

Once my horse came closer to the emperor's box, it wasn't hard to find the area near where she should have been. Magic rose in me, more than I wanted, and though none was allowed for the race, I had no hesitation about using magic for her.

And suddenly, I saw her there, taking her seat exactly where she should have been. She wasn't really watching me, but then she wasn't really watching anyone. Just staring forward with her back straight and tall, her hands in her lap, and completely indifferent to the noise around her. That was enough. The Praetors would keep their eyes on her. I could only hope that they would leave her alone while I raced. If they didn't, it would ruin everything.

Or more accurately, ruin everything more than it already was. It hardly seemed possible for things to get any worse.

I waved up at her, just to test her reaction, and she waved back. She looked more confident than anxious, and even if it was faked emotion, it still made me feel better to see it.

"Is that your sister?" the racer to my right said. "She's a pretty little thing."

"She's the granddaughter of a Roman general," I said. "Who would gladly gouge out your eyes for looking at her that way."

The racer laughed nervously. And stopped looking.

The man at my left caught my eye and then glanced at my hands, holding the reins. "All we're allowed to do is keep you from winning. But if you're not tied in, you might do even worse to yourself."

"*You* won't stop me from winning." I looked over at him and smiled. "Maybe one of the other men here, but not you."

He grinned. "Listen, boy, I'll get to you first."

"I can smell you from here," I said. "Your fleas will consume you before you've had a chance to catch me on this track."

And the man next to him laughed, starting an argument between them, which I much preferred to any attention on me.

With six chariots between us, it was difficult to see Aurelia from here, though Callistus was perfectly visible and was getting plenty of attention from the crowd. At one point, I saw Aurelia's hair blowing in the morning breeze, but that only reminded me I had let my team of horses fall behind and needed to straighten our line.

I looked into the spine too, but couldn't see Radulf. He should have been there already, but wherever he was, it wasn't out in front watching me.

The man at my left called my name. "You can always forfeit, you know. There's still time."

"Why would you suggest that?" I asked. "Are you frightened of me?"

"No." But his tone hinted otherwise.

I wasn't looking at him, but I said, "Perhaps you are the one who should forfeit. I'm going to win this race."

"What about the girl? Did you forget about her?"

I smiled over at him. "Aurelia? No, I never forget about her." Which were the truest words I had ever spoken.

And with that, we had completed the procession. Normally, the soldiers should've ridden off at once, but this time, they remained in their places. And then from the spine, I heard a familiar voice. Radulf.

"Citizens and friends," he called out. "Give me your attention!"

The audience quieted so they could hear him. I certainly could, though my heart was pounding in anticipation of what trick he might try next. If he had been sincere before, in the feelings he had so awkwardly tried to express, he might've come to think of me as a true grandson. After all, he and I had gone through a great deal together, more than I had ever thought possible within such a short time. The battles he and I had fought against each other were easy to comprehend, but I didn't know how to deal with an enemy who wanted my affection. Or maybe we weren't enemies anymore. I genuinely didn't know how to think about my grandfather.

But as it turned out, the announcement was not about me, or even for me.

Once Radulf had the ears of the people, he said, "I have terrible news, something that is unwelcome and untimely on this great morning. As you all know, nearly three months ago, Emperor Tacitus was killed on his way to battle in Gaul."

I gritted my teeth and looked down. Radulf should know about that assassination. He was the one who had ordered it, as he had ordered the deaths of other emperors before that. Then I realized what this announcement was likely to be, and I looked up at Radulf, dreading his next words.

"The emperor's reign fell to Florian, who continued the fighting in Gaul and has been there ever since. Sadly, my friends, Emperor Florian will never return to Rome. He has been killed by his own soldiers. A search will begin at once for a new emperor."

Silence fell over the entire circus, out of respect for a fallen emperor. Off in the distance, an eagle was released, Rome's tradition for sending the emperor's soul to the gods. And though everyone around me followed the eagle's path in the skies and whispered to Pluto to carry him safely into the underworld, I only stared up at Radulf, letting him see the blame in my eyes.

Radulf had ordered Florian's death as well. I knew it just from looking at him. Only a few days ago, we'd learned that the emperor was sending his soldiers to bring Radulf to Gaul. Radulf had replied that the soldiers were loyal to him, far more than the emperor. Now I knew what he meant by that. When Radulf looked back at me, his first expression was one of pride. Yes, this was the Radulf I knew and understood. The one who would do anything, and destroy anyone, to get what he wanted.

But Radulf's expression quickly changed once he found me in the group. There was a brief moment of confusion while he looked at my horses, and then at Aurelia in a chariot behind Callistus. And then he knew exactly what I had done. His face twisted in fear, or anger, or whatever emotions were running through him.

"Stop this race!" Radulf yelled. "Out of respect to the emperor, we must not race today!"

No, the reasons for his panic had nothing to do with respect to the emperor. This was about me now. And nobody would stop this race.

Ignoring Radulf's words, as they had to do, the soldiers directed us to back up into the gates, which closed in front of us. A metal grille above the wooden doors let in light and would allow us to hear the trumpeter's warning that the doors would be opening, but I could no longer see the crowds and that helped me calm down. I backed my team of horses to the rear wall, which also put me farther away from everyone. It looked unwise, but I knew what I was doing.

Crispus came forward, calming my horses just as other workers were quieting the horses for their charioteers.

"You're going to start this race from behind?" he asked me.

I didn't answer. My eyes were on Aurelia, whom I could easily see from here. She stared back at me with an expression I couldn't understand. There was worry, and sadness, and even a spark of anger. Maybe other emotions too. I only winked back and gave her a smile that made the creases of her brow deepen.

I wasn't sorry for what I'd done and wouldn't pretend to be. This was the best chance either of us had.

Decimas Brutus was speaking from the staging area above us. Though I couldn't hear his exact words, he had excited the crowd again. He didn't want them in mourning for an emperor who had been in power for only a few months, all of it at war in Gaul. He wanted them cheering for the race and distracted from the larger issues of treason that were everywhere in the circus. Rome was a mob. Everything Rome did seemed to be about distracting the mob.

I did not see Brutus drop the white cloth to begin the race, but I heard the trumpets, and the noise of the lever turning to spring open the gates. My horses were already in motion when the door flew apart. I had given myself nearly five feet to build up speed first. The others did not.

The chariot race for my life, Aurelia's life, and for the future of the empire, had begun.

⊰ · FORTY · ⊱

Perhaps it was a small thing to have started moving even before the gates opened, but it was already working to my advantage. My horses were second out of the gates, only by a fraction of a hair perhaps, but I could use that. Callistus was faster and was already in the lead, but I had expected that. If nothing else, I was grateful to Radulf for forcing me to spend so long working on these precious first few seconds.

The first part of the race was to get to the break line, which was nearly even with where the spine began. We were required to stay in our lanes until then, thus avoiding a mass collision in the first few seconds of the race. Once there, I knew what to do.

As I had practiced so many times, my most important job was to work toward the inside track. But there were ten teams around me who didn't care about winning. Their only job was to see that I didn't get to the finish line.

The trouble started early, as the player to my right, the meanest-looking one, began edging me inward with his chariot while the man to my left matched my chariot's speed. I knew it was deliberate because when I slowed, so did he, and when I slowed yet again, so did he.

Although I'd been furious a couple of days ago with the racers who had cheated, I realized what a useful lesson it had been. Because now, I recognized the look of conspiracy between the men on either side of me. I understood the expression of warning from the one on the right, to prepare himself. Something was about to happen.

All three of us had been slowing, but without giving any warning of my own, I urged my horses to speed forward, so suddenly that the man to my left could not keep up, and the man on my right had already turned his team inward, intending to career his chariot directly into mine. Instead of hitting me, as I raced past them, their chariots collided. Both men flew into the air, but their horses were left in a tangle, which probably saved the riders' lives as they cut free of their reins. A roar rippled through the crowd. The people wanted violence from any of their games, but with me on the tracks, they also wanted a show, and I regretted knowing I would have to provide one to survive.

Slaves ran onto the tracks to clear the fallen chariots. Now there were eight teams against me, and I hadn't yet completed my first lap.

Though I was glad to leave those two teams behind, they had also cost me time. Because of having slowed down, I was in very last place. I cut toward the center in a hard angle, sharper than I should have done, but I kept my footing and moved ahead. Most of the men here had never ridden a chariot before, and their inexperience was showing. The ones who had raced were keeping pace with Aurelia, though she was still ahead of them all. But they clearly wanted to win too. It would earn them a dual reward, from the Praetors for keeping me away from victory, and the sack of gold from the empire. The rest of these men, the ones meant to frighten and intimidate me, they were just bumps in my road. Literal bumps if they didn't stay in their chariots.

Following that turn, my first lap was complete. The first bronze dolphin overhead was already pulled downward, signaling to the cheering crowd that the second lap had begun. Ahead of me, the second carved wooden egg had already been pulled, meaning the lead chariot was that much farther ahead in the race.

I was nearer to the inside than before, though a charioteer now on my right and slightly behind me was whipping his horse to increase his speed. It was Kaeso, the chunky man who had drawn first for his gate. I felt a sting on the back of my arm and without even thinking, yanked my arm away from the sting, which pulled the reins even farther to the inside. My chariot bumped against the team of horses next to me, which caused us to rock up onto only one wheel. I threw my weight down to steady my chariot, and only then had a chance to look at what had caused the sting.

The whip.

Instantly it snapped again, this time catching me across the back with a cut that I knew had drawn blood. The crowd had seen it, but there were as many cheers as jeers, both directed at me. They were no doubt hoping I'd respond with magic, and in fact, I heard chanting about it coming from somewhere in the stands.

I merely pushed forward, hoping to stay far enough ahead to avoid that charioteer's whip. The sting was still burning on my arm and back, but I couldn't use magic to heal myself. With the pain, it was harder to hold on to the magic protecting Livia. I could not risk losing her while I raced. Whether I won or lost, I had to protect her for as long as my magic held out.

Cutting so tight to the center had given me a huge advantage. I had narrowed the lead between myself and the racers ahead of me, and three teams were behind me now. There were only three chariots between me and Aurelia, and another two had pushed ahead of her. From one look at her driving, I understood why. Aurelia kept looking back for me and was deliberately slowing Callistus in an effort to increase my chances of winning.

No, that wasn't the plan. She had to keep going as fast as possible. The worst of everything would be if we both lost. But from here, I had no way to communicate that. Even if I yelled it to her, I knew she'd ignore me.

I was approaching the next turn, the final one before the third lap would begin. A chariot to my right was pressing in on me, hoping to force me too close to the spine.

The Romans had a word for the crashes that happen here: *naufragia*. The same word also meant "shipwreck." The dual use of the word was no coincidence.

The charioteer pushed in until our chariots met, and he threw a punch at my arm holding the reins. It hurt like he'd clubbed me, and I nearly dropped the reins, which would have been disastrous. But I didn't drop them and, instead, realized that he had done worse to himself. For he had punched so hard that it cost him his balance, and as we rounded the spine, he crashed.

Naufragia.

Moments later, the bronze dolphin marked the third lap's beginning. I was as close to the inner track as anyone could be, enough that at some point I heard Radulf yelling at me. Or yelling *for* me, rather. He called my name with such hope and encouragement that I truly believed it was possible to win this, somehow.

I used my position to gain speed on the others. With superior teams of horses, they were far ahead, but they were also farther from the spine, so at least for now, I was keeping up with them.

Aurelia was the third chariot ahead of me now, and I was in sixth place. A total of nine competitors remained.

I urged the horses to go even faster. They must've believed they were already giving everything they had, but I knew otherwise.

When I had been a slave in the mines, there were many times when I had thought there was no way I could continue working. I had known exhaustion to the point of my very soul begging my body to lay in the dirt and give up. But I had reasons to keep going, and always, somehow, I found more strength.

These horses would find more strength too. I needed them to run faster.

By the beginning of the fourth lap, I had a stroke of luck. A chariot just in front of me was moving fast enough that I could not gain on him, but his position on the track also prevented me from edging around him. One of his horses kicked up enough dirt to reveal a curse tablet that had been buried on the track. This was supposed to be illegal, though it sometimes happened. Some Romans had faith in the gods to curse a charioteer. Others had even greater faith in the power of a lead tablet to trip a horse.

The horse stumbled against the lead tablet and brought the rest of his team down. The charioteer flew over the front of his chariot and landed on his horses, but immediately cut himself free. I expected him to run for safety, but instead he leapt for my chariot and got a hand on the rim. "You cursed boy!" he shouted. Which was a fine irony. Odds were that the tablet had been meant to trip my horses.

I veered my team in a sharp turn to avoid running over his, and the man fell without harming me. But his words stuck in my head. That I was cursed.

And with that thought, I looked up to see the fifth dolphin fall for the chariot farthest ahead. Two and a half laps remained for me, and I was now in fifth place out of eight competitors. That wasn't nearly enough time for what I needed to do.

❧·FORTY-ONE·❧

When it came to their competitions, the Romans' definition of cheating was fairly lenient. As far as they were concerned, as long as the charioteer completed all seven laps, anything he did to destroy his competition was a fair race. So from the perspective of the audience in the stands, any violence on the circus track was great entertainment. If there were deaths in here, then the race was even better.

Avoiding the fallen chariot had cost me in the race. The team of horses directly behind me had caught up again, carrying the man with the whip. He came at me with a vengeance, slashing his whip in every direction, hoping to hit me.

When he finally did, my back arched with the pain, and I leaned backward, nearly losing my balance again.

Aurelia must've seen it. Above the crowd's noise, I heard her yelling something about what would happen to that man if she had her bow, and despite the sting in my back, I smiled and encouraged my horses to go faster and stay toward the middle. I took the reins in my right hand alone and turned sideways.

Though I wouldn't use magic to help me in the race, there was no doubt that magic had sharpened my reflexes. When the whip snapped again, I caught it in my hand. Where it hit bare skin, the whip cut my wrist and palm, but I swallowed the pain and yanked hard, pulling the man forward.

"Let go," I yelled. "Or I'll pull you to the ground."

"I'm stronger," he said. "I'll pull you off instead."

That was true enough. One quick tug on my end confirmed that. So I gave in and released the whip.

It happened just as the man tugged on his end, throwing his entire weight into the motion, intending to pull me down. Without my weight to balance him, he rolled backward off his own chariot, effectively pulling himself to the ground. His horses continued running, and the man was dragged by his reins. I looked back and saw his knife had fallen from his toga. He wouldn't be able to cut himself free. And I knew from personal experience how that felt. This man would be dragged to his death or run over first.

I shot out enough magic to snap his reins free from his chariot. Technically speaking, it was a small cheat, though not for myself. And I doubted anyone but me and that man knew what had happened. Neither of us would tell.

I was just beginning my fifth round, half a lap behind the leader, and I was no farther ahead than before. The horses of the man who had whipped me were a finer team than my own. Strong enough that it was worth the risk to get them. So I matched my speed with theirs and got as close as possible, until my chariot was even with his empty one. This was the reason I could not be tied into my chariot. I released my reins and grabbed the side of his chariot. Taking a deep breath, I leapt sideways.

There was a huge reaction from the crowd, but I was far from safe.

The instant I leapt, our horses parted and I clung to the side of the chariot with all my strength. I had less than half the length of the circus to get inside this chariot, because I'd never survive the turn.

The reins that had been snapped free by my magic were waving wildly in the air. While keeping hold of the side of the chariot with one arm, I reached for the reins with the other. The end of the spine came closer.

As the team of horses started their turn, the reins fell in the wind, and I got hold of one, and then the other, then used them to brace my weight as I dragged myself into the chariot.

And immediately I urged them forward. This was a faster team, every bit as strong as Radulf's stolen horses. In less than half a lap, we had overtaken the chariot team between me and Aurelia, and I was gaining on her.

"That was completely insane!" she shouted to me. "Never do that again!"

"Let me get closer!" I shouted back at her. "Because I must do that one more time."

Aurelia's eyes widened as she understood what I had intended all along. She had to win the race, and so did I. But only one chariot could cross the finish line first.

Ours.

✣·FORTY-TWO·✣

I t had been extremely difficult for me to cross from my chariot into this one. And in truth, it hadn't gone as well as I'd
expected. There had been only a whisper of a difference
between my making it safely inside and falling to the track
below. Perhaps the only reason I didn't fall was one of the gods
had nudged me inside. Nothing else could explain it.

In comparison, Aurelia was helping me this time. She
slowed Callistus until I drew up beside her and then pushed her
chariot as close to mine as she dared. Callistus would match his
speed with my team of horses, which would help a great deal. If
I was careful, I wouldn't even have to leap. I could simply step
out from behind my cart, and onto hers.

"Give me your reins," I told her.

She obeyed and stretched her chains enough to hold to my
chariot with both hands, determined to keep them together.

I took one step over to hers, just as she screamed my name
and told me to stop. It was too late.

One of the chariots that had been ahead noticed what we

were doing and had gotten directly in front of my horses, then halted his.

We crashed directly into his chariot, sending him flying, but also ripping me entirely off my cart. I landed in the dirt behind Aurelia. My helmet flew off my head and the pads protecting my legs came off as well. I could take the scrapes to my legs but I kept my head as high as possible — that would be much harder to heal.

I still had Callistus's reins, and Aurelia cried out for me to let go before it killed me, but I couldn't. Instead, I used the strength that had been built in me from five years in the mines, muscles formed from carrying rock and scaling chiseled walls, and from being forced to remain on my feet from dawn until dark. Slowly, I inched forward on the reins.

Aurelia leaned out, trying to help me. "Take my hand!" she yelled.

"I'll pull you out." If she fell, she'd be dragged by her chains, unable to cut herself free.

"You won't!" Then her eyes focused directly on mine. "Nic, I trusted you. Now please, learn to trust me too."

I nodded, inched forward once more, and then reached for her with my hand that had taken the whip.

It stung again when she clasped it but not as much as being dragged behind the chariot, and it was only for a moment before she had drawn me closer to her, and now she had my forearm, and then both arms. And then she pulled me into the chariot with her.

"Can you stand?" she asked.

I had to, though my legs were shredded from the fall. Aurelia put her arm beneath my shoulders and helped me to my feet, and I tugged on the reins to tell Callistus that it was time to finish this race. We had lost time in that fall. Two teams were ahead of us, and another two teams were behind, but both of them were too far back to catch up now.

And trumpets sounded as the final dolphin fell. We had one more lap.

With me at the reins, Callistus knew I had come back to him and likely had known this was my strategy from the moment I exchanged chariots with Aurelia's. So he burst forward, running as if racing for the gods themselves. I was grateful for it; no other horse could've had this much energy so late in the race, but the speed was hard on me and I was having trouble keeping my balance. Sensing my weakness, Aurelia crossed behind me. She held to both ends of the chariot and then braced me with her weight. Without her there, I would've fallen, but she wouldn't allow me to fail now.

We quickly passed the chariot in second place, and rather easily, for he obviously had not seen us coming. But the one in first place was well aware of us. As he neared the first turn of the final lap, he pressed in even closer to the spine. It was the strategy any leading charioteer would take. He had no one to pass, and all he had to do was run out the final lap while keeping us trapped behind him.

A few days ago, I had joked to Radulf about using Callistus for this race. My attitude had been that with only one horse, I could squeeze between the other teams. Radulf had laughed then.

But I had been entirely serious.

I pressed Callistus to go faster, and toward the center of the track.

"We're going to make a sharp turn," I said to Aurelia. "Get ready to lean."

Callistus pushed forward until his nose was in line with the other chariot. Then I yanked on the reins and pulled him hard to the left. We hit the spine, tipping our chariot against the columns, but with two of us inside to shift our weight, we quickly came down on two wheels again. And emerged from the bend in the lead.

"We're ahead!" Aurelia screamed in my ear. "There's only a half lap remaining. We're going to win!"

She let go of the chariot and instead wrapped her arms around my waist. And I held the reins with one hand and folded my other over her clasped hands.

The crowd's roar grew as we neared the last bend. Aurelia and I released each other to brace ourselves for the tight turn, but we were far enough ahead of the other two chariots that nothing remained to stop us.

Or so I thought, until I heard a cracking sound beneath us. As we straightened out toward the finish line, the ground beneath Callistus collapsed like a ramp into the underworld. We had no choice but to run down with it.

"What's happening?" Aurelia cried.

Before I could reply, she had her answer.

The ramp was raised up again over our heads, and in the sudden blackness beneath the circus, all we had to rely on was dim torches on the walls.

Which revealed the hundreds of Praetors who had been waiting here, their final insurance that I would not win the chariot race.

Win or lose, they had never planned for me to finish.

❧· FORTY-THREE ·❧

I immediately raised a shield around me and Aurelia, and then sent out a burst of magic that dropped most of the Praetors to the ground. It shook the earth, and dirt rained down upon us.

"Can you get us out of here?" Aurelia asked.

Truthfully, I wasn't sure. Though I hadn't used magic for myself, I had been using it throughout the race as a protection for Livia. The bulla was working to rebuild my strength from what had been lost while on the track, but I was worried. The magic I'd just sent out should've collapsed the ground, not merely shaken it.

My next use of magic was to free Aurelia from the chains. Once I had enough magic gathered together, I would disappear with her, though that left Callistus with the Praetors and I hated the thought of that.

Praetors were already unhitching him from the chariot. I continued repelling those who tried, but more took their places. And they were getting closer to Aurelia and me, waiting for my shield to fail, which it eventually would.

I released more magic, aimed at collapsing the ground again. A lot of dirt fell, but then I also felt the shield weaken.

"You need to let yourself heal first," Aurelia said. And I realized that although my arm was around her in a show of protection, really, she was the one still bracing me up. She put her hand on the bulla and pressed it against my chest. I felt its warmth, and that strengthened me but I could not find the Divine Star's magic, which I needed for healing. One of the whips had sliced directly across it, and I supposed in its own way, the Divine Star itself had to heal before I could.

By then, the Praetors had released Callistus from the chariot though he was fighting their attempts to get control of him. I sent magic to help him, and shot out more at other men who were getting close to us again. Then I tried to find Radulf with my mind. He would be directly overhead. Why didn't he come? I regretted what I had told him earlier, that I would no longer call for his help. Because I needed him now, and I didn't know whether he would answer me anymore. Not after the way I had behaved, and the things I had said. Even when he had tried to express concern for me, the most I had done was to stare dumbly back at him. For all my unwillingness to forgive him, I needed his forgiveness now.

"We know the Malice is hidden somewhere in Valerius's field," a Praetor said. "You lost the race, and now you must fulfill your promise!"

"You took me from the race!" I shouted. "You broke the bargain we made. This was not a fair race!"

"When has Rome ever been fair?" That was Brutus, coming through the tunnel with a torch in his hands. I wanted to erase that smirk on his face with an entire ball of magic, but I was saving up what I could for when I'd need it most.

"If nothing is fair, then we never had a bargain," I said. "You can search for the Malice all you want, but you will never find it. By the time you figure out where it was once hidden, I'll have already destroyed it."

"You'd never do it, no more than you'd destroy that bulla around your neck," Brutus said. "Above ground, we have men in the circus on their way right now to grab your sister. Surrender, or she will pay for your stubbornness."

I grinned. "Go get her, then."

"Nic!" Aurelia scolded.

I kept my expression even, hoping it wouldn't show that keeping Livia protected came at a high price to me. Even now, it was wearing my magic far too thin.

"So it's a trick," Brutus said.

It was a very good trick, one I'd have loved to see them discover. I still couldn't do Radulf's trick of fighting in a place where I really wasn't, but I could make it appear that Livia was in the circus when in fact she was nowhere near us.

There was no point in maintaining that illusion any longer, and with a deep breath, I released her image. Keeping it in place for so long had drained me, though I hoped it would prove to be worth it.

Finally, I felt my magic growing again. Even with my injuries and the shield around me and Aurelia, it was growing.

But what I did not expect was for Praetors to grab the axle of the chariot. We jolted forward, and then at once, they lifted it high over their heads, working their way up the axle. Aurelia and I rolled off the chariot and onto the ground with hard thuds.

The shield fell when I landed. I released magic in every direction while I scrambled to raise it again, but with so little light, it was easy for the Praetors to hide in the shadows. I got the shield in place for her, but instantly realized my mistake. Even if it seemed like a selfish thing, I had to protect myself first. I *had* to, because all that a Praetor had to do was get a single hand on me.

And one did.

Aurelia's shield failed a second time, as did all my magic. I struggled to get free, but they pounced on me like hungry lions.

"Nic!" Aurelia screamed my name and began cursing at the men who had grabbed her.

Brutus knelt beside me and pulled my tunic back, revealing the Divine Star, with the whiplash across it. "The whip is reserved for disobedient slaves," he said. "Is that who you are, still, after all you've done to prove otherwise?"

"I am a slave to no one," I said. "Let me go!"

"Nearly two hundred years ago, Emperor Domitian wanted a way to connect his palace to the circus, but few people ever knew where his tunnels were." Brutus smiled. "*I* know about these tunnels, though. And, I suppose, now you do too."

I fought hard and knew Aurelia was fighting too. Then above the noise, a Praetor said, "We don't need the girl."

There was the slice of a sword.

And Aurelia screamed again.

✠·FORTY-FOUR·✠

Everything seemed to have gone silent. Only Aurelia's scream remained, like a horrible echo in my ears.

A new power emerged in me, something that could not have been magic, but which was even stronger. Praetors scattered around me like unwanted garbage, and I escaped their grip, then leapt to my feet and ran over to her.

Aurelia was still alive, but only barely. Blood seeped out of a deep wound in her side, and with it, life was leaving her too.

"Stay away from me," I warned the Praetors. "Stay away or I promise to destroy you all."

Brutus stepped forward. "You can't fight us off and heal her."

I knew that. Worse still, I wasn't sure that I could heal her. *I* hadn't recovered from the race, and my magic was already depleted. The bulla was helping, but the Divine Star gave me nothing. Without the mark in my shoulder, I had no powers to heal.

"So which do you want the most?" Brutus asked. "To destroy us, or to save her?"

Aurelia grabbed my hand. Her face was pinched with pain, an image I knew could not be the last I ever saw of her. I could never bear that memory. "There's not enough magic for me anyway," she whispered. "Don't waste it."

"Where's Callistus?" I asked Brutus. "The unicorn? Where is he?"

"Under our control. But don't try calling him here. Trust me, he won't get far if you do."

"Give me the unicorn and my friend."

"And in exchange?"

"I will ride with you to that field."

"No, Nic." Aurelia's life was slipping away like smoke through my fingers. "Please don't."

I pressed my hand against the wound and began pouring magic into her. I didn't have enough to save her, but hopefully it would keep her alive until they returned Callistus.

"Are you begging me for her life?" Brutus asked. "Here, on your knees, are you begging me, as I predicted you would do?"

"Yes, if it helps, then I am begging." Sweat dripped from my brow, stinging my eyes, yet I only gave her more of what I didn't have. "But I am also threatening. If you refuse to return my unicorn, things will not go well for you."

"We can ride this tunnel and exit near the amphitheater," Brutus said. "No crowds are there. We'll go to the field together."

I nodded. "Let Callistus come now. Hurry! I need him to save her."

Aurelia's eyes were closed, but she shook her head. Even this close to death, she still wanted to fight me.

"Give me the bulla," Brutus said. I started to protest, but he added, "You'll get it back when it's time to use the key. But if I'm holding the bulla, then that ensures you won't try any tricks on the way."

It also ensured my magic wouldn't return as strong as I had hoped.

"Where's Callistus?" I asked.

He grinned and shook his head. "Give me the bulla, Nicolas. I have as much time as I need to bargain. But how much time do you have with that girl's life?"

I closed my eyes and kept one hand on Aurelia while I removed the bulla with my other and placed it in Brutus's open palm. Fury rose in me, but not magic. Everything I had left was going to her.

Instantly, Brutus snapped his fingers and two Praetors came forward with Callistus.

"Get on," Brutus told me. "Then we'll give you the girl."

I didn't argue. Aurelia was so close to death that every second mattered. So I left her side and quickly climbed on Callistus's bare back. I would've preferred his saddle, for Aurelia's comfort, but nothing could be done about that.

Aurelia didn't respond at all when they put her in my arms, and once she was secure, I instantly put one hand on Callistus's horn, then my other as close to her wound as possible.

Magic began moving through me, entirely different from anything I'd felt before. This magic wasn't part of me or even for me; I was only the connection between the unicorn's powers to heal and the person in need of healing. It was the purest magic I'd ever felt. It gave without asking and built without destroying. If I could feel magic like this for the rest of my life, I would never feel cursed, and I would never take any risk of losing it.

Aurelia was already breathing more easily, and the wound had sealed. That wasn't enough, though, so I continued holding on to the horn, using anything left in me to send thoughts of gratitude to Callistus.

"Let's go," Brutus said. "Remember, Nicolas. No tricks."

Some of the men had horses and mounted them to ride on either side of me. Others loaded into wagons and followed behind us. The rest would be walking or had rides waiting for them outside the amphitheater, I assumed.

But none of that mattered. Aurelia was moving again, just light twitches of her hand or flutters of her lashes. And she was closer, molding herself into my arms.

After several minutes of traveling through the darkness of the tunnels, we emerged into open air on a hillside within view of the amphitheater.

Brutus rode even closer to me now. The bulla was around his neck, and though I knew he couldn't feel its magic, it still angered me to see it there.

"Nic," Aurelia mumbled. A tear escaped her eye, but I knew she wasn't in any pain.

"I'm here," I whispered.

Looking around us, Rome seemed to have emptied, which was an odd sight. I figured everyone who had the option of going to the circus was there.

Sensing my desire for privacy, Brutus rode forward a little. It was an unexpected show of respect from him, and I appreciated it.

Aurelia's eyes opened a little. "You never listen to me. Never."

"I always listen," I said. "I just don't obey."

"You should."

"I will when you stop giving ridiculous orders."

She smiled and closed her eyes again. "Where are we going?" she asked.

"I'm going to take the Malice," I said.

Her eyes snapped open, and she tried to sit up. "You're what?"

"You said that you trust me, remember?"

The smile returned. "I might change my mind."

"I saved your life."

"I knew you would." Her eyes shut again. "I know you love me."

❖· FORTY-FIVE ·❖

urelia remained asleep for the rest of the ride, but I had never been so awake. Every sense in my body was focused on understanding what had just happened. If what she said could be understood at all, which I doubted.

Because somehow, Aurelia knew my feelings, in words I couldn't even figure out how to form on my tongue.

Stranger still, she didn't seem to object. Whatever that meant, I couldn't keep the smile off my face.

If Livia were here, I'd have asked her advice for what to do next. And I already knew how she'd answer. She'd giggle and tell me to figure it out for myself, suggesting the answer was within me. Well, it wasn't. Magic was in me, and right now there wasn't room for anything else.

I was no longer holding on to Callistus's horn. Aurelia had clearly healed from the wound, and, I realized, so had I. The Divine Star was as strong as ever and with it, I searched for Radulf.

"I know where you're going," he said into my head. "Do not open the door for them. Do not awaken the Mistress."

"My options are narrowing," I thought back to him. "Please come. I need your help."

He didn't answer, but I felt him then, why he wasn't here. It was fear that caused him to hesitate, and not fear of the Praetors when they got close enough to him. No, he was afraid of the Mistress. Just knowing that Radulf trembled to think of her, my heart pounded harder too. I would do what had to be done at Atroxia's temple; indeed, there was really no choice at this point. But I would not awaken her.

Once we left the smoother main road to head into Valerius's vineyard — or Crispus's vineyard now, I supposed — the canter of the unicorn changed, and Aurelia awoke. She yawned and smiled up at me until she realized that I had been holding her in my arms. Then she sat up straight and mumbled an apology. She clearly did not remember the words she had spoken before. How odd that was, considering I would never forget them.

"It feels like I've been in a bad dream," she said. "How much of it was real, after the chariot race?"

"All of it."

"Did you tell me that you're going to take the Malice?"

"Yes. We already had an entire argument about it, and I won. You admitted it yourself, that I'm usually right."

She smirked, and then said, "I'd never be delirious enough to say that. I remember saying that you never listen to me. And I told you that —" Now she went silent for much longer, an uncomfortable few seconds that might've been hours for the way my breath had lodged in my throat. Finally, she said, "I thanked you for saving my life, I think."

"Something like that, yes."

No, it was nothing like that. But it was a lie we could both agree to remember. For now.

When I told Callistus to stop, Aurelia looked back at me. "What's wrong?"

I slid off Callistus's back, saying, "This is as far as you go."

"I can still help you."

She started to get off too, but I shook my head. "No, you can't help me now. And you won't."

"If you're alone with all those Praetors —"

"I'd rather be alone than try to figure out how to protect you."

"Protect me? How many times have I saved you from them?"

"Far too many. If you do it one more time, I will be in so much debt to you that I'll never be able to pay it back. So please, stay here. Please, Aurelia."

Brutus wasn't that far ahead, and when he heard our argument, he looked back at Aurelia. "Nicolas goes on with us alone."

Aurelia glared at me, even though I could've continued the argument with another dozen reasons why I was saving her life.

I gave Callistus a pat on his neck and said, "Don't let anything happen to her."

Callistus tossed his head in agreement, but I knew even an animal of the gods could not stop Aurelia from doing as she wanted.

"Leave now," I said to them both, then turned my back to walk the rest of the way to Valerius's field.

It was empty when we arrived, and with every step I took toward the ruined temple, Atroxia's tearful voice seeped into my mind. Diana had saved her from death, but saving her had also cursed her, much as saving me from Caesar's cave had cursed me with the bulla. And I understood now what the curse had done to Atroxia. It gave a simple vestalis the title of Mistress, and for reasons I doubted Radulf fully knew, he was convinced that she must remain asleep.

If she really was asleep. No sleeping person I'd ever heard could cry like this. Then again, I'd never heard anyone who could cry for such a long time either. If Valerius was right about Atroxia, then she had been buried here shortly after Caesar's death almost three hundred years ago. This had to be a memory of her tears, and nothing more.

Brutus dismounted and walked up to face me. He cocked his head as a reminder that he had won, but I kept my expression blank. I didn't want him to read anything from me.

Brutus had his hand on the bulla still around his neck, but not in the obsessive way I always seemed to hold it. He just wanted me to be aware that it was in his control right now, and that I had to cooperate to get it back. I didn't need to cooperate — a burst of magic from the Divine Star would get it back for me. But that wouldn't solve anything. I needed to open the door.

"Before I do this, I want to see my mother," I said.

"I had the very same idea." Brutus motioned for a couple of men behind him to do as I had demanded. When his attention returned to me, he asked, "What is it like, to care so intensely about others that you forget yourself? It makes you such an easy target, do you know that? Whatever I want from you, all I have to do is choose from those you love, and I know you will give in."

"And I might ask what it's like to care for nobody but yourself. Is your world cold? Your heart nothing but a crusty rock and your soul a bitter wind? It makes *you* such an easy target, because the only person I have to go after is you."

He leaned in. "I care nothing for other people, that is true. But I will serve the goddess Diana forever, even into the afterlife."

"Be careful," I warned. "You may get there sooner than you think."

"Nicolas?"

The Praetors were escorting my mother into the field. She had been cleaned up since I saw her last; she looked tired, but still healthy and strong. There were no chains on her wrists, and though her feet were bare, her clothes were nicer than most slave women wore. She looked much improved from when I'd seen her in the caged wagon.

I nodded at her and she smiled back, but with an audience around us now, I couldn't think of any words to say. There was so much to tell her. It felt like a hundred lifetimes since I had spoken privately to her in that cage. How could I describe everything that had happened in only a few words? Years ago, before the mines, I could have communicated every thought in my head from only one look between us. But I had changed since then, and maybe she had too. Though I loved her and remembered how it had once been to have a mother I could depend on, I just didn't know her anymore. And so I didn't know what to say.

"Nicolas," she whispered again. "My son." And that told me enough of the emotions in her heart. Her love for me, her fear, and her worries that I was making a great mistake now.

I started toward her, but Brutus stepped between us. "Open the door first."

I looked back to my mother, who shook her head at me.

"I'm sorry," I said to her. "But I have to do this." Then I reached out my hand for the bulla, and it lifted from his chest in obedience to my call.

Brutus took hold of it. "No tricks, Nicolas. Do not risk your mother's life."

"The risk is yours if you continue to threaten her," I countered. "Now give me that bulla, and let's finish with this."

He handed it to me, and I put it back over my head. I was already anxious enough that when the magic flooded into me, I gasped with the pressure inside.

"Are you all right?" Brutus asked.

"Hush, or you'll get your answer." I walked to the pile of rubble, closed my eyes as I knelt before it, and called the wolf.

☙ · FORTY-SIX · ❧

There was a reaction when the Praetors saw the wolf of Mars. For many of them, it was probably the first time they'd seen the wolf here, and this one was larger and fiercer than those in the wild. If I had asked him to attack, he would have, and probably could do far more damage than I'd ever done with my magic. But that wasn't my purpose.

The wolf came to sit beside me, and I put a hand on the back of his neck. Above the sound of Atroxia's tears, Mars's voice came into my head.

"You've come again to open this temple."

"I've come to see it again," I silently replied. "But to open it for the first time."

"Very well."

"I can hear the Mistress. Is she awake?"

"No," Mars said. "And if you are wise, you will not disturb her."

That would be a problem. Because if I'd learned anything over the past several days, it was that I lacked wisdom, or any good sense, for that matter.

"Do you have the key?" Mars asked.

I nodded, and under my breath whispered, "*A caelo usque ad centrum.*" It was the last thing Horatio had said to me before he sent me into the amphitheater, and what Crispus had said in memory of his father.

From heaven to the center of earth. That was the meaning of the words. When Horatio had spoken them, I had thought he was beginning to understand that his life was in danger, and it was a sort of prayer to the gods. Maybe it was, in his own way, but it was also the key. The power of the gods came from the heavens and much of it had been stored at the center of earth: in Caesar's cave in the mines, and here, in the catacombs of a former vestalis.

Crispus had reminded me of it last night, when Livia and I talked with him in his fields.

And upon my words, a light formed in front of me. Whereas before, only I could see the temple, this time I knew it was visible to the Praetors because they gasped and fell on their knees.

When I stood, a door appeared directly in front of me. There was no handle, but it was open, beckoning me inside.

No, I was not going in there. The Praetors would, while I got my mother to safety. Then I would use magic to destroy the temple, sealing the Mistress inside the tomb forever.

I turned to Brutus, who had come near me, his jaw open wide as he gazed over the temple and its beckoning door. "Release my mother," I said. "Now."

"Your mother has one last job to do," he said. "As my slave, I order her into the temple to get the Malice. When she brings it out and puts it in my hands, then she may go."

"No, I will not agree to that," I said. As long as he controlled my mother, he controlled me. I was willing to risk my own safety, but never hers.

"I don't need you to agree," Brutus said. "Those are my orders, and she will obey them."

"No, she won't." I glanced over at her, but she was too far away to hear us or to have any idea of the danger she was still in.

"Are you challenging my authority, slave?" he asked. "Because if I recall, the last time you started a fight with us, we nearly killed that sewer girl. The time before that, we did kill Valerius. Do you doubt that I will harm your mother, if necessary?"

"I'm not challenging your authority," I said. "I'm denying that you have any authority, at least over me. I will go in my mother's place. I will go into the temple."

And collapse it from within. And hope to survive.

He smiled. "I thought you would offer that. And I accept, though I don't trust you, no more than you trust me. So you will not go in alone."

"You want to come in with me?" I said. Fine, he could remain in that temple forever, keep the Mistress company while the walls crashed in on them both.

"Yes, I will come." Brutus nodded to the men still holding my mother. "And so will she."

"No!" I raised a hand, and then heard Crispus running toward us, completely out of breath and calling my name. He must've left the circus the moment I disappeared.

"I need to speak with Nic!" Crispus said. "In private, before anything else happens."

"Whatever you have to say should be for everyone," Brutus said.

Crispus turned to him, almost violently. "You murdered my father and dare to stand on my land! I will have my revenge on you, Decimas Brutus. You and Nic are *not* on the same side of this quest, and so if I want to speak to him in private, then I will!"

Brutus chuckled, giving off every impression that he was unconcerned, but the look in his eyes said something else entirely. He knew with one hand on my flesh, he could stop me. But Crispus was a judge now within the empire. He had ways of stopping Brutus that were far beyond what I could do.

Brutus nodded, and Crispus pulled me aside. I had no doubt that it was important — the tense expression on his face told me that. But with my mother only a short distance away and magic filling me, his timing couldn't have been worse.

"What is it?" I hissed when we were alone. Not *alone* really, but at least we were out of earshot from any of the Praetors.

"The temple was here all the time?"

"Did you come here to chat? Because I'd rather do this later."

"No, I came to help you. I owe it to my father to fight them."

"Not this time. I'm either about to end a war on this earth or start one in the heavens. Whichever it is, I don't want you here."

"It's my property!"

"This land belongs to the gods! They've let you stay here, that's all. You have to leave while you still can."

"I can, but I won't," Crispus said. "Not yet anyway. Aurelia is here, hiding in the vines. You can't see her from the field, but she has another bow."

I cursed and didn't care if the gods heard it. "Again?" Was there an entire storehouse of bows in Crispus's fields that I didn't know about? "Where could she possibly have gotten a bow?"

"From Radulf, I assume. He's hiding there with her."

So he would keep her safe, which would've been comforting except that if he gave her a weapon, then he was expecting her to use it.

I made a turn, pretending to survey the Praetors just as Crispus had done, but my eyes were searching elsewhere. I didn't see Aurelia or Radulf, though I had no doubt they were here. But what I did see made my heart lurch into my throat.

Livia was hiding beneath some bushes with tears streaming down her face. By now, she was supposed to be miles away from this place. But she was here, and obviously terrified of being found. I couldn't let that happen, not at any price.

"What are we going to do?" Crispus asked.

"You're going to get out of here with Aurelia. And Livia. You'll see her hiding behind us." I was less clear about my own plans. I couldn't destroy the temple with my mother inside.

"Let me come in there with you. I can help."

"You can help by getting my sister out of here. That's going to be hard enough."

"I'll try, Nic."

"Let's go." Brutus had my mother by the arm. "Give me the Malice, and then you will have your mother."

"Just give him the Malice," Crispus whispered. "It's not worth the risk."

I nodded, but it only deepened the pit in my gut. I could not give Brutus the Malice, even if I wanted to, for it was no longer inside the temple.

The Malice was with Livia. I had given her the key before the race, just as Horatio had given it to me. Then today, while I raced and put up a trick of light to make it appear that she was in the circus watching me, she had come back here and entered the temple, something which, until now, only she and I would have been able to see.

But she was supposed to have been back at Radulf's house by now, not hiding beneath a bush. The Malice was easily within the Praetors' grasp and not one of them knew it.

I needed the Malice to get my mother back. But revealing where it truly was would cost me my sister.

❧·FORTY-SEVEN·❧

I walked past Brutus to enter the temple, but stopped long enough to give my mother a kiss on her cheek. She touched my shoulder when I did, her fingers digging into the skin with worry, which made it even harder to pull away and walk toward the temple. They would follow behind me.

Before we entered, Brutus called out orders for his Praetors to remain exactly where they were until we returned. I glanced back at Crispus, motioning with my eyes to where Livia was hiding, but I wasn't sure if he understood. Even if he did, I doubted there was any way for him to get to her without the Praetors noticing. Still, if there was a way, I trusted Crispus to find it.

Strange emotions rushed through me when I entered the door of the temple. It was different from how I'd felt when Aurelia and I had taken refuge in Caesar's temple in the forums. Back then, I had felt the guilt of being a thief who'd stolen the bulla from his cave, and the unworthiness of being an escaped slave. Now I considered the bulla mine and no longer thought of myself as an escaped slave. Instead, I felt a belonging in this temple, as if I had earned the right to stand here.

Which was a good thing. Feeling acceptable in this temple gave me courage to step forward. And right now, I needed courage more than ever before.

The temple was far larger than what it appeared to be on the outside. Indeed, from what I'd seen outside, it should have only barely fit me and Brutus, but then two Praetors stepped inside with my mother between them, and a dozen more Praetors could have followed and stood comfortably with us. Not that I wanted them here. I didn't even want Brutus here, and especially not my mother. This would've been much easier if I were alone.

Just as Livia had done this, alone. And I took extra courage from that.

At the far end of the temple was a narrow ladder leading underground. Atroxia's cries were coming from there. Nothing else was on this main level, no vase or statue or even a layer of dust as I would've expected to find after being buried for three centuries. The Malice was not up here, and probably never had been.

To retrieve it, Livia must have gone underground, into the temple's catacombs.

Before going down the ladder, I reached for Radulf with my thoughts and told him where Livia was hiding.

"You must take my sister back home," I said. "Aurelia too. Make her go with you."

A moment later came his response. He was connected to me through magic, but not to Livia. He could not find her without revealing himself. "If the Praetors know I'm here, a fight will start," he said into my head. "Nobody can fight while that temple is open. Do you understand?"

I understood. But understanding the risk did not mean I could control it.

It was decided that Brutus and I would go into the catacombs alone while my mother was held near the temple doors. I glanced back at her and forced a smile to my face. It was the complete opposite to how I really felt.

"May the gods go with you," she said.

And I nodded, again without saying a word. I could fake a smile, but every phrase of comfort seemed hollow, and might've given us both false hope. I turned away, regretting that I hadn't at least tried to say something.

As I descended the ladder, I debated whether to tell Radulf that Livia had the Malice. He would take a greater risk to find her if he knew that, but at the same time, his refusal to help right now made me angry. He should take the risk because Livia was his granddaughter. That should be enough of a reason.

"Can you create a light down here?" Brutus asked me. He held a torch in one hand, but it was flickering from the breeze coming down the ladder hole and had become dim.

I shook my head, which probably was a sort of lie. Of course I could create a light, but I wouldn't. I needed time for Radulf to get to Livia. So that meant, if necessary, I'd wait in here until dark, because then he'd easily be able to get closer to her. But I doubted Brutus would let me stall for that long. I probably didn't even have three minutes before he'd lose patience with me.

"Where do you think the Malice is?" I whispered to Brutus.

Because I had no idea where I should look, or pretend to look in this case. This underground room was vast and very dark, and thanks to my refusal to use any light, it was mostly bathed in shadows. Like on the main floor, there was little of anything down here. This temple was nothing but an enormous tomb. A place for Atroxia to die. No wonder she cried in my head the way she did. Of all the punishments I'd faced as a slave and all the violence in the amphitheater or events of the circus, nothing in Rome seemed more cruel than to have locked her in this room, dead to the world long before her body knew it.

"The Malice is meant to be worn. I'd expect to see it on the statue of a warrior, perhaps one of the god Mars." Brutus motioned to his forearm. "It will be made of silver and for the person who wears it; it'll extend from the knuckles halfway to the elbow. The carvings on it will be very fine, but most prominent will be a carving of Mars's wolf."

What he described was very similar to the armband Radulf had wanted to use as a trick. Maybe that had been a good plan before. Of course, even if we had fooled them, it wouldn't have lasted long.

I started to walk away, to search in any other part of this temple for what I already knew was no longer here. But Brutus grabbed my tunic. "If you think you can steal the Malice for yourself, then know this. I do not fear awakening the Mistress. If you try to get away with the Malice, I will wake her."

I shook my head at him. "If I find the Malice in here, I will give it to you. I don't want it."

"Call me *Dominus*," he said. "I am about to hold a most powerful possession. I have earned the right to be called by a superior title."

"Tell that to your dogs outside," I muttered. "You haven't earned that title from me." Then before he could answer, I moved deeper into the shadows of the temple, alone.

It was cold down here, and damp, but I shivered for entirely different reasons. The cries in my head were growing louder, so much that I knew I was walking toward Atroxia, or the Mistress. I tried not to go forward, but it was as if my body had become chained to her will.

Somewhere in my thoughts, Radulf was trying to break through, with warnings or information or I didn't know what. But I couldn't hear him, not anymore, not while the cries for help were so much louder.

I needed to see the Mistress, to reassure myself that she was still asleep, or better yet, that I really was only hearing an echo from three centuries ago, from before she died in here. Because soon, Brutus would give up his search, and he and I would leave the temple. I couldn't leave without knowing what had become of the vestalis.

There she was, just ahead, her body laid out on a small bed that was really only cloth stretched across a wood frame. A thin blanket completely covered her, but it couldn't have kept out the cold. I was already chilled and had only been down here for a few minutes. She'd have likely frozen to death long before she felt the effects of hunger or lack of air.

Her cries were pounding inside my head, ripping at my heart for their sadness, their desperation. And yet in some ways I felt better. Because she lay there so perfectly still, not even breathing.

Valerius had been right. The cries were nothing but an echo in my head.

I wondered how in three hundred years, she had not yet decayed into dust. Perhaps that was the curse Diana had given her, to preserve her body, forbidding her spirit to ever rest in the afterlife. Looking her over, I realized one hand had fallen out from beneath the blanket. For as long as she had been gone, the skin should have long rotted away, but her hand looked perfectly whole. I leaned over to cover it with the blanket, simply out of respect.

Then I caught my breath in my throat. Her hand was warm.

Atroxia was as alive as everyone had warned me. Alive, but asleep. I started to pull my arm away, but in an instant, her hand turned and caught my left wrist in her grip.

My breath released in a sudden gasp of pain. This was no ordinary grip, far beyond the worst that had been done to me by Sal or his brute guards, or even by Radulf in the fiercest of our battles against each other. The pinch of her fingers around my wrist had instantly broken the bones like they were nothing but brittle twigs. A wave of nausea swept through me as I fell to my knees and tried to stay conscious, more locked to her than any chain had ever been to me.

There was no other movement from her, not even a flutter of her eyelashes, as far as I could tell in this dim light.

Only her voice in my head. No longer crying, but saying with the deepest feeling of sorrow, "Help me."

⊰ · FORTY-EIGHT · ⊱

With the pain in my wrist, I couldn't hold my thoughts together enough to answer her cries for help, but then, I wouldn't answer either. Clearly, there was a connection between us, just as Radulf and I were connected, but I didn't want to hear her. I never had. And giving her any reply would only strengthen that bond.

I froze in place, hoping as her body relaxed back into a deeper sleep, her hand would also release my wrist. I needed her to release it because I wanted to cry out for my own help, and I knew I couldn't. Whatever else happened, I had to keep her asleep.

Finally, footsteps were behind me, and Brutus brought his torch. "It's not anywhere," he was saying. "What are you — oh!"

My head was down, trying to manage the pain. I didn't look up at him, but it wasn't necessary. He could see her hand locked around my wrist. He immediately understood.

"The Mistress is alive," he whispered. "I knew it!"

"We don't know what'll happen if she wakes," I said. "It could be bad for both of us."

Brutus pulled the blanket away from her face, though I couldn't see it. "She's just a woman," he said, obviously disappointed. "The stories I've been told of her greatness . . . well, this isn't what I expected."

She wasn't an ordinary woman. If he could've felt the grip of her fingers, he'd have known that. In a better light, he might've seen the strain on my face as I struggled to keep breathing. With the bulla, I was stronger than I used to be, but even that wasn't enough to make her release me. Maybe she looked like a sleeping vestalis, but she was holding the strength and power of an angry goddess. Diana.

"I'm going to awaken her," Brutus said. "The Malice is nothing compared to her power. And when she wakes, she'll find the Malice for us."

"You will not wake her," I said. "I will destroy this temple over our heads if you try."

Brutus laughed, and even that bit of noise caused the Mistress to clench her grip. It might as well have been around my neck for the way her grip was suffocating me. Enough of this.

I had to get free and stop Brutus. If the Mistress awoke, none of us would leave this temple. I might not be leaving anyway. Even if I got my wrist free, I wouldn't be able to climb the ladder now.

I closed my eyes and pictured the temple's entrance, where my mother was. I saw it as clearly as if I was there, then felt the pressure on my chest as the room faded around me. My arm was released, and when I opened my eyes again, I was there, directly beside my mother.

The two Praetors who had been holding her started to react to me, but I had the advantage of surprise and dropped them both with a small burst of magic.

My mother pulled me into a hug, and though it was torture on my wrist to be pushed against her, I didn't protest. I had missed the presence of her love, and wanted it and needed it in more ways than I could count.

"Nicolas," she whispered. "If your father could see you now —"

Her tone was kind, but she didn't finish her sentence, and I wasn't entirely sure I wanted her to. This was not the kind of life my father would have hoped for me; I already knew that. And yet at the same time, I knew he'd never have wanted me in chains, slowly dying in the mines outside of Rome. I wanted to think he'd be proud of me for having come so far in my life. If where I stood was proof that I had come far.

"You have to run," I said to my mother. "I will shield you long enough to get past the Praetors, but once you get into the vineyard, a unicorn will be waiting there."

Her eyes widened. "A unicorn?"

"He'll take you to Radulf's home."

"Your grandfather's home?" Mother asked. "If you know about Radulf, then you probably know he was never . . . happy to have me for a daughter."

"But he will protect you," I said.

"I won't leave you here," she said. "We'll go together."

I glanced back toward the ladder hole. Brutus was still in the catacombs with the Mistress, and I had no doubt of his evil intentions. "There is more for me to do here," I said. "But I won't be far behind you. Now run. Go!"

The moment she left the temple, I raised the shield for her, at the same time as I called Callistus to the vineyards.

The Mistress was no longer crying in my head. In fact, I no longer detected any feeling of sadness from her. That would've been good news, except that the emotion was being replaced. With rage.

With my left wrist held against my chest by my other arm, I crept back to the ladder.

"Come with me now," I called to Brutus, speaking no louder than necessary for him to hear me. "Or you will be trapped in here forever. I'm going to collapse the temple."

There was no answer from him, though I knew he could hear me. Softly, his voice rose to my ears. He was chanting. He was waking her up. There was no choice but for me to leave them both in here.

I sent out enough magic to cause the ladder to fall apart in splinters. Then I braced my wrist again and started running toward the door. Sunlight beckoned me out, but I needed no encouragement. Although it hurt to release my wrist, I aimed my good hand toward the entrance. The moment I was out, I would destroy the door and let the rest of the temple fall with it.

Just before I reached the door, it slammed shut, turning everything into perfect darkness. Darker than Caesar's cave had been. Darker than the mines ever were on the blackest nights.

Any magic I had offered for my mother's protection was shut off with the door, and I could only hope she'd had time to reach Callistus. Then I dug within me for all the magic I had left.

I released it in every direction I could, certain that the bulla was capable of penetrating the walls and giving me a way out. It had to be strong enough, for the same magic that had cursed this tomb also powered the bulla. One could not be stronger than the other.

Unless it wasn't Diana's magic. The Malice belonged to Mars, and Jupiter himself had ordered Atroxia to be buried here. If that was true, then this situation might be far worse than I'd realized. I was trying to counter magic that I couldn't even begin to understand and which was certainly far more powerful than me.

The Mistress was more powerful than me too. Surely she had attempted to escape this temple many times before and failed. I needed something stronger.

A sound like thunder began rolling beneath my feet, and then came a scream such as I never could've imagined. It tore through my head like fire, but also pierced my ears and into my heart, and I was certain the scream reached to the ends of the empire. I wanted to raise my hands to my ears to block it out, but my injured arm wouldn't help. There was nothing I could do but fall to my knees and let it echo throughout this room.

"Help me, please," I whispered to Radulf. But I knew already that he couldn't hear me. That within the closed doors of these temples, I was as isolated as she had been for almost three hundred years.

"It's been stolen!" a woman cried. "The Malice has been stolen from me!"

I crawled until I reached a temple wall and crouched as low as I could get. It wouldn't give me much protection, or really any protection, but I didn't know what else to do.

The Mistress was awake.

⋈· FORTY-NINE ·⋈

The thunderings that had begun at my feet were rising, shaking the floor and even the temple walls. The best of my magic had destroyed a wooden ladder, but nothing else I'd done had even left a scratch on the walls.

I was using the Divine Star to heal my wrist and it was having some effect with the pain, but I still couldn't move it or feel any magic in it. I had to heal it, and fast. I needed some way to fight against her.

Then the marble floor began to crack like it was at the center of an enormous earthquake. I expected the temple walls and ceiling to come down on me as well, but for now, only the floor was in danger.

I started to stand, although I had nowhere to go, but before I could get to my feet, the floor crumbled beneath me.

I fell back into the catacombs amidst a heap of rubble and dust. If my wrist had been healed at all, it was worse now. My entire left arm where I had fallen felt like it was on fire.

"Nicolas Calva, why did you come here?" That was the Mistress's voice.

I didn't answer. Instead, I put up a shield and tried to do what I could for healing. Then I sent a little magic into the air, asking for light. I didn't need much, but at least I wouldn't be blind down here.

Brutus was supposed to be around here somewhere, and then I saw him unconscious in the corner of the room. Whether she had done that or pieces of the falling floor had hit him, I didn't know. But it was hard for me to feel any sympathy for him since he was the one who had caused this trouble.

As I had caused it too. I could not excuse myself so easily.

With my magic, the room had lightened enough to see the Mistress walking toward me. Her white robes had grayed, perhaps from natural aging, or from her corruption. But her face was that of a young woman. She had narrow eyes that sloped upward at the outside corners and her crimson hair was in a braided bun with ringlets on either side of her face. When she spoke, her voice was low and commanding.

"Kneel before me, Nicolas."

I shook my head as I stared at the ground. "You are beautiful, Atroxia, and I have great respect for your power. But I will not kneel to you."

She waved her hands, and I felt myself hurl backward through the air and I crashed into the catacomb wall. Without the bulla, a collision like that would've knocked me unconscious too, and I almost wished that it had. Dirt crumbled behind me when I fell back to the ground, landing on both knees, one arm, and a partially healed left wrist that collapsed beneath my weight. The pain it caused made my head swim with dizziness.

"Where is the Malice?" she asked. "You stole it from me!"

"The Malice is gone," I said. "It's out of your control now."

If she was enraged before, then that made it worse. She flung her arms apart, and it felt as if claws had scratched my chest, though when I felt for blood, there was none.

"I will find it," she said. "Weak human, you cannot hide it from me, not for long."

I didn't need that long. Only enough time to get the Malice from Livia, and use the bulla to destroy it. After that, the Mistress would lose too much of her power to be any threat to me, or to Rome.

She hit me with something that punched against my gut. I felt the pressure, but not the pain from it, but then I realized pain had not been her intention. Whatever she had done had collapsed my shield. I scrambled to raise it again, but couldn't find it within me. And I would've fought back, except I needed to preserve my magic for one last attempt at destroying this temple.

Behind her, Brutus was beginning to stir. He raised his head and then slowly got to his knees.

"Get on your knees," he muttered to me. "Nothing else will save you today."

"I will not be saved on my knees to *her*." Then I turned my attention to the Mistress. "You were a vestalis, the holiest of women. You betrayed that when you helped in the assassination of Julius Caesar. You are a traitor to the empire and to your vows."

A growl emerged from her now, a sound I had never heard from anyone. And with that growl, she threw a wave of magic that passed right through me, one that tried to steal my soul as it exited.

I punched back, but it only came at her like a breeze, and now she laughed. "Did you think you were strong, slave boy? What Diana put into that trinket around your neck is only a little play magic. But what she gave me, to keep me alive all this time, is real power. And once you return the Malice to me, I will show you the worst of it."

While she spoke, I had been looking around the temple for any hope of escape. Though it was still dark in here, my eyes had adjusted somewhat. Above me, I saw claw marks on the walls and attempts to scratch between the marble blocks, but nothing to suggest there was a way out.

Except I knew better, because I had spent too much time in the mines of Rome to believe this was sealed up forever. She might have Diana's powers, but she did not have Diana's lungs to breathe. The Mistress needed air.

And if air had found a way in for the past three hundred years, then I had a way out. For that, I didn't need the strength of the bulla. I needed the quiet magic of the Divine Star.

Using it meant I would not have its powers to continue healing my wrist. But I braced my arm against my chest and then used magic from my shoulder to feel for the flow of air.

Ahead of me, Brutus was groveling to the Mistress about the Malice, about all he had done to protect it, and promising to find it again for her. It was pathetic, but I supposed this had been the entire purpose of his life thus far, to hope to grovel at her feet.

He did that while I detected gaps between the stone walls. There hadn't been any before. Indeed, the workmanship of this temple was perfect, or it had been until Atroxia collapsed her own floor. That destruction had created gaps that I could use to escape.

Using my good hand, I sent the Divine Star's magic through the gaps, wearing away at the mortar and worming out even larger holes.

"What are you doing?" Atroxia snarled.

Invisible hands clutched at my shoulders and threw me high into the air and against the temple wall, above even where the main floor had once been. I expected to fall and tried to brace myself for the impact, but instead she held me there.

"You stole the Malice," she said. "If you want to live, then tell me where it is."

I shook my head. "If I want to live, the last thing I can do is give you the Malice. I know your plans."

At this height, and with my own magic, I was feeling air

begin to move between the marble blocks. Enough air that I could get a grip on the real world outside. And I used it.

"Give me the Malice!" The angrier she became, the deeper Atroxia's voice rumbled.

I created a rumbling of my own, in the vibrations between the blocks. All I needed was a good burst of magic and they would tumble like stacked dice.

Atroxia's eyes widened — even from as high as I was, and pressed far against the temple wall — I saw them redden with anger.

"Not to my temple, you won't!"

"This is *not* your temple!" I yelled. "This is your tomb, you traitor!"

She threw a ball of magic at me, but I used my own magic to push it away. There was so much power in the combination that I was forced harder against the temple wall, which shuddered at first, and then blocks began to fall.

I landed on some stone blocks that fell outside the temple, not far from the Praetors who had obeyed Brutus's orders and were still on their knees. But upon seeing me, they leapt to their feet, startled, and unsure of what to do.

I wasn't much more clear on what should happen next. The temple's collapse was massive, stones falling upon one another and sending up a storm of dust.

Choking on it, I backed away, still keeping my injured wrist against my chest. Once again, it had started to heal. Until I careened through several feet of marble. Surely there would come a point when the Divine Star would refuse to heal me anymore.

There was silence amongst the Praetors until the last brick fell. Then all eyes turned to me, realizing I had entombed their leader, trapped the Mistress, and destroyed any chance they might have had to get the Malice.

From far in the back, someone yelled, "Get him!"

⊰ · FIFTY · ⊱

I was in no condition to fight, or at least, no condition to fight well. But I'd come this far, and I would not let the Praetors win now. Rather than send out any attack, I did as I had done before and collapsed the ground in a circle around me, creating an impassable ditch so no one could get close to me. It wasn't useful for my escape, but it prevented them from laying a finger on my magic.

From there, I worked to heal my wrist while I used my right hand to throw magic wherever I could. Outside of the suffocating bounds of the temple walls, my magic was stronger and easier to access, and I took full advantage of that. Without their leader, or really, even a purpose left to them, the remaining Praetors didn't put up much of a fight.

Livia was no longer hiding beneath the bushes, so I hoped either Radulf or Crispus had gotten her away somehow. I wanted to search for her, but arrows had started flying from the vineyard. Aurelia was still here too, obviously.

I should've been angry with Crispus for failing to get Aurelia away, but I wasn't. We both knew how impossible it was to make Aurelia do anything against her will. Aurelia would never willingly leave me behind.

So I closed my eyes and pictured the vineyards, and Aurelia standing in them, and then prayed I would not have the bad luck to reappear in front of her just as she was firing an arrow.

I actually entered the vineyards far behind her. She was on a rock that gave her a better view into the field, and was taking advantage of that position with every arrow she released. I started forward, then Crispus ran up beside her with a handful of arrows. Neither of them knew I was here.

He leapt onto the rock beside her and stuffed the arrows inside the quiver on her back. I noticed his hand lingered on her shoulder when he had finished, longer than was necessary. And when she looked over at him, I had hoped she would smack him with the wooden edge of her bow, but she didn't. She just smiled and thanked him for the arrows.

"Nic isn't there anymore," Aurelia said when she looked back into the field. "He was just there a moment ago."

As if they sensed the answer to their confusion, both Aurelia and Crispus turned back in unison to see me behind them.

"Nic!" Aurelia jumped off the rock and caught me in an embrace. "You terrified us, going inside that temple! We thought you would never come out!"

I grimaced as my wrist bent between us, but let her hold me anyway.

"Are you all right?" Crispus asked.

"Is my sister all right?" I countered, pressing back from Aurelia. "Where is she?"

Crispus looked from Aurelia over to me. "I don't know. We can't find her, not without the Praetors seeing us search for her. Maybe Radulf found her."

"Where is he now?"

Crispus and Aurelia shared a look, and then Aurelia said, "When the temple collapsed, he vanished. He muttered that he needed something from home, but he hasn't come back."

"He probably won't come back because Radulf's afraid of the Mistress." I didn't blame him for that. I understood his fears now in a way I hadn't before — her magic had overwhelmed anything I could do. Fortunately, she was trapped inside the temple.

"So she's awake?" Aurelia asked.

"She was." I nodded to the temple ruins. "But it's all destroyed. Even if she survived the collapse, I doubt she can get out from beneath so much rubble."

"The Praetors won't continue to fight. Why would they?" Crispus smiled broadly. "You did it!"

He clapped me on the back and Aurelia gave my arm a squeeze, but I couldn't feel the same relief. Despite what I had just said, Atroxia's magic was much stronger than mine. I had not been able to use the full strength of my magic within the temple walls — what if hers was the same way? What if her punishment wasn't being buried alive? What if it was burial without the full use of her magic?

Radulf's voice returned to my head again, icy cold but not from anger. He was still afraid, but this time, it was for my life. "Nic, this is not over. Leave right now, please."

"Where's Livia?"

There was silence, and I felt his fears intensify. He was her grandfather too. "I can't pull her away from there," he said. "I know she has the Malice. It's stronger than my magic, and it wants to stay with the Mistress."

"I won't leave without her," I said. "It's my fault she's here at all."

"What are you talking about?" Crispus asked, then Aurelia shot him a knowing look.

"Get out of there." Radulf was pleading with me now. "I will come find Livia."

That wasn't good enough, and he knew it.

Aurelia put her hand on my shoulder. "What is Radulf saying?" she asked.

I shook my head at her and tried to keep my thoughts straight. Since destroying the temple, I was stronger. If she survived, then maybe the Mistress had grown in strength too.

I stood and started walking back to the field, calling to Crispus and Aurelia, "You both need to leave right now."

To my dismay, they followed. "Why?" Aurelia called. "Just tell us why!"

I used magic to raise another shield, only this one prevented both Crispus and Aurelia from crossing into the field.

"Nic, don't go back there alone!" she cried.

I turned. "I can't save your lives and mine. Run from here, please!"

Aurelia started to follow me, but Crispus put his arms around her and held her back, then they ducked into the vines. He wouldn't get her to leave; I knew that already, just as I knew Crispus would not leave without her. I hoped they would at least find a good place to hide.

Once I got to the field, the Praetors had grouped together, probably deciding whether they still had any strategy to defeat me and if it was worth it to continue the fight.

It wasn't.

"Surrender now!" I called to them. "It is your only chance to walk out of here alive."

"You cannot kill us all!" one man shouted.

"I don't intend to kill any of you," I replied. "But that does not mean you are safe. For the sake of your own lives, leave while you still can."

Another discussion started amongst them, with some obvious disagreements. But it didn't take long before a few men backed out of the group and hurried away, and then others followed, and more followed after that.

"Now *you* leave," Radulf said into my head.

"Only two days ago, you scolded me for refusing to fight," I said. "Now you'd have me leave?"

He drew in a breath, one I could hear in my head. "Nicolas, you are not entering a fight. This will be a slaughter. Listen to what is happening around you!"

And I did. The field was emptying of Praetors, and Crispus and Aurelia were out of sight, hopefully out of reach, so I took a moment and listened.

At first I had expected the sounds to be coming from the temple, or from the Praetors who'd refused to leave. But it wasn't — these sounds were in my head, the same way as when Radulf spoke to me, or when I heard the crying of the Mistress.

But this time, it was laughter. Atroxia's harsh, wicked laughter, though the voice was deeper than before. She had growled at me then, in an almost inhuman way. Her laughter was even less human.

The fallen marble blocks were shifting from their place, from movement deep below the surface. Movement in the catacombs.

Atroxia was only a vestalis, one buried alive as punishment for supporting Caesar's assassination. That was who had cried, who had begged me to help her. But it was not who I heard now.

Diana's curse changed the vestalis into the Mistress. This was who Radulf feared, and who wielded the angry magic of a vengeful goddess. The Mistress was about to reveal herself to me once more.

The marble blocks burst from their resting place in a fierce explosion that rattled the skies themselves. I shielded myself to prevent any blocks from landing on me, and felt grateful for the shield already protecting Crispus and Aurelia. And it was a good thing, for I felt an impact over that way and knew the shield had been tested, and had held strong.

"Livia, run!" I cried. I didn't want to expose her presence here, but I couldn't find her anywhere and I needed to warn her away. My warning had come too late.

Emerging from the rubble, I first saw the end of a massive tail, as red as blood. It beat through the rocks to separate them, and as they did, the tail continued to stretch forth from the ground. Next a claw emerged from the rubble, each tip like a sword. It pressed against the ground to allow the head to rise up with a savage growl. I knew this creature. A draco. The dragons of Rome. Little different from the images engraved on the columns of Radulf's home.

The serpent's front teeth were as long as daggers and doubtless twice as sharp, and when she spat at me, saliva dripped from her fangs and smoke flared from her nostrils. Her eyes were yellow with slits of black that seemed as deep as the mine pits. Nothing about her seemed to ever have been human.

As she pulled herself to freedom, her second claw unfolded with Brutus in her clutches. She dumped him on the ground, where he immediately fell to his knees and praised her for rescuing him.

She turned to me and spoke as clearly and plainly as she had before, with the voice of the vestalis from the catacombs, but deeper and more commanding.

"There is Decimas Brutus, my servant. Do you see that I saved him from the fate that was nearly mine, that of being buried alive?"

"You should have left him there," I said. "He earned his fate by his betrayal of Rome. Just as you betrayed it."

"The Praetors have always served me, and in turn, I will always protect them. Join us, Nicolas."

I shook my head. "Not today, Atroxia." Not ever.

Fire spat from the serpent's mouth, setting everything around me aflame, including the vines. Crispus and Aurelia ran from the vineyard but were stopped by the shield I had created. Though it wouldn't make them much safer, I lowered the shield now to allow them a way out. Rather than run, Aurelia immediately fired off each of her arrows, searching for any weakness in the dragon's hide, but they were as useless as if she'd tossed feathers at the creature.

Crispus took Aurelia's hand and they ran safely away from the fire, but only to a worse problem. They were closer to Atroxia now.

"Where is the Malice?" Brutus said, on his feet again and coming closer to me. "The time for games is over."

"I don't have it," I said.

"Just as you denied having the key," he said.

"Yes, well, I was wrong about that," I said. "But I am not wrong about the Malice. It's out of your reach now."

Another lie, though I never flinched while telling it.

"Are you sure about that?" the Mistress asked.

I readied myself for whatever she might bring. If she as much as coughed up another ember, I would call in enough rain to put out her flame forever. For my own safety, I didn't want to, but I would. The clouds were already gathering, in fact.

The Mistress paid no attention to the skies overhead. Instead, her golden eye went from me to Aurelia and Crispus, who were trying to get up the hill to Crispus's home.

Faster than I could react, she snatched them each into a claw and raised them high into the air.

I sent everything I had at her chest, hoping it would force her to release them. Yet like Aurelia's arrows, nothing registered even a scratch.

She squeezed them tighter, enough that both Aurelia and Crispus reacted with cries of pain. "Now will you deny having the Malice?" she said to me. "Because if you do not give it to me, I will crush your friends!"

⚔·FIFTY-ONE·⚔

I used magic to launch all of Aurelia's fallen arrows back into the air. Had Atroxia been anything other than a dragon, they'd have been driven through her. But the arrows and my magic combined failed to even get her attention.

"I'm telling you that I do not have the Malice!" I yelled. "Search me for it if you must."

"You lie!" she said. "I can sense it nearby. I can feel its power."

She tightened her grip on Crispus, and he cried out again. I understood his pain as if it were my own. It *had* been my own less than an hour ago, when she had crushed my wrist in her hand. No matter how that had felt, I knew it must be so much worse for him now.

"Wait!" I said. "You cannot harm him. Those are your own words."

She loosened her hold a little, or at least, Crispus seemed able to breathe again. "Why not?" she asked.

"He's a Praetor now," I said. "And you just told us that the Praetors serve you, so you are bound to protect them."

Atroxia turned to Brutus, who until now had seemed relieved to be forgotten in this conversation. "Well?" she asked.

His irritation was obvious, and he clearly was pained at having to answer her. But he did. "It's true, Mistress. Only days ago, this boy was made a judge in Rome. He is a Praetor, though he's not really one of us. His father served the empire, not you."

I stepped closer. "But you cannot punish him for his father's loyalties. Crispus is a Praetor and must be granted your protection."

"Yes," the Mistress said. "I suppose he must."

And she dropped him to the ground. I released enough magic to cushion his fall, but there was still the problem of Aurelia. She had no similar claim of protection from Atroxia. Nothing she could offer for her life.

But there was my life.

I got to my knees and lowered my head. Not in humility to the Mistress but because I knew how Aurelia would react and I didn't want to see it. "Take me instead," I said. "Take me and not her."

"No!" Aurelia struggled to break free, and Atroxia squeezed her again.

I heard her cry and looked up, yelling, "You want me!"

"Let her go!" Crispus stumbled to his feet and crossed between us. "The Praetors of Rome have the protection of the Mistress."

"That privilege does not extend to the friends of Praetors," Brutus said.

"I know that." Crispus looked back at me for a moment, offering a silent apology. Then he turned to the dragon. "But the wife of a Praetor would be protected just as he is."

He was right, of course. Marrying Crispus would save Aurelia's life. But it still came at me like a knife.

"Is this true?" Atroxia said to Aurelia. "You will marry this boy?"

Crispus stepped forward again. "I have already made her the offer. All she must do is accept."

If I had offered when Aurelia first wanted me to, or at any moment since then, she would have agreed to marry me. But I never said a word. And instead of hating myself for my silence, I should've been happy now, because this was her only chance to live.

Yes, that's how I *should have* felt.

Aurelia cried out from the crushing pain of the dragon's grip, then said, "Yes, yes, I agree to his offer. I will be his wife."

Atroxia let her fall to the ground. Though a new and different sort of ache had flared within me, I summoned enough magic to give her a cushion as well and immediately ran to her side.

I brushed the hair from her face and whispered, "Are you hurt?"

She tapped her side, at the ribs, and I placed my hand there to give her healing. She ran her fingers over mine. "I'm so sorry, Nic."

"You did what you had to do."

"This isn't what I want. Do you understand that?"

I did. Nothing else would've saved her life, so it obviously had been the right decision. I understood, but I didn't want to.

"Wait for me," I said. "When this is over, I will come back for you."

She arched her back as my magic continued to heal her. "It's too late. The deal's been made." Her words echoed what I'd said to her only four days ago, and they pierced me with sadness.

"Come along." Brutus touched my shoulder before I'd even realized he was speaking. All magic instantly dissolved from within me. I shrugged him off and reached for Aurelia one last time, but he pulled me to my feet. Crispus stepped forward to defend me, but Atroxia let out a growl and he stopped.

Aurelia wasn't fully healed, but she was better than before and Crispus helped her stand. They would protect each other, strengthen each other in ways I could not. As Brutus pulled me away, Crispus took her in the opposite direction. Their hands were clasped together in a familiar way I never had dared with her. They were already together.

"You are ours now, Nicolas," Brutus said. "Every other part of your life is over."

"She cannot force me to make a Jupiter Stone," I said. "I'll let her kill me first."

"Death is not the worst thing she can do to you," Brutus said. "The Mistress always gets what she wants."

The dragon's massive tail swiped Brutus away, then I was snatched up into her claw, the same as she had done to Crispus and Aurelia. More than the pain of it, I became aware of how odd I felt here. She was no Praetor, so some magic had returned to me already, but though I could feel it, I understood the uselessness of my abilities compared to her power.

"The scent of the Malice is nearby," she said. "Tell me where it's hidden."

"I've destroyed it already," I said. "You only detect its memory."

She gave me a squeeze, forcing all breath from me and crushing me in her grip. I cried out, then tried to focus again on creating a storm. If I could direct a bolt of lightning straight at her, it might pierce her thick hide. Would it kill me too, if she was still holding me? I was pretty sure it would.

Above all other ways in which I never wanted to die, lightning was the worst. But Livia was still here, somewhere. If this was my only chance to save her, I would accept my fate as bravely as possible. Or if I died like a coward, I hoped no one was watching.

Brutus saw what I was doing, but rather than take cover from the coming storm, he shouted up to Atroxia, "This is the boy's power, Mistress! See the storm? He can create the Jupiter Stone for you!"

She dropped me to the ground. I landed hard on my side, and I was pretty sure the fall broke my wrist. Yet again. I wouldn't even bother healing it this time. By now, it felt like a waste of magic since my bones were clearly determined to remain in pieces. While gritting my teeth, I moved my arm to my chest and rolled so that with my other hand I could pull the darkest clouds directly over our heads. The growl of thunder echoed throughout Valerius's fields and the first drops of rain began falling. This would be a mighty storm.

Atroxia's tail encircled me and slithered in tighter and tighter. I stood to avoid being crushed, and when I did, for the first time, I saw Livia.

She hadn't gone far from the bushes where she had hidden before. Instead, she was deeper within them and in a cavity of earth where little but her eyes were visible. I suspected that the only reason I saw her was because she had wanted that. And when she held up her arm and I saw the Malice in her grip, I understood her message. She intended to give up the Malice to save my life.

I couldn't allow that. Livia had to understand why.

I shouted up to Atroxia. "If you get the Malice, what will you do to me?"

The serpent laughed, and its echoes rumbled like waves through the air. "When I get it, you will make me a Jupiter Stone. I will give that stone to Diana, and with it, she will make war against the gods."

I glanced back to where Livia was hiding, but she was no longer visible. I hoped she had her answer. And hoped even more that she would forgive me for putting her in this terrible situation.

Rain was falling harder now. My storm was ready. Atroxia's tail widened again, and I took my chance to run. When I did, her tail rose up and careened against the hard earth. It missed me, but I fell back to the ground. Her tail slithered around again, catching me back within its fold. I struggled until I got my good hand free, and then raised it high, ready to call in the lightning. The charge tingled in my fingers, ran down my arm, and sparked inside my chest. This would be a powerful bolt, hopefully enough to kill the evil creature.

Certainly it was too powerful for me as well.

Atroxia reached for me with her claw. When she lifted me up, the sharp talons dug into my flesh, and I cried out. I had to focus on the lightning, which would've been easier without claws cutting into me.

"Stop!" a voice commanded.

We turned to see Radulf walking through the lingering fire in the vineyards, completely untouched by the flames. It was him, not a trick of the light. Despite the terror I knew he felt for the Mistress, he had come back.

Atroxia dropped me yet again, and Brutus rushed forward to grab my arm. His efforts wouldn't make any difference now. Too much of my magic was already spent, and the injuries had made me weak. Still, I shook my head at Radulf, hoping to make him leave, but he didn't seem worried. His hands were clasped behind his back as if he'd been on a casual afternoon stroll. He merely smiled back at me and nodded, perfectly calm.

"General Radulf, you are late to our party," Brutus said.

"Hardly," Radulf said. "No, actually I was hoping not to attend this particular gathering. But you have forced me to it."

"What do you want?" Atroxia asked.

His voice never wavered as he looked up at her. "I want the return of my grandson, obviously."

She laughed at his boldness. "The boy is mine now. He will give me the Malice and then he has a job to do."

"Even if he wanted to, he cannot obey," Radulf said. "Nic was telling the truth. He does not have the Malice, and he will not be able to get it."

"Why not?" Brutus asked.

Radulf smiled and raised an arm that had been clasped behind his back. The Malice was wrapped on his forearm. Not the real one, but the fake one Valerius had created when he hoped to trick the Praetors in exchange for my mother. It would never work.

But it was our only chance.

"No, not the Malice!" I yelled, trying to sound as desperate as possible. Atroxia had to believe my performance.

The dragon sniffed, trying to get a scent for its magic. I wondered how keen her senses were, because Livia had the real Malice here. Could she tell the difference?

Radulf raised his arm, and the Malice lit as with flame. I knew it had no magic, so it was his Divine Star at work here. But it certainly looked convincing enough. He gestured forward and from the Malice, a wave of magic punched through the air and traveled all the way to the forest beyond the field, toppling every tree there.

Radulf gasped, then stumbled from the release of so much magic. As strong as he was, even he had his limits, I supposed. Brutus ran from me, taking cover from the branches that were falling into the field now. One should have landed on me, but it merely rolled sideways through the air and fell on the ground. Radulf was shielding me. The Mistress still stood above me, though. She hadn't even flinched in the explosion, because none of its fallout could harm her.

"The Malice's magic is too powerful," I yelled to Radulf, though it wasn't him who needed to hear me. "We cannot give her that amulet."

"Release my grandson now," Radulf said. "Because if I count to three, I will disappear with this Malice and you will never find me again. One."

No, he was supposed to make her target the Malice, not himself. He was supposed to offer it to her and escape.

But he hadn't come just to trick her. He had come to make a trade. His life for mine.

"No, I caused this!" I said. "I have to fix it."

"*I* must fix this, Nic," Radulf said. "This war began long before you received your magic, and it's my fault for failing to stop it. Two!"

"Get out of here!" I yelled. My magic was returning, but there wasn't enough to fight Atroxia. I couldn't save him.

"Radulf has the Malice," Brutus said to the Mistress. "Take it!"

"No!" I yelled. "You want me!" Even if he fooled them for a moment, it wouldn't take the Mistress long to know she had been tricked. In her anger, she would destroy him.

"You must leave." Radulf was more firm than before. "I am your *pater familias*, so this is my decision. Besides, your magic is stronger than mine, so I need you to get out of here." Then he looked at Brutus. "Three!"

"We accept," the Mistress said. And with that, she snatched Radulf into her grip.

Instantly, I shot a bit of magic into his arm to make it feel as if the Malice had power of its own. It was all I could do. If I called the lightning back, the strike would kill Radulf. And for everything he had done to me once, I was surprised to find that all I cared about was saving his life, just as he was saving mine.

"Leave now!" Radulf said.

I rushed into the bushes, diving for the place Livia was hiding. She pressed the Malice into my arms, and the moment she did, the Mistress let out a fierce and angry growl. It hurt my ears, and Livia pressed her hands to either side of her head, obviously in pain too. Atroxia knew she was being tricked.

"I have to get away from you," I whispered to Livia. "Wherever I go, the Mistress will follow."

Unless. Unless I went to the one place she would never return to. I needed to go there and recover my strength. Then I could figure out what to do about Radulf.

I brushed one hand against Livia's arm. "Once I go, the Mistress will leave too. She'll try to find the Malice. Stay in hiding until she's gone."

Livia's eyes widened and she shook her head. "Please don't leave, Nic."

"I'll see you again soon. Take care of Mother for me."

I closed my eyes and pictured the room beneath the collapsed temple, where Atroxia had slept for three hundred years. Getting there took the last of my magic. It took nearly everything I had left, but at least I was safe here.

I landed beneath thousands of pounds of stone and brick, in a small pocket of space that could hold me, and perhaps a fly or two, *if* we all squeezed together. But nothing more than that.

Above me, I was sure I could hear the Mistress's screams and the vibrations of the earth with every stomp of anger. Even if she sensed where the Malice had gone, she would not follow me here, and it would take the Praetors a year to pull all of this stone away. Whether that was good news or not, I knew that my leaving would have consequences for Radulf. I couldn't imagine what was happening to him now.

I was bruised, badly injured, and could barely move. But . . . I had the Malice.

I rolled to the side that hurt the least and gripped the Malice with my good hand. Once I had strength enough to heal the other arm, I would wrap the Malice around my wrist and claim its magic for my own.

Even now, holding it, I understood the greater power in this amulet. Though I only held it in my hand, it was already flooding my senses and sharpening my instincts in a way that made the bulla seem like a toy. With the Malice, I heard every shift in the stones above me and perceived each grain of dust that fell between their cracks. I was holding magic that was not only capable of creating a Jupiter Stone, but magic that *wanted* to create it.

I returned to my back, but the movement caused an unfortunate shift in the stones. One dropped directly on my legs, pinning me to the ground. In sudden pain, I thrust the Malice toward the stones, which instantly crumbled them into dust. It saved my legs, but the burst of such intense magic took my last measure of strength.

No! I needed to save Radulf.

To destroy the Mistress.

I needed air. And soon.

The Malice fell somewhere away from me. I knew it was lost, but I'd search for it once I woke up. *If* I woke up.

The rocks shifted again. There were loud cracking sounds above me, and dust crumbled over my head. As the first rock began to fall, only one thought remained with me:

This was never the way I wanted to die.

❧·ACKNOWLEDGMENTS·❧

Warmest thanks go to the amazing Scholastic family for all you do for me and for my books. There are few endeavors as rewarding as bringing books into young readers' lives, and it is a privilege to associate with each of you and to share in the excellence of your work. Special kudos to my editor, Lisa Sandell. You are priceless to me, both professionally and personally, and I am eternally grateful for the privilege of associating with you.

Thanks also to my wunderkind agent, Ammi-Joan Paquette. I don't know what I'd do without your exceptional guidance, support, and wisdom. Oh, wait, I do know. I'd panic.

Final thanks to my family, who are my foundation and the greatest blessings of my life. To my three children, you are better than I deserve and more than I ever could have hoped for. To my husband, Jeff, you are stuck with me forever, and I enjoy every single day of deserving someone like you.

⫷∥·ABOUT THE AUTHOR·∥⫸

JENNIFER A. NIELSEN is the acclaimed author of the *New York Times* and *USA Today* bestselling Ascendance Trilogy: *The False Prince*, *The Runaway King*, and *The Shadow Throne*. She also wrote the historical thriller *A Night Divided*; the sixth book in the Infinity Ring series, *Behind Enemy Lines*; and the Underworld Chronicles, a humorous middle-grade fantasy series. Jennifer collects old books, loves good theater, and thinks that a quiet afternoon in the mountains makes for a nearly perfect moment.

She lives in northern Utah with her husband, their children, and a perpetually muddy dog. You can visit her at www.jennielsen.com.